LEGENDS OF FIRE

ARCTURUS ACADEMY, BOOK 4

A.L. KNORR

Edited by

NICOLA AQUINO

Edited by

VICTORIA KNORR

PART ONE
A PATTERN ESTABLISHED

ONE

SAXONY THE SPOON

Elda had been right. Whatever was happening in Enzo's life, it was stressing him out. Fear leached from him, and the cold tentacles of his anxiety seemed to crawl across the floor toward me, making my skin want to creep off my body.

The old boss fixed me with a smile, but it had none of his former confidence or superiority. He'd aged a decade in the year that had passed since I'd last seen him. His skin, formerly lined but plump and dewy, was dry and flaky. A net of wrinkles had closed in on his over-large brown eyes, and the skin under his chin sagged. He looked like a caricature of his former self, one drawn by a malicious cartoonist.

With his hands stacked over the top of his cane, Enzo tilted its silver handle in the direction of Basil's largest sofa. An invitation to sit down, or maybe a silent command. In spite of his elderly appearance and fearful energy, he maintained the physical bearing and habitual gestures of someone used to being in control.

With a glance at Basil, who only raised an

eyebrow in curiosity, I headed for the sofa and sat down, heart drumming a steady rhythm against my breastbone. There was only one reason Enzo would leave his Venetian palace to come and see me in person. It was time to pay off the debt I owed. My palms felt clammy and my stomach tightened. I pressed my hands between my knees to keep from fidgeting.

"Grazie for the use of your office," Enzo said to Basil with a voice full of gravel, thick fingers gripping the head of his cane tight enough to bleed the knuckles white. Maybe he was just as nervous as I was. I wondered if he was implying Basil should leave. The idea doubled my anxiety.

"Prego," replied Basil, not making any move to vacate his chair. He did glance my way again, the question in his gaze as clear as if he'd spoken it: Did *I* want him to go?

Gratefully, I gave him the smallest shake of my head. I never wanted to be alone with any Barberini again, if it could possibly be helped.

Enzo lifted his shoulders in a shrug, the classic Italian 'whatever' gesture. He swung his chair to face me more directly. "I hope my visit finds you well, Ms Cagney, and that you've enjoyed your time so far here at Arcturus."

I forced a smile as a lonely thought rattled in response: *and I hope you choke.*

"You know why I am here," he said without waiting for a reply.

I held eye contact with the don. "You're cashing in your chit."

He paused. "I don't know this saying, but I understand its meaning well enough. Yes. It is time for you to repay."

"What do you want?"

I didn't miss Basil's surprised glance at my abrupt tone, but Enzo didn't even blink. Perhaps he appreciated the opportunity to get to the point.

"Let me tell you una piccola storia to begin," he replied.

Okay, so maybe he was going to take his time getting to the point. I let out a sigh and waited.

Enzo dropped one hand from his cane, curled his fingers and gave a few dry coughs into his pudgy fist. Thumping himself on the chest, he looked to Basil and began to ask something but struggled to get it out.

The headmaster was already out of his seat and moving toward the table with the carafe of water and the stack of glasses. He poured two cups full and delivered one to Enzo and one to me.

Thanking him, I took the glass and took a sip before setting it on the coaster nearest my knee, using the moment to settle myself emotionally. My heart was beating madly. Just seeing Enzo again had resurrected the unpleasant memories of what his son had done to me. Dante did not share many of his dad's features, he must have taken his good looks from his mother, but it was enough to know that this man had fathered the person who'd tortured me for a number of hours I'd never be able to tally accurately. But more than the desire to get as far away from Enzo as I could, I wanted him not to see any fear as a result of his presence. That would only make him happy.

Enzo thanked Basil and sipped the water. Appearing to be to his taste, he took two larger gulps before setting the glass on Basil's wooden desktop, either not seeing or simply ignoring the coaster Basil had pushed across the desk.

"I know many people in Napoli," the don began, scratching at two day's worth of salt-and-pepper beard growth. "I have business interests in all of our largest cities. More than this you do not need to know, but it *is* important for you to know that six days ago, I sent my son to negotiate a contract in Napoli. Did you ever visit?" He slanted a sly look in my direction, taking me off guard with his question.

"Naples? No. I've only ever been to Venice."

He waved a hand and pulled on the end of his nose, a nervous gesture perhaps. "Just curious. It would have been helpful if you knew the style of the city, but no matter."

I blinked. Enzo's funny way of talking might have been charming under other circumstances. I assumed by 'style', he'd meant layout.

"There is a beautiful piazza called Vittoria in front of the Baia that is very popular with tourists," he went on, wiping the sides of his mouth with a thumb and forefinger. "My son's favorite bakery is there. The Neapolitan are famous for their baba."

I arched a brow. Dante had never struck me as much of a pastry lover. Then again, such a leaning went well with his penchant for pastel colored clothing. But what did baked goods have to do with me?

"I know, I know. Dante is very fussy." Enzo chuckled affectionately, but he was chuckling by himself as Basil and I stared at him. I had forgotten how meandering Enzo was in conversation. He acted like we were old friends catching up. It was the kind of artificial warmth that left one feeling more chilly than before the encounter.

"I hope when you are there you take the opportunity to sample the baba yourself," he said with that same foxlike glance, making sure I hadn't missed the smoke signal he'd sent up between the words. I would soon find myself visiting Naples.

I felt like wilting but I forced my shoulders back and my expression into neutral. I *really* didn't need this right now. What I needed was to get on a plane and go home to Canada. I needed to sleep beneath my childhood duvet, play cards with Jack and RJ, and razz my mom about her latest self-inflicted dye-job. I needed to meet Gage at Flagg's, if only just to have him smile at me. I needed to fill the cracks in our relationship with mortar, even if it was friendship mortar.

"My son has disappointed me," the old man went on, putting counterfeit sadness over genuine fear. The effect was grisly. "Dante has not put aside his foolish ambition, as I had hoped he would, after the... adventure with you last summer. If he had been moved away from his goal, he would have made me happy, but... what do they say in the English stories? Alas. He has not."

The only ambition I'd ever known Dante to have was that of becoming a fire mage. I bristled but waited out the silence for Enzo to get to the point. I didn't like the direction this was headed, but what Enzo wanted from me, I had to do my best to give him.

In a way, now that the shock of Enzo's appearance (softened thanks to Elda's warning) had worn off, I was surprised to feel an eagerness I had not expected. Perhaps getting Enzo's debt paid off sooner rather than later would be better than having it hanging over my head for years.

"Having grown up with a magus"—Enzo paused and looked at Basil, meandering around the point the way satellites orbit earth—"Nicodemo." He swung back to me. "Dante can easily spot the small, hardly noticing details that mark your kind."

Enzo had been doing quite well with his English up until this point. "Hardly noticeable?" I supplied.

"Si, si. Hardly noticeable. As you say." Enzo chuckled. "Dante prouds himself to recognize a fire magus at forty meters. I agree with such claims. What Dante believes to be unpayable, I would pay to eliminate."

It took me a minute to discern that one. "Priceless, you mean? What Dante believes to be priceless?"

"As you say." Enzo nodded, the chair's leather squeaking beneath him. "When he phoned me to relay that he had spotted two of you, I understood he was not lying."

The small hairs at the nape of my neck raised themselves. It was only with great effort that I didn't gape at Basil in rising alarm. Dante had spotted two fire magi in Naples? What were the odds? If Basil knew the magi population of Naples, he could make a deduction, but he obviously wasn't going to say anything in front of Enzo. The headmaster's gaze merely twitched in my direction briefly.

"I commanded Dante to leave them alone and come home directly after the negotiation." Enzo shook his head.

I crossed my arms over my chest and hooked one knee over the other, sitting back against the sofa in a movement that clearly relayed my cynicism. "Let me guess, he defied your orders."

"No. He did come home, but only to fetch something and leave again."

"Back to Napoli?"

The don nodded as he fished a small pocket handkerchief from an inside pocket and mopped his brow. "My son is not normally so disrespectful, but I fear he is starting to see me as..." he paused. A flash of the same kind of panic that consumed someone lost in miles of wilderness flashed across his face, then it was gone.

"In the way?" I guessed.

"Perhaps. Time, it seems, takes everything from us. Little by little. Including the respect of our children." He returned the handkerchief to his pocket.

I didn't agree with his assessment, but wasn't interested in launching a philosophical debate. If Enzo was losing Dante's respect it was because Enzo had raised an inconsiderate brat and also hadn't done much worthy of respect. "What did he come home to fetch?"

"Strangely, I can't tell you what it was, only that he took it from Nico's things—items left in our private safe before his death." The don paused to take another sip of water after this enigmatic announcement.

I narrowed my eyes. Nicodemo had gone to a lot of trouble to record videos for Isaia. He'd wanted to teach his son how to live with his fire, tell him things that any normal father would want his son to know. It was highly likely that the things Nico had left in the safe had been set aside for Isaia as part of his inheritance. I didn't doubt that the Barberinis would never honor their dead employee's wishes, especially if the items were valuable. What Isaia didn't know about, he would never miss.

"You have no idea at all what it was Dante came to get?" My tone was flat and disbelieving. I wanted Enzo to know I didn't trust for one second that Nico had left property to the insanely wealthy crime family.

Outside Basil's window, the thin sunlight dimmed further as clouds moved in front of the sun. Enzo pulled out a small leather spectacle case. Unsnapping it, he pulled out a set of thin glasses, unfolded them and put them on, taking care to tuck the wire behind his ears and fix them well. His breathing seemed to be heavier than it had been when I'd first sat down. There was a whistle in his lungs that didn't sound friendly.

"I had Karim look through the items to see what was missing," he continued. "A bit of parchment is all, very fragile, rolled and held in a cardboard tube."

"Parchment," I repeated. "And you want it back? Is that why you're here?"

Enzo peered at me through his glasses, his already big eyes doubled in size. He was still for a while, as though absorbing my English words and slowly translating them into Italian inside his antique but still-sharp mind.

"No." He shook his head but didn't take his gaze from mine. "I don't want you to bring back the parchment. I want you to bring back my son."

It was harder to contain my surprise this time, and my dismay. So much for never seeing Dante again. "Are we talking about a rescue, or the art of persuasion here?"

"Perhaps a bit of both. My boy is in need of saving from himself, and I am hoping you can achieve this with simple persuasion. However, it may come that you are required to use force. If you are, you have my blessing, just do your best not to hurt him."

"Why can't you send Karim or a couple of your other"—I wanted to say 'goons', but Enzo didn't appreciate implications that he was mafia—"hired hands?"

Enzo shifted in his seat, rocking back and forth as he settled his bulk anew. "It is not my practice to use a fork where a spoon is needed."

I pointed at my breastbone. "And, I'm the spoon?"

"I fear Dante has gotten himself tangled with these magi in pursuit of his goal to become one of them. I want you to convince him to give up and come home. In the event he refuses your persuasions, then I'm giving you permission to knock him out, throw him in a sack. I will even supply a helicopter delivery."

"You mean pick up?"

"Just so."

I cleared my throat. "I see."

My mind tumbled with questions and suspicions. On the face of it, either persuading Dante to go home or forcing him didn't appear to be too difficult a task—setting aside the fact that kidnapping someone is illegal and I'd already told Enzo I wouldn't break laws. I suspected there was something he was not telling me.

"As enjoyable as it would be to knock your son out and throw him in a sack, I still don't understand why me? Surely one of your men would be enough? Why use up the favor I owe you on this particular errand?"

"Your skills may be necessary," Enzo said. "Your experience at the hand of my son, and your understanding of what it means to live the life of a fire magus may all come into play. You are the only one who can convincingly express to him how dangerous it is, how painful."

"With all due respect, Senor Barberini," I said, my lips twisting with an ironic smile, "Dante already knows it's dangerous. He killed Nicodemo and he almost killed me too when he tried to manipulate me into giving him Isaia's fire."

Strictly speaking, I understood there to be less danger for a mage who was to receive the fire than any mage undertaking a Burning, but Enzo took my point anyway. Dante didn't need to be told that he was playing with his life.

The don nodded. "Dante understands some of the danger, but coming from you, I believe he will take it more seriously. The reason I want to send you is not only because I happen to know from personal experience that you have negotiation skills, I think there may be a possibility Dante has some kind of agreement with these unknown magi. They may come to his defense, and if they do, I want to be able to fight fire with fire. Is that clear enough?"

I gulped and slid a sideways glance at Basil, who was listening with a narrowed, calculating gaze.

If the two magi Dante had involved himself with were Nero and Ryan, then I didn't need Enzo to ask me to go to Naples and I thought I could deduce that Basil's thoughts ran along a similar vein. Whatever was going on over there in Italy, we needed to understand it and more than likely stop it. I hoped the agency knew more than Enzo did, because I didn't feel like going in as blind as I currently was.

"What do you know about these magi?" I took a sip

of water, hoping it would soften the ball of nerves filling my stomach.

"A little. When Dante came home to get the parchment, he seemed very excited. Too much for my comfort."

I nodded, putting my glass down. I knew the manic look Dante could get.

"He told me that he was buying baba in the Piazza Vittoria when he saw a young man with eyes like Nico had. The kind that look red in some lights. *Your* kind." Enzo leaned forward, his expression full of meaning. "The young man was seated at a table in front of the café. He appeared to be waiting for someone. Dante ordered an espresso and sat at a table not far from the magus. That someone came along a short while later. The other man, also with the eyes, was older than the first. Perhaps mid-fifties, was Dante's guess. They spoke in English. The younger was American, and the other was a local, the Neapolitan accent is quite particular. They spoke and Dante listened, pretending to read a newspaper. He learned from their conversation that the two had an agreement. The young one was newly Burned, the older was in charge, perhaps the young one's employer? My son could not clearly hear all that was said, as they kept their voices low. You can imagine my son's enthusiasm at finding these magi, for he has desperately missed Nicodemo."

I resisted the urge to roll my eyes. I highly doubted Dante missing Nico had anything to do with friendship or brotherly love. He missed the only supernatural in his father's employ. Dante had so wanted to be a mage that he gave himself a fake mage mark, a tattoo.

"When the young one left the table and walked

away, the older one stayed and ordered breakfast. When he was finished, he went in the opposite direction. My son followed him, but not very well, because the old magus turned on him and demanded to know what he wanted."

Enzo paused here for another coughing session and a drink, leaving me nearly writhing with impatience. Senor Barberini was slow and pedestrian in his speech. It was enough to drive one mad.

"Dante told him the truth, not about who he is, in case this magus belonged to one of our enemies, but that he loves the magi and desired to become one of them. The older magus grew angry and told my son to go away, but Dante did not."

"He's nothing if not tenacious," I muttered sourly.

"Si, é vero. Dante proposed a deal. In exchange for helping him acquire a fire, perhaps even the younger magus's fire, he could pay a lot of money. He took a great risk offering this, making an assumption that the magi were not loyal to one another, but Dante is not risk averse, as you know. However, money did not interest the magus, but when my son brought up the fact that he once knew a magus and that he'd inherited some interesting artifacts, this older magus became interested."

My skin felt oddly cold, even as my fire licked up and down my spine.

"After the magus agreed, my son promised to bring the parchment to him and give him time to discover for himself its authenticity. After that, he would help Dante get his fire." The corners of Enzo's lips quivered at this, in fear or anger, I couldn't tell.

Heart beating as rapidly as a bird's, I cleared my throat. "Let me see if I understand. After this agreement was struck, Dante returned to Venice, collected the parchment, filled you in on the situation and then left against your command?"

Enzo nodded. "Si. Esattamente."

"He has returned to Naples with the parchment, he will allow N–this older mage to inspect it, and if he's happy with it, the older mage will facilitate the passing of the younger mage's fire over to your son?"

"I can't speak to whose fire Dante expects to acquire, that is speculation. It is also possible the parchment will be of no interest to the magus and he will not agree, but it is just as possible that they will strike a bargain. I am afraid for my son's life and want him to abandon this plan and come home. Even if he was to receive a fire successfully, you and I both know what his next step will be."

I nodded. "He'll attempt a Burning."

"And you and I both know that he will not survive that. So I want you to bring him home before he gets to a place where he can try it. Do this, and you will fulfill your promise. You will owe me nothing and I will never approach Isaia or his family. You have my word, and all of your expenses will be covered."

The room fell into a heavy silence as I tried not to think about how Enzo had given me his word that he wouldn't bother Elda, and yet he had. An antique clock on Basil's shelf of oddities ticked quietly along, watchful but unaffected by the tension.

My voice came out reedy. "And if I fail?"

Fear filled Enzo's brown eyes again, giving them a glassy sheen. His brows slanted down over his tired gaze. "Then I may be short my only son, and you will find that the next assignment is much more difficult."

"I told you I didn't want to break any laws."

Enzo waved a hand. "It is up to you how you reach success in this matter. In my view—and I am the one who says whether you have succeeded or not in this task —my son at home in Venezia, safe and alive, is the goal. Make this happen and you will be released. You never have to see me or Dante again. Do you agree?"

I glanced at Basil, who remained unhelpfully impassive, then back at the don. As far as I could see, I hadn't much choice in the matter, and I had my own reasons for wanting to go to Naples now, anyway. "I agree."

"Bene." Enzo thumped his cane on the floor twice, as if to seal the deal. "I will have Karim send you Dante's contact information, cell number and email address. I'm afraid he has not told me where he is staying in Naples. He knows his padre is not above having someone pluck him from his bed in the middle of the night." He lifted a brow in question. "Presuming you do not have these details already?"

I couldn't stop a bark of indignant laughter at the idea of keeping Dante's contact information in my phone after what he'd done to me.

Enzo smiled and shrugged. "Young women do strange things. Many of them are very attracted to dangerous and impulsive men like my son. If you are an anomaly among your kind, I congratulation you."

"Thanks," I said, my tone thick with derision. "But it would be helpful to know where he is staying in Naples. He may not agree to meet with me and if I can't track him down in person, this task may have already failed."

Enzo pulled out his handkerchief and dabbed at the

corners of his mouth, nodding. "If and when Karim has that information, he will send it to you. How soon can you fly? I can offer you the use of a plane and one of our villas in centro historico." He tucked the handkerchief away. "I hope you mark how good I am to my employees. Whatever resources I can give you, I will."

That was not such a subtle way of suggesting that should I be successful, I could take Nicodemo's place on Enzo's roster, if I was interested. I was not and never would be, but I didn't feel the need to rub it in his face.

Enzo got to his feet, leaning heavily on his cane. "Can you be at the airport later today? You can fly with me to Venice, and my pilot will carry you on to Napoli."

My heart did a roll. "I would prefer a little more time to prepare. My family is expecting me in Canada, I will have to update them, and I would also like some time to do a little research."

"Time is not your friend right now, signora," Enzo replied, almost gently. "I have a car outside. You should take the opportunity to ride with me. No?"

Feeling like steam might blow from my ears from the sheer pressure of the situation, I scrambled inwardly, though Enzo was right. Still, I was completely unprepared and desperately wanted to discuss the situation with Basil. "Let's meet in the middle. I need a couple of hours to pack. Can you send a car for me at six?"

"As you like." Enzo nodded, fishing two cards out of his pocket he set them on Basil's desk then turned for the door.

"Did Dante tell you the name of these mages?" Basil asked, getting to the door before Enzo and pulling it open for the older man.

"Dante knows me well. Give me too much information and I will take control. I do not know them by name."

Basil watched the don pass into the hall and followed him out, possibly to make sure the elderly Signor Barberini didn't fall down the steps.

I watched them leave, wondering. If Enzo knew who Dante was getting involved with, he probably would have sent a hitman instead.

TWO
SPECULATIONS

I trailed behind Basil and Enzo as the don made his way down the stairs, rocking from side to side and bumping against the paneling from time to time. He couldn't be much older than sixty-five but he moved like he was in his eighties. If it was just stress from what Dante was up to, then what they said must be true: stress is a silent killer.

Basil held the front doors open and Enzo crossed the gravel to the waiting car, a medium-sized SUV with no apparent branding visible anywhere. Sliding into the rear seat, he tapped the edge of his cane on the window. The motor turned over and Enzo gave us a final nod as the car rolled away to tackle the hill leading up to the road.

Basil and I returned to the front foyer.

"That was interesting." He adjusted his glasses and gestured to one of the nearby sofas. "I'm hesitant to ask just how dangerous this mission will be, and whether your family knows about this deal you made."

Sinking into the sofa, I nodded. "They do know. I

told them everything not long after I returned home from Venice. I had to tell them how I knew about Arcturus, and I couldn't explain how I got the fire without telling them about Isaia, Dante and Enzo. But they won't be expecting the debt to be repaid so soon. I—we—thought Enzo would let me finish school first, at a bare minimum. Letting me hit my mid-twenties would make even more sense, but I guess Dante's actions forced Enzo's hand."

"Do you think you can succeed?" Basil asked. "Without force, I mean."

I realized as I studied the headmaster at a closer range, that his brow was shining with a thin layer of sweat. It was in both his nature and his occupation to want to protect students, although he knew he couldn't forbid me to uphold my end of the bargain. But now I could see the headmaster was dismayed by the whole thing.

"I don't know," I said, answering honestly. "Dante and I didn't exactly part as friends, so it's not like I have rapport going for me. He's a lot like Ryan in his single-mindedness, only..." I paused, not sure if I should continue.

"Only what?"

"Only, Dante is worse than Ryan. Ryan is crafty and manipulative, but he was still raised by decent people, especially his mom. According to Gage, Angelica always kept them on the straight and narrow. But Dante is willing to kill to get what he wants. He doesn't care who he hurts."

Basil's Adam's apple bobbed. "I'm having an idea but I'm hesitant to share it, because I'm not sure I can come through on it."

I found a smile. "Clearly you're going to share it, otherwise you wouldn't have mentioned it at all."

He nodded and cleared his throat. "Yes, but I don't want you hanging any hopes on it, not until I can speak to the Agency. I'd like to see if I can get an asset reassigned to help you. Best case, I'd ask to have them take over your task and get it done in record time without Enzo any the wiser. Worst case, they would assist you as silent backup, only there in case of emergency."

My heart gave a grateful pulse and some of the feeling of fishing-line tightening around my chest loosened. Even if Basil couldn't come through, I loved that he would try.

"Enzo did say that I could use any means needed to achieve the goal, but I have to be careful. I don't trust him. I wouldn't want us to get Dante safely home only to have the don claim I still owed him because I didn't execute the task myself."

Basil's brows pinched. "Do you think he would do that?"

I chewed my lip. "He didn't get to where he is by being honest and law-abiding, so yes, he might do that, incurring my wrath be damned. He also gave me his word that he would never bother Elda, but then he contacted her anyway. Even if you can get me help, it has to appear as though I'm doing the lion's share of the work. Enzo might have people watching."

The headmaster stared at me in horrified wonder. "You are far too young to be so cynical, but I suppose it happens when we are taken advantage of, no matter our age. And I think it's wise not to trust him."

"Are you as certain as I am that the magi Dante ran

in to were Ryan and Nero?" I got up to pace. My thighs were quivering with nervous energy.

"I wasn't certain until Enzo mentioned the parchment. I believe we are safe to assume that's who Dante is dealing with."

"Why would the parchment make you certain?"

Basil's lips formed a flat line for a moment. "I'm not permitted to say."

I turned to gape at him, pausing my trek around the ottomans.

He put up a hand as though to fend me off. "Not because I don't want to tell you, but because it's the Agency's intel and until they give you some kind of security clearance, I can't say anything more."

I brightened at the suggestion. "Can you get me security clearance?"

Basil shrugged. "I've no idea. It might be tricky just getting you an asset. It depends on what missions they have going and their priorities. When fires went out back in March, we lost several agents and have not managed to replace them. They're running short-handed. That said, they've been watching Nero for years and have compiled quite a dossier on him. All without ever finding out where he lives, incredibly."

I gaped at Basil. "If the agency has so much intel, why haven't they taken him into custody?"

"You mean for the murder of my brother?" Basil slid his spectacles up his nose. "They never gathered enough solid evidence linking Nero to Bellamy's death. Nero is sly. Very careful."

I sank onto an ottoman, dumbfounded. "In all these years? You mean to tell me they can watch Nero go about his business, buying street food or going to concerts, and they've never been able to arrest him?"

"I'm afraid so, although I don't think Nero attends many concerts," Basil replied with a wry twist of his lips.

I almost asked if that infuriated Basil, in spite of his calm appearance, but it was a stupid question. Of course it did. Bellamy had been killed in the eighties, so although Basil had had a long time to adjust to the reality of what had happened to his brother, it had to eat him up inside. It would if it had been my brother. I wondered if Basil had ever attempted to get revenge outside the agency's knowledge, then dismissed the idea. He was too much a stickler for procedure.

We sat in silence for a minute, my mind turning like a top.

"Do you think Nero can facilitate a plenary endowment?" I asked.

"From Ryan to Dante, you mean?" Basil asked.

I nodded.

Basil frowned. "I'm not convinced Nero could make such a thing happen."

"Because Ryan is Burned?"

"Yes. I do think a Burned mage's fire can be *given*, but I also think the process would take days and would be extremely difficult. But I'm not so confident it could ever be *taken* by force."

I worked my lower lip with my teeth, thinking. "When Dante tried to take my fire, he was relying on the pain being too great for me to bear, that I would willingly give it to him in exchange for water. But Ryan would never give away what he had worked so hard to amplify, even under duress."

"True. But we have little understanding of the mechanics. The agency has no record of fire being either given or coerced out of a Burned mage. Who would be strong enough to do such a thing? Nero is Burned, but even he wouldn't be strong enough to force Ryan to do anything against his will."

I agreed, but there were also many unknowns. Maybe we were wrong about what Dante wanted from Nero. We knew he wanted fire, was desperate for it, but there could be many factors at play of which we were unaware.

My thoughts circled back to Gage, and then to my family, who were waiting for news about when I'd be landing in Halifax. I had to bring them all up to speed before I left for Naples. Even though I'd flown to Venice by myself at the age of sixteen, and had been excited to have some freedom and independence, I was having major nerves about getting on a flight to Italy with Enzo. This time I wasn't going to babysit some cute kids, I was going into known danger to rescue an old enemy from a new one.

"See if you can swing me some backup then, would you?" I asked Basil with a nervous smile. "I'd better get on the phone and pack a bag."

"I'll do what I can. You have my word." Basil stood.

"Thanks. Can I leave my stuff in my old room?"

"Of course. You don't even have to ask, though you'll have to move it all to the second-year's wing for the new school year."

I nodded. "No problem."

"You'll see me before you leave, yes? I may not have an answer by then, but I would like to see you off regardless. I'll give you my private mobile number so we stay in touch."

I agreed and headed to my room as Basil went back to his office.

Part of me wanted to laugh about the exchange we'd had over my stuff having to be moved to the second-year's wing. I was about to become the youngest, least-experienced and most unwilling participant in a game that had a lot of unknowns and a lot of moving parts. His confidence that this would all work out and my second-year at the academy would begin without delay or hiccup warmed and comforted me.

When I got back to my room, I sent a text to the group chat I shared with Georjayna and Targa, asking if we could have a three-way video call sometime soon. Georjie texted back that she was in downtown Blackmouth at a noisy café, but she could be back up at the castle and in a quiet room within the hour.

While I waited for Targa to answer, I sent a text to my parents. It was still early morning in Saltford, but both of them were early risers. Mom responded immediately—as was usual for her—reporting that my dad was in the shower but would be able to talk in fifteen minutes.

Targa's response came in just after Mom's, saying that she was in the middle of a meeting at the shipping office and wouldn't be free for another hour and forty-five minutes.

I sent a message to Gage that we needed to talk, but knew he wouldn't receive it until he'd landed later today. Then I rapid-texted Georjie and Targa, solidifying our time to talk.

Phone in hand, I made my way to the first-year's

lounge to grab a coffee. I'd have to make an order online for real food and eat it between the call with my folks and the call with my friends.

Coffee in hand, I headed back to my room to begin a marathon of updating people and trying to answer the million questions I knew my parents would have without alarming them too much.

THREE
CONFESSIONS

By the time it was late enough in the day for Gage to have landed, I was seated in the back of a black, unbranded SUV, on my way to the London City Airport to join Enzo. The afternoon had passed with a frenzy of stressful conversations, some mediocre pizza, and a black hole of time while I tried to figure out what one would need when executing a directive given by a mafia boss. One thing was certain, I didn't own enough black clothing. Somehow running around Naples in flip-flops and a spaghetti-strap sundress didn't seem to fit my task—not that I had any to pack. Then again, Dante had liked me in dresses. The thought of wearing anything for Dante's pleasure made me feel like gagging, but my dad had a saying about catching more flies with honey than vinegar, so I decided to try and find some summer clothing when I arrived in Naples. Not just for Dante's sake, but to blend in. Summer in Naples could border on unbearable in terms of heat.

Before the SUV was even out the academy's driveway, I checked the text I'd sent Gage earlier, looking for a confirmation that he'd received and read the message. He had. Hitting dial, I lifted the phone to my ear.

Gage answered, sounding tired. "Saxony?"

I smiled, not because I felt like it, but because I knew he would be able to hear it in my voice. "You know it. Sorry to harass you so soon after landing. How was your flight?"

His tone was withdrawn. Understandable given our breakup. "Good. I slept so it went fast. What's up?"

I took a deep breath through my nose and went straight into it. "There's been a development. I can't come home yet, so I won't be able to meet you at Flagg's any time soon. I'm actually headed to the airport myself right now, but I'm flying to Naples."

There was a heavy pause, then a drawn out, "Okaaaay, I'll bite. Why?"

Guilt sent a thin blade into my heart. I'd never told Gage about Enzo. I never thought Enzo would cash in his chit so soon, and when Elda had come, dropping hints, I'd told Tomio the story because he'd been here when Gage hadn't. After that, what had happened with Eira, and the confession of kissing Tomio had made everything else seem unimportant.

"It's a long story, but here's the fast version. I owe a favor to the don of a Venetian family named Barberini. I have to convince his son to leave Naples and go home to Venice before he gets further into trouble. From what Enzo told me, his son—Dante—might have made some kind of deal with someone who sounds a lot like Nero, and Enzo is worried for Dante's life."

I paused, letting Gage absorb this. My heart pounded as he took his time answering.

"This Dante, he's a mage?"

"No. He's just a regular guy, but that's what Enzo is worried about, that he's made a deal to receive a fire. I'm supposed to stop that from happening." I braced a hand on the SUV's door as the driver took a corner a little too fast.

Gage was quiet for too long.

"Hello?"

"I'm here. Do you have any idea how nuts this sounds?"

"Yes, and I'm sorry I'm blind-siding you with it. If you'd been here when Elda had visited, I would have had a chance to explain."

"Who is Elda?"

"The mother of the kid who gave me his fire."

"She visited you?" He sounded incredulous. "At the Academy?"

I was quickly feeling worse and worse for never having told Gage. Why *hadn't* I told Gage more when I'd had the chance? Gage was the first mage I had ever met. Had I been swept into a love-bubble with him because I'd had nothing else to compare our relationship to? We had enjoyed one another's company but Gage had never drawn me out the way Tomio had. Maybe because Gage hadn't inquired much about my background, I thought my history was boring and irrelevant to him. Some people were like that, solely focused on the present.

"Yes, while you were in Italy with your mom," I explained, fiddling with a curl and feeling embarrassed.

"Why didn't you tell me? Why didn't you tell me about the favor you owed? Why do you even owe a favor? Why is this up to you?" His voice cracked and filled up with an edge of anger and something else. Concern?

"I... it didn't ever seem important, and then the games happened, and then..."

"Tomio."

"Yes."

"My God, Saxony. *Who are you?* I feel like I don't even know you. Maybe I've never known you."

I closed my eyes in guilt and frustration. I felt bad, but didn't have time for this. Sighing, I opened my eyes and told myself to find patience. None of this was Gage's fault either. "I am sorry I never told you and I promise, when there is time, I'll tell you everything. But right now, I'm on my way to Naples and I think Ryan might be in trouble. Again."

Gage sounded bitter, and totally unlike himself. "Isn't he always?"

I ignored his tone, even if it raised a red flag. Gage was stretched thin, and maybe whatever he'd learned in Naples was starting to reveal his twin's true character to him and he didn't like it. I hoped this was the case, though it made me sad to hear him sounding so disheartened.

"You said you learned some things when you were in Naples, things that you were going to tell me when we met at Flagg's. Can you tell me now? I feel like I'm flying in blind here and need all the facts I can get my hands on."

He let out a breath. "Yeah, okay. Well, I'm not sure that Ryan will even be in Naples when you get there."

My head snapped up. "Really?"

"He never told me directly, but when he met me and Mom one night for dinner, I managed to steal his phone and take it to the washroom with me. I didn't have much time with it but I saw some text exchanges with an unknown number about rushing a tourist visa for Iran. Someone gave him a travel authorization number from a contact at the Iranian Ministry of Foreign Affairs. With that number, he was supposed to be able to fast-track a tourist visa. He was told it normally takes two to three months for an Iranian tourist visa to come through, but this contact could rush his application and get one for him in a matter of days."

"Iran?" I breathed, feeling dizzy. What was Ryan up to?

"Yes. A coastal place called Ramsar. The message said that Ramsar was outside of the Free Trade Zones and so he needed a visa to visit. That was all I learned, I had to get back to the table before Ryan realized his phone was missing."

"I don't know what's more shocking," I said, "the fact that Ryan is going to Iran, or the fact that you broke in to your brother's phone. How did you bypass his security code?"

Gage sounded cynical again. "How do you think?"

It took me a second. "Face ID."

"Yes. See what my brother is turning me into?" He let out a harsh breath. "Anyway, I think he's going as part of his deal with Nero."

"Do you know if Nero is going with him?"

"I don't know, but I don't think so. There was only talk of rushing one visa, and maybe the unknown number was Nero himself. It's not like Ryan knows anyone else in Italy."

"Any idea what he's going there to do?"

"None whatsoever but whatever it is, it can't take

too long. His rushed visa will only be good for twenty days."

"I don't suppose you took photos of this info?"

"Of course I did. I'll text everything I have to you. And I'll do my best to be on a flight to Naples as soon as I can."

I froze, my eyes wide and sightless. I must have misheard him. "What did you just say?"

"I'll meet you in Naples, Saxony. There's no way I'm letting you do whatever the hell it is you're doing all alone."

"You only just arrived in Canada!"

He bit out his reply, sounding frustrated. "So? If I had known you'd be getting yourself into trouble like this, I wouldn't have left in the first place. I only came home because Ryan stone-walled me and you and I broke up. Now I know a little bit of what's going on, thanks to you finally sharing something with me, so I'm coming. What am I going to do in Saltford? Get a job landscaping with the town? I'll go crazy waiting for news from you. Why be here when I could be there helping?"

My heart drummed wildly, hardly knowing what to do with this information. I was relieved, frightened, excited, shocked. "What will you tell your parents?"

"The truth, or a sanitized version of it, anyway. Don't worry about it. I know how to handle them. I'm not a kid anymore."

I stared out the window at the blur of green countryside flying by, old stone cottages bristling with roses and wisteria. "Thank you," I said, sounding hoarse. I didn't know what else to say and I was so grateful my muscles felt weak.

"You're welcome. Listen, I'd better go. By the time you've landed in Naples, I'll have travel plans. Call me when you're settled. Where are you staying?"

"They're providing me with a villa."

"A mafia house? Bloody hell, Saxony."

"I know." I brushed at my eyes, feeling full of emotion.

"Please, be careful."

"I will. You too."

He snorted, then: "Bye."

I hung up the phone and tucked it into my pocket, hardly aware of what I was doing. Gage felt like he didn't know me, that maybe he'd never known me, and I was starting to wonder if I felt the same. I considered what Gage had recently been through. His brother had excluded him from whatever was going on in his life. That would be bad enough for any pair of siblings who cared about one another, let alone twins. On top of that, I'd broken up with him after kissing someone else. Or had he broken up with me? I didn't even know anymore, and it didn't really matter. It was hard to guess which of Gage's relationships might be the biggest disappointment for him. I should count myself lucky that Gage was so eager to hop on a plane, but I knew it wasn't just for my sake that he was coming back to Europe.

Up until recently, I'd always felt so close to Gage. I felt love for him and loved by him. But pressure applied to the cocoon of our relationship had popped it like a soap bubble. I'd had ample opportunity during the school year to explain my deal with Enzo. After Basil had outed me on stage, the door had been propped wide open. There was no need to keep secrets any more. But

Gage had never pried and I had never volunteered the information, thinking that paying back Enzo would happen years in the future. But was that really the reason I'd never told Gage? When I examined my true feelings baldly and without excuses, I could admit that there was more to it. In some dark place in my heart—shadowed not because it was wicked but because it was vulnerable—I didn't fully trust Gage. Not because he wasn't a trustworthy person, but because I knew just how strong the ties were between him and Ryan, and I could never compete with that.

And what of our fire coming between us? Did my fire have some consciousness of its own? Did it know that Gage would always prioritize Ryan even before I'd seen proof of it myself? But Gage's fire had a problem with me just as much as mine had a problem with him. What did *that* mean? Did it mean Gage didn't trust me fully either?

So where did that leave things? It left me heading into an unknown situation, an ally at my side with whom I had a relationship that was riddled with complexity. Maybe it was a bad idea to let Gage come along, but at this point I'd take what help I could get. I didn't fancy facing Dante, Nero, or Ryan, let alone all three together. Italy was quickly becoming a nest of enemies and I was headed straight for it.

FOUR

MEETINGS

Less than twelve hours after I'd landed at Naples International Airport I was back in arrivals. I checked my phone for what felt like the millionth time as butterflies brushed against the walls of my stomach. It was fourteen minutes after ten. Gage's plane had landed, but he was either stuck in a customs line or waiting for luggage. He had basically gotten home, unpacked, repacked, and returned to the Halifax airport. He'd taken an overnight flight to Amsterdam, then a smaller plane to Naples early this morning. His internal clock was going to be so screwed up.

I'd landed late the night before, taken a cab to the villa Enzo had provided (a small two-bedroom flat with a loft which had been divided from the rest of the old house) and gone to bed. When I woke, I grabbed breakfast at a nearby bakery then found a street vendor who sold cheap cotton dresses and hand-made leather flip-flops. Even in the early morning, the sun was powerful. Heat didn't bother me the way it had before my Burning, but jeans, sweaters and closed shoes would draw attention.

On my way to the airport to meet Gage, I texted Dante, which had gone pretty much as expected:

Me: *Hi Dante. It's Saxony.*

He received the message, but twenty minutes passed before he replied. I could imagine the shock of hearing from me cracked his usual suave and smooth exterior, but it was back in place by the time he answered.

Dante: *Well, well. Here's one redhead I never expected to hear from again. Missed me, did you?*

Me, after an eye-roll so violent it almost gave me a headache: *I'm in Naples.*

Another twenty minutes passed before Dante deigned to answer. Shock number two had thrown him for another loop. Again he reassembled his James Dean cool before answering. Instead of asking me what I was doing there or how I knew he was in the same city, he oozed that all-knowing, flirtatious superiority that I so despised.

Dante: *If you want to see me, you have to ask nicely.*

I'd rolled my eyes again, then bracketed my next text with flower emojis while my teeth were clenched: *When can we meet?*

In spite of his demeanor, I was the fire mage here and Dante was obsessed with magi. He wouldn't be able to deny himself the temptation of setting eyes on any mage, let alone the one he'd created. But he'd also be suspicious, because he was right, I never wanted to see or speak to him again. He'd know something was going on.

I wished I'd asked Enzo if he'd told Dante about me owing him a favor, but it was too late for that now.

Dante had suggested the afternoon at a gelato shop in front of the bay. The irony wasn't lost on me. Dante had taken me to a gelato shop on a date before he'd revealed his inner monster. The timing worked for me. It meant that Gage could observe our meeting from a distance, be my backup in case things got weird.

Dante had sent me a GPS pin for the shop and I'd returned a new pin for a nearby café, stating that it was better than the gelato shop because it had seats outside. I suggested we meet at two. He'd agreed.

Gage's appearance, arriving among a cluster of tired looking tourists, brought me back to the present moment. Incredibly, he looked as bright-eyed as he always did, even if he didn't give me as big a grin as I had been hoping for.

I put my arms around his neck and he wrapped his around my waist, but he didn't squeeze me close against him the way he had before our breakup. He also held his head and neck away so that our skin didn't touch. What else should I expect? But somehow, the distance between us and his appropriately withdrawn behavior still stung.

We parted and walked toward the exit.

"How can you look so fresh? Did you sleep on the plane?"

"I was exhausted after the flight from London. It made sleeping on the flight to Amsterdam easy." Gage looked around as we emerged from the terminal. A line of taxis stood waiting for customers and we headed for the one at the front.

"I just need to get some cash." Gage gestured to a nearby ATM.

The taxi driver loaded the luggage into the trunk while I waited for Gage to return. Three girls rolling expensive-looking bags stopped outside arrivals to take selfies. They looked younger than me. I wondered if this was their first trip away from their parents. One of them spotted Gage as he tucked his wallet into the rear pocket of his jeans. The girls giggled and made kissy-faces for their cameras. Either unaware of them or ignoring them, Gage slipped into the seat behind our driver. I took the one behind the passenger seat.

While we rode to the villa, I caught Gage up on my history with Dante and Enzo and why I had to pay off this favor. Which meant it was time to give him more detail about Elda, Isaia and Nicodemo. I told him the story using the baking and cooking code words Arcturus students used in Dover so as not to alert the taxi driver.

He listened quietly, not looking at me. I was surprised to find I was grateful for that. His disappointment was apparent even without looking into his eyes. He was still hurt, I could tell by the way he sat with his arms crossed and his head down. He nodded on occasion, and asked me a question here and there. When I told him I had the meeting with Dante scheduled for that very afternoon, he told me he wanted to be there, as I knew he would.

"It would be best if you remained unseen," I suggested. "I have to convince Dante to abandon whatever it is he's doing. Another chef in the kitchen would be a distraction."

Gage looked out the window, chewing the inside of

his cheek. "And it would be better if you appeared to be single in order to do it," he murmured some time later.

I didn't feel the need to confirm that.

NERVOUS APPREHENSION MADE my fingertips feel cool and tingly as I walked across the flat stones of the open piazza. Dante hadn't seen me yet. He was seated at a small outdoor table, typing something into his phone. If I hadn't seen his profile, I might not have recognized him. He'd let his hair grow long. It hung in a straight, glistening sheet of pale brown. His hair might have changed, but his taste in clothing hadn't. He wore a butter-yellow polo with a white stripe encircling the chest and a pair of fitted chino shorts with tiny yellow suns embroidered all over them. A thick gold Rolex glittered from his wrist.

My sandal scuffed against the stones as I approached and he lifted his gaze. Looking into the eyes of the person who'd nearly killed me in his attempt to steal my fire made me feel like I'd swallowed a bunch of rocks. I forced my lips into something smile-like as I sank into the spindly metal chair across from him.

"Saxony." He studied me intently, his lips curving upward in a wolf's grin.

Dante had the skin, bones and hair of a very attractive young man. When I'd first laid eyes on him, I'd been so drawn to him. We'd flirted on a party boat, me giving as good as I'd gotten. How many times had I looked back at that moment and cursed myself for being foolish? I'd been so easily lured by a pretty face, thinking him trustworthy and kind, maybe a little dangerous, but never toward me. I hoped never to be so naive again. Though Dante's features had only improved in the last year, I found him repulsive. The mind that lurked behind those eyes was without scruple or empathy.

"Dante," I replied, mimicking his tone exactly.

A waiter wearing a black vest and carrying an empty tray wove through the tables to reach us. He knew a foreigner when he saw one.

"Coffee, signora?"

"Una macchiato," I replied, unearthing my rusty Italian, "per favore."

"Un altro, per piaceré," added Dante.

The waiter nodded and moved away.

It took great effort not to look the short distance into the piazza where Gage sat on the edge of a fountain, pretending to read an Italian book he'd borrowed from the villa. He'd have an ear cocked in our direction, listening to every word we exchanged, if not watching every move and gesture. I couldn't see him without looking over my shoulder but I could feel his presence.

"What are you doing in Napoli?" Dante asked casually, leaning back against the chair and crossing his arms. Long locks of hair framed his cheekbones and swayed in the soft breeze.

After talking through some alternatives with Gage before this meeting, I had decided to take a line that was as close to the truth as it could be. Lies followed half-truths the way blossoms followed buds.

"I'm here on behalf of your father. He is very worried about you."

Dante didn't even flinch. "I know, but he can wait.

When this is all over, he'll be happy I didn't come home before it was finished."

"What exactly is 'it'?"

I'd raked my hair into a topknot hurriedly, my fingers not as steady as they usually were. Dante's eyes followed the movement of my hand and lingered on my ear for a moment, but he didn't answer my question.

I tucked a stray wisp of hair behind my ear as my heart bumped. "I know about the parchment you took from Nicodemo's things."

I sat back and lay my hands in my lap as the waiter returned with our coffee. We were silent as he set the two espresso cups and two small glasses of water down. He unloaded a little box containing packets of sugar.

"Would you like anything else?" he asked.

We murmured we didn't and he moved away.

"You can't know that much about it." Dante's expression was smug. "It's not just any old parchment. It's a rubbing, taken from some old tablet found in Turkey. It's been in Nicodemo's family for generations. Did you know his grandmother was Turkish? I always knew it was worth something."

"What does it say?"

Dante shrugged elegantly, uncrossed his arms and ran his hands through his hair, tucking both sides behind his ears. "How should I know? I don't think anyone knows what it says. The language is so old it's obsolete."

I frowned. Skipping over the admonishment I wanted to deliver for not having passed Nico's things on to Isaia, I reminded myself why I was here. It was time to get to the point.

"Don't sell it to Nero. I know someone else who will

buy it, someone much more honest. Go home to Venice, and I'll arrange a meeting."

Dante, who had started at my use of Nero's name, laughed. "I don't need money." His eyes glittered, he leaned forward and lowered his voice. "I need fire. Is your buyer willing to give me that?"

"And kill you?" I snorted. "Of course not."

"Rich, coming from you." He cocked a brow. "You don't look very dead to me."

"No thanks to you," I snapped, then closed my eyes and took a breath before opening them again. "Listen. You need to give up this insane pursuit. Enzo knows that even if you survive endowment, you'll only die when you try to Burn. On top of that—and this is something he *doesn't* know—even if you did survive, the chances that you'd end up a psychopath are through the roof." I didn't need to add my personal opinion that he already was one.

"If he wanted to convince me that I was in real danger of anything you just mentioned, he shouldn't have sent someone who survived both endowment *and* a Burning, with her sense of right and wrong intact," Dante responded calmly.

We stared at each other. I had no idea what Dante was thinking, but I was roundly cursing Enzo because Dante was right. Seeing me would only bolster Dante's desire for what I had. Maybe this would end in me kidnapping Dante and forcefully delivering him to his father in Venice after all, but I would try a different tactic first.

"I wasn't to say this except as a last resort, but he'll disown you if you don't go home immediately."

Dante blinked, his mouth flattened and his eyes narrowed. "Did he tell you that?"

"Yes." *So much for not outright lying,* I thought, my heart rate picking up. But was I making headway?

"What exactly did he say?"

The words came out confident, before I had time to appear like I was making everything up. "That if he couldn't trust his son to follow orders, he couldn't trust his son to manage the Barberini wealth."

My gaze clashed with Dante's as he scrutinized me. I didn't blink and I didn't look away, though my heart felt like rolling thunder behind my sternum.

Dante took a deep breath through his nose, looked down, smiled at the table, then looked up at me again, the smile still in place. He leaned forward slowly, resting his elbows on the metal surface. His face came uncomfortably close but I refused to back away.

"You're lying," he breathed.

Shrugging, I returned his smug smile. "It's your future. See if I don't enjoy watching you destroy it."

I downed my coffee in one gulp, returned the cup to its saucer and fished a few euros out of my bag. My heart was in my throat as I lay the money on the table, feeling Dante watch my every move. I got to my feet. So much for using feminine wiles to convince Dante to do what his father wanted. My acting skills needed work. Time to try apathy.

"I've done as your father asked," I said, turning away. "Arrivederci, Dante."

I just caught a glimpse of the fountain where Gage should have been sitting when Dante's hand snaked out and grabbed my wrist. He tugged me back to my seat and I let him, hope surging in my chest that my charade of indifference had worked. I settled my gaze on Dante but I was processing the vacant fountain. Where had Gage gone?

Dante kept his hand wrapped gently around my wrist, his fingers were cool in spite of the heat of the day. When his thumb stroked the back of my hand it took everything I had not to yank away.

"Come with me," Dante whispered suggestively. "I know you haven't forgotten the chemistry we had. You can feel it, even now."

My surprise was nearly as strong as my urge to gag. I hid both and waited. If I spoke, my voice might give away my disgust. Letting him rub the back of my hand with the pad of his thumb, I made a face I hoped looked more interested than ill.

"I know you're angry about what I did to you. You have every right to be. But surely you can see now that I did you an enormous favor. In time, I know you'll forgive me. When I have fire, you may even grow to love me. My father will never disown me. I'm his only son, and when he passes—" Dante crossed himself hurriedly, but didn't elaborate, as if realizing that he was saying too much and I hadn't said anything at all.

My stomach tightened when he closed his mouth. *Go on*, I thought desperately, *spill your plans*.

But he only held my gaze, then released my hand. He shifted his hips forward and reached into his pocket, producing a small jack-knife. The gesture was so familiar that it felt like a déjà-vu. He opened the knife. With a confident movement, he lifted the blade to my topknot. I felt a tug, then all of my curls tumbled down around my shoulders in a red curtain.

"Bella," Dante said as he closed the knife and put it

back into his pocket. "I always liked you better with your hair down."

I had opened my mouth to form a flirty response I hoped would get him to trust me when a shadow fell over our table.

Gage materialized at my elbow. He was panting a little, like he'd run from somewhere. There was only time for me to catch the look of shock on Dante's face before Gage swooped in and planted a long kiss on my lips. Curls of fire spiraled from his touch, warming my cheeks and chin. I was too surprised to do anything but sit there. I could feel Gage's exhales against my cheeks and hear his elevated heartbeat, tension radiating from his body.

Gage pulled away and looked at Dante, his expression open and earnest even as he took a deep breath. "Sorry to interrupt, I thought you'd be finished by now. I was starting to get bored."

He thrust an open hand toward Dante, the movement a little aggressive. "I'm Saxony's boyfriend, Gage. You must be Dante. She's told me all about you."

I had to give it to him for not allowing even a hint of sarcasm into his tone.

Dante leaned back in his chair, staring up at Gage with wide eyes. He didn't shake the offered hand. He was too shocked to even try to hide it behind his usual veneer. "What are *you* doing here?"

"What do you mean? Where else should I be?" Gage left his hand in the air over the table, while the other gripped the back of my chair protectively.

Dante's gaze flashed to me and back to Gage, stunned. I could almost smell the smoke as he tried to figure out what was going on. His amazement spoke volumes.

He thinks Gage is Ryan.

My initial reaction to Gage's interruption was one of irritation, any momentum I'd had with Dante was now lost, but I'd gained something else instead. Confirmation. Still, maybe Dante had been about to tell me something important.

He recovered himself enough to swallow his shock but he couldn't tear his eyes from Gage.

Gage withdrew his hand, tucking it into his pocket. He looked down at me. "Are you finished here? I want to get to Pompeii with enough time left before closing to actually enjoy it."

I was about to ask for a few more minutes when Dante got up in a hurry. His expression inscrutable.

"Yes, we're finished." He pushed his chair in and dumped a few euros on the table.

I got to my feet, accidentally stepping on Gage's foot. "Wait, where—"

But Dante was already moving across the piazza, his back to us as he fished his phone out of his pocket.

I watched him disappear down a narrow alley before turning to Gage, who now had both hands jammed in his pockets. His fake smile was gone and his eyes were filled with thunder.

"I don't know whether to thank you or throttle you," I said.

"He pulled a knife on you, Saxony," Gage snapped, "or hadn't you noticed?" He yanked a hand out of one pocket to gesture angrily at my face. "Did you expect me to stand back and watch while a lunatic cut your throat?"

"The knife bit was something he did once before, cut my hairtie. I wasn't in any danger. I think he was about to tell me something important."

Gage's mouth flattened. "Do you have any idea how idiotic you sound?"

I let out a growly exhale of frustration and dug in my bag for a spare elastic. I began to rake my hair back up into a bun with sharp, fast movements. "Come on. I need to call Enzo."

FIVE
TAKEN

A cheerful conversation happening in the street below my window roused me to consciousness. It took several seconds before I remembered that I was in a villa in central Naples and not in my bedroom back at the academy. I opened my eyes and sat up, kicking the sheet off my legs. I blinked blearily at the clock: just past nine. I hadn't set an alarm and stress often made me tired so I'd overslept.

The events of the day before surfaced like some gruesome creature of the deep. I rubbed at my eyes and let out a long sigh.

The villa was quiet. If Gage wasn't asleep I was surprised he hadn't knocked on my door. Not that we had a lot planned for the day. With Dante's outright refusal to go home, all we could do now was try to get a hold of Ryan and come up with a new plan, one that might involve a night-stick, a black breathable sack, and an unmarked van.

I stumbled into the bathroom and splashed cold

water on my face before peering over the edge of the loft and into the small kitchen. "Gage?"

No answer. But from my vantage point I could see a note on the kitchen table. Taking the narrow steps down, I snatched it up, smiling as I read Gage's messy handwriting.

Since you've obviously gone into hibernation, I went for croissants and cappuccino. If you're not awake when I get back, I'm eating yours.

-Gage

I left the note on the table and returned to the bathroom, stripping off my pajamas and cranking up the shower. Morning sun slanted through the stained-glass window over the toilet, promising another retina-shattering day. I hurried through washing my hair and soaping, not wanting to let my cappuccino get cold. The shower was loud, so I wouldn't be able to hear Gage when he came in unless he shouted.

Turning off the spray, I stepped out and snatched two towels up from the shelves by the tub. I turbaned my hair up in one and vigorously scrubbed at my skin with the other.

Putting my hair up in a wet and messy bun, I slapped sunscreen on my freckled chest and shoulders and pulled on one of my new sun-dresses and sandals. Gage still hadn't returned by the time I was ready. I frowned, wondering if he'd gone to the bakery across the square instead of the one at the end of our alley.

Poking my head out the door, I looked down the steps toward the piazza. He wasn't in sight. There was only one direction he could come from. Going left led up to a church and more villas and flats. Going right led down to the bustling piazza.

I looped my long-strapped purse over one shoulder and grabbed a pair of sunglasses and the keys to the villa. Taking the steps down to the piazza, I passed closed doors festooned with trailing wisteria. The shadows were cool but as I stepped into the square and the sun hit my skin, it was so warm the sudden contrast lifted goosebumps across the back of my neck and arms

The piazza was large, bordered with many restaurants and café's but only two proper Italian bakeries. One was on the corner nearest to our flat, the other across the piazza and halfway down the block going toward the Bay of Naples. Gage wasn't at the first one so I headed across the piazza toward the other, wondering why he'd gone to the far one instead.

I passed over to the shadowy side of the street as I closed the distance to the other bakery. Just beyond it was a tourist shop, the kind with racks of postcards and Napoli-branded knick-knacks sitting out on the side-walk. A spray of keychains, postcards and fridge magnets covered the sidewalk and spilled into the gutter. A man in a flattened fedora was in the act of standing up a postcard rack that had been knocked over, muttering to himself. A few people stood together talking in Italian too fast for me to make out, but they looked unhappy. I wondered if someone had tried to steal something from the shop.

Gage wasn't in the bakery and the woman on staff was tucked into an alcove behind the cash register, talking rapidly into a phone. She also sounded upset. There was no one else in the café. Half-eaten pastries, half-drunk espresso, and a couple of overturned chairs meant something had disturbed her patrons. Frowning, I turned the chairs upright and waited for the woman to get off the phone. She was leaning against the door to her little office with her back to me.

Feeling uneasy, I returned to the street. The tourist shop was well on its way to order again but there was still no sign of Gage. A petite lady with a tiny dog held in one arm entered the café and went to the front counter, rubbing the little dog's ears as she waited for service.

The baker hung up the phone and served the woman, unsmiling.

When the woman moved to a table, I approached the counter.

"Buon giorno, parle Inglese?"

She nodded, brow wrinkling. "Si, certo. What can I get for you?"

"I'm looking for my friend and was wondering if you've seen him. He might have ordered breakfast here. He's young, about this tall." I held my hand up to just under the six-foot mark. "Dark blond hair, clean-shaven and good-looking. He's Canadian—"

I trailed off as her face clouded. "Someone like that was taken from the street, only fifteen minutes ago."

My stomach tightened. "What do you mean, taken?"

She pointed a finger at the sidewalk to the right of her front door. "Just there. A small van came onto the pavement and two men came out. They pushed a young man inside, he was a tourist for sure because I heard him speak. They took him away." She lowered her words to a whisper. "The mafia do this sometimes. They don't care that our businesses hurt because people are afraid and stay away. They go to places in the north instead, like Rome and—"

I shook my head. I fumbled for my phone and found a picture of Gage. I zoomed in on his face and showed it to her, interrupting her complaints about the mafia hurting tourism.

"Is this the man you saw?"

Her eyes widened and she took my phone, staring at it. She looked up, nodding. "This is him! I called the polizia. They will come. You should wait outside."

She handed the phone back and waved me off, like she didn't want anyone associated with crimes, even a victim, in her bakery.

Not feeling my body, I floated outside on a wave of shock. I studied the street, now looking like any busy sidewalk in any Italian city on any summer morning.

My vision shifted as the realization that Gage was gone, that someone had taken him, penetrated my brain. Details in the center of my sight grew sharp while my periphery blurred.

A fruit vendor stacked crates of lemons and oranges. People wandered up and down the street, talking and laughing. A trio of tourists with their phones out headed for the piazza, speaking in German. A young couple with golden tans and glossy hair cuddled and kissed as they leaned against a wall.

"Signora?"

I turned, the back of my quivering hand pressed to my lips.

The man with the flattened fedora was there, studying me with a furrow between his brows.

"Are you ok, signora? You look like..." he paused, struggling for the right word. "Una phantasma."

"Did you see what happened here?" My voice trembled. I hadn't felt this alone and frightened since I'd been locked in Dante's basement. I grasped the kind stranger's compassion like a drowning person grabs at the nearest floating thing.

His concern deepened as he reached for a back pocket. He produced a phone, nodding. He pulled up a video clip and showed it to me.

Chest and head throbbing with every heartbeat, I watched the short video. It opened on action already in progress, taken from the vantage point of inside the gift shop. A small blue van was partially visible where it had pulled up on the sidewalk. It had already knocked over a rack of postcards.

I caught a flash of Gage's hair and the side of his body as he was shoved in through the van's open door by two people dressed in dark colors. I saw no faces and not enough of the bodies to be able to describe the kidnappers to anyone.

"They are mafia," whispered Flattened-Fedora. "They will ask for money. Is your friend rich?"

I shook my head, biting my lip so hard I tasted blood. I watched the short clip again and again. It was all over in a few seconds.

"You know the faces along the piazza?" Flattened-Fedora continued.

It took me a second to register what he meant. I had seen them. The enlarged photographs of people hanging along the top of a columned facade. Most of them were smiling. Names printed beneath each face, and a span of dates—birth dates and death dates.

"All mafia victims," he said. "The photographs are our way of protesting. We try to remind the polizia who they work for."

"Where are the police?"

"They will come, but always too late. That's how we know it's mafia." Flattened-Fedora made a face of disgust. "They care more about filling their own pockets than they do about their people." He turned his head and spat to the side, putting all the anger and frustration he had about this into the gesture.

"My friend only arrived yesterday. Why would they take him?"

He gripped my shoulder. It was a gesture too familiar for one stranger to give another, but under the circumstances I appreciated the feeling of fingers pressing into my flesh. It helped me focus.

"They watch new arrivals at the airport. Think. Did your friend withdraw any money or give any other signs of wealth?"

My heart spasmed. "He took money from an ATM."

His fingers gripped harder. "The one across from the taxi stand?"

"Yes."

He clucked his tongue and swore in Italian, releasing my shoulder to hit the top of his own head. It explained why his fedora was so flat. He removed it and began to wring the poor hat like washing. "No one warned you not to take money near the airport?" he almost wailed, gesturing at me in a very Italian way with his crumpled headwear. "Napoli is not like Firenze. All of us know the airport is where they target people. How did you get from the airport to your hotel? By taxi?"

I felt dizzy and stepped sideways to put a hand on the nearest wall. How could this happen? "Yes, we took a taxi. If someone followed us, they hid themselves well."

"No one had to follow you, signora. The taxi driver is part of it. Now, the polizia will come. They will take our statement, they will look at my film, and they will do nothing."

The look on my face made him regret his words. He softened his tone as I bent to put my head between my knees. I wondered if he knew how in danger his spotless wingtip shoes were of being vomited upon.

"Mi dispiacé, signora," he said, apologizing as I took deep breaths. "I am sorry. I am ashamed for my city."

He went on about the mafia kidnappings but I was hardly listening as I sat on my haunches with my head down and my eyes stinging.

The whole thing seemed too coincidental. Had Gage really been targeted for a kidnapping based on the hundred euros he'd taken from an ATM? He never wore brand name clothing. He looked clean-cut and cared for, but he needed to replace his sneakers and he hadn't even brought much luggage. If I were going to hold a tourist for ransom based on who had been at the airport when Gage had arrived, it wouldn't have been him. There had been that trio of glamorous looking young women taking selfies in front of arrivals. Why not one of them instead? Or all three of them, for that matter. Why Gage? Unless they'd marked all possible targets and our taxi driver had made it apparent Gage was the easiest.

But did staying in a little side street along a piazza rather than in a hotel along the water front make him more accessible or more appealing? I would have thought it would be easier to nab someone from the bay where kids went to smoke and socialize at night. But what did I know? This was the first time I'd ever considered the business side of kidnapping.

What should I do now? Wait for the kidnappers to contact me? Or would they get Gage's parents' number from his phone and call them directly, leaving me out of it?

His parents. The nausea climbed my throat with a vengeance as I thought about Angelica and Chad. I put a hand over my mouth. If the kidnappers contacted me, I was going to have to tell his parents what had happened, and Ryan too, if he bothered to answer his phone when he saw who it was.

Before I did that, though, I had to call Basil.

Interrupting Flattened-Fedora mid-complaint, I stood and asked him if he would forward the video of Gage being taken. He agreed and I gave him my number. Thanking him, I moved into the bakery away from the noise of the street as I dialed Basil. Flattened-Fedora moved away, a troubled expression on his lined face.

Basil answered on the third ring. "Saxony. I'm glad you called—"

He took a breath to continue speaking but the words poured out of me like a torrent. "Listen. You're not going to believe this, but Gage has been kidnapped. Two men shoved him into a van this morning in front of a bakery. Only minutes ago. One of the locals caught part of it on camera. I'll send you the footage but it probably won't help much. He thinks it was mafia, because Gage took money out at the airport—"

Basil's voice invaded my ear. "Whoa! Slow down. *Who* thinks it was mafia? *What* happened? I can hear you're in a panic but you're talking too fast. I can't understand you. Where are you?"

The sound of Basil's voice centered me. I took in a breath and closed my eyes, keeping them closed to shut out the world. "I'm in a bakery across the piazza from where we are staying. When I got up this morning, Gage was gone."

"What is Gage doing there?"

Right. I hadn't updated Basil about Gage's movements. "I called Gage on my way to the airport," I explained. "He got on the next plane he could and met me in Naples. He didn't want me to face Dante alone."

"Good man," Basil said. "So you woke up this morning and he was taken?"

"No, he left me a note saying he was bringing back breakfast but when he took too long, I went looking for him. When I arrived at the bakery, it looked like there'd been a fight on the street. But it wasn't a fight. There are people who saw Gage get shoved into a van and taken away."

My phone chimed as the video appeared in my messages. I looked for the man with the fedora but he must have returned to his own shop.

"I'll send you video that one of the locals took. Hang on."

Fingers trembling, I forwarded the video to Basil. It felt like it took forever, but it finally went through.

I could hear Basil watching it on the other end of the line. There was a distant shout, a flurry of sounds, the slamming of a van door. A gunning of the van's engine. A tire screeched.

"My God," Basil breathed. "Have the police been called?"

"Yes, but no one has arrived yet. That's another reason it could be mafia."

"What were you saying about the airport?"

I told him what Flattened-Fedora had said about targeting rich tourists at the airport, and about the photographs of victims the locals had put up in protest. "But it doesn't seem right to me," I added, my hand pressed to the base of my throat. "If I wanted ransom money from someone at arrivals, I wouldn't have picked Gage. You'll send someone from the Agency now, right? How soon can they be here? I don't trust the police and time is ticking. Arcturus must have solid protocols for kidnappings?"

There was a tense moment of silence and a long exhale.

"Basil?" My gut twisted into a knot. "What is it?"

"Under normal circumstances, I would ask them to send a team immediately, but I can't."

"*What?*" Indignation and anger roiled to the surface, my face flushed with blood and my voice came out on a sneer I couldn't stop. "Why the hell not? You don't think that now might be a good time to finally unleash the supposed power of the Arcturus Agency? So far, they're more zero than hero."

"More fires went out last night, Saxony," Basil replied gently. "If someone was available to send, I would send them."

My eyes flew open, my jaw dropped.

"The Agency is in an uproar," he continued when I didn't immediately reply. "I've never seen such panic. We lost three agents in March when the first fires went out. We lost another six, last night. Current projects have halted. All agents, with or without fire, have been recalled to headquarters, just outside of London. I'm on my way there now, in fact."

I tried to apologize but it came out on a wisp of air.

"That's alright," Basil replied, understanding me. "I'm sorry, too. I'm afraid you're on your own until the Agency rights itself. I can't promise anything, not until I know the extent of the damage and who we've lost."

Voices in the background of Basil's call sounded urgent. The world around me seemed to spin. I sank into a seat inside the bakery, my knees feeling too weak to hold me up.

"I have to go, Saxony. I'll call you as soon as I can. At the very least, I'll have an authority on kidnappings call you with advice."

Advice. That was the best he could do?

"Okay," I croaked, massaging my forehead where my brain felt swollen. My thumb headed for the button to end the call when Basil's voice came through again.

"Oh, and Saxony?"

I drew the phone back to my ear. "Yes?"

"Don't call Gage's parents. Leave that to me."

"Okay. Should I try to reach Ryan, though?"

Basil paused, then: "You can try."

SIX

AN UNEXPECTED ALLY

A duo of police officers finally arrived ten minutes later. One short and portly and the other tall and lanky. They interviewed me, Flattened-Fedora, the baker, and any other witnesses who'd remained around to be questioned. They asked me the same things that Flattened-Fedora had asked. When had Gage arrived? Had either of us taken money out or made any expensive purchases at the airport? What had we done immediately after meeting in arrivals? They showed me a couple of photographs of men and asked me if I recognized them. I didn't. They exchanged a look (when I told them Gage had indeed withdrawn money at the airport) that said more loudly than any words would have, that they thought I was a stupid teenager who had been irresponsible and deserved whatever happened. By the time they moved on from me to grill Flattened-Fedora, I was ready to cry or throttle the short, portly officer.

I waited for them to give helpful advice but they told me in halting English that there was nothing to do now but wait to be contacted by the kidnappers. When they asked me for the Wendig's contact information, I had to give them Basil's because I didn't have any way of reaching Chad and Angelica. I also gave them Ryan's number, but told them I didn't think he'd answer any number he didn't recognize.

While the police were taking the baker's statement, I stepped aside and took out my phone. Calling Ryan's number was more than a failure. It didn't even ring. There was no recording that the number had been discontinued, it just ended itself before any connection had been made. I didn't know if that meant Ryan had turned off his phone, taken out his SIM card, or was out of range or out of the country. Giving up trying to get through on the phone, I recorded a voice message for him instead.

"Hi Ryan, it's Saxony," I said, the phone shaking a little in my hand. "I'm with the Neapolitan police. They will probably try to call you. Gage was kidnapped from a street-front this morning. I don't know if he told you that he returned to Naples to help me with something, but he did, he arrived yesterday. The police think that kidnappers targeted him because he withdrew money from an ATM, but I think he made an unlikely target for a few reasons. You have to call me back. Better yet, you need to stop whatever it is you're doing and help me find him. I don't have much faith in the police here. Gage needs you and so do your parents. Basil will have called to tell them by now and they'll be distraught. Please don't ignore this message. I'll be waiting to hear from you."

I sent the message and watched as it uploaded. The phone gave no indication that it had been delivered, but neither did it give me the little red message saying it had bounced. I frowned at the screen and waited, but nothing changed.

Clenching my teeth, I growled. "Where are you?"

My cell rang. I gasped, thinking my voice message had gone through successfully after all. Until I read the number. It was the headmaster.

I lifted the phone to my ear. "Basil?"

He dispensed with greetings and got down to business. "I've just gotten off the phone with a Neapolitan inspector. How are you?"

I was freaking out, but I didn't think he'd appreciate hearing that. "I've given a statement to the police. I'm still on the street where Gage was taken. I haven't been able to get through to Ryan. What's going on there?"

"I've spoken to Angelica Wendig, so they know that Gage has been taken. They will connect with the police. They're in the middle of their busy season and have a whole bunch of events and bookings they have to cancel, but they'll be on the soonest flight to Naples they can manage. You won't be alone for much longer. Have you talked to your own parents?"

"Not yet. There hasn't been time, but I will. As soon as I figure out what to say. My mom is going to want me to come home."

"She'll understand that you can't though, right? Not until Gage is found?"

"Yes. But what should I do? I can't sit around the villa waiting for the police to find him, or for the kidnappers to get in touch with the Wendigs. I have to do something."

"I don't think the kidnappers are going to get in touch with the Wendigs," Basil replied. "I don't think we're dealing with someone who wants money."

My head snapped up as he voiced the suspicions that I had been unable to convey to the police. I sidled into the shadow between buildings, away from the noise of passing traffic.

"I don't think so, either. Dante and Gage met yesterday."

Basil was quiet for a moment. "And how did that go?"

"Dante mistook Gage for Ryan, so they've obviously met, or at least, Dante has seen what he looks like. Then I think he realized he was dealing with twins because he got up and left in a hurry. Here's my theory: Dante spotted Nero and Ryan, just like Enzo said, he took the rubbing from Nicodemo's things—"

"Rubbing?"

"Yes, Dante said the parchment was a rubbing, it's text but in an ancient language that he couldn't read. If that rubbing is of interest to Nero, then Dante will trade it for assistance in acquiring fire."

"So Dante was still a natural when you saw him?"

"Yes."

"That's good. You can't forcefully take a mage's fire, it has to be given. Ryan will never give up his fire, but maybe they think Gage could be... convinced."

Hope surged in my chest. "Exactly, and when they can't convince him, they'll let him go."

Basil was quiet so long that I thought our connection had been cut. Then he found his voice. "Why would they let him go?"

I felt like someone had swung a marble tile at the back of my head. My breathing came in shallow. "You think they'll kill him if he doesn't play along?"

"I don't know this Dante kid, Saxony, but I do know

Nero. You think they'll just shake Gage's hand and let him walk out of wherever they're keeping him?"

"No, but if Ryan is part of this, he won't allow them to hurt Gage," I croaked, feeling slow.

"Are you sure about that?"

I wasn't.

"Has Ryan responded to you?"

"Not yet. Gage told me that he found out Ryan was in the process of trying to get a visa for Iran."

"Iran?" Basil sounded surprised. "So he might not even be in the country?"

"Maybe not. That's probably why my messages aren't getting through. Can you come? Please?" My voice quavered.

Basil let out a long breath. "I can't tell you how much I wish I could, but the Agency is in full-blown emergency mode. I've learned that this most recent snuffing is not the second but the third. It's affecting more mages than I feared possible. We're setting up a database now to compile the numbers who've lost their fire and it's not looking good."

The hair on my forearms lifted into spikes.

"Reports are pouring in, all of our resources are being redirected, which is why I can't leave yet. One of our superior officers has been working on a digital map. When a new report comes in of a fire that has gone out, they input the data with a view to pinpointing the date of the snuffing and the location of the mage. Now that we've got the cooperation of agencies on every continent, who are also inputting data, what is emerging is a very interesting pattern."

"What pattern?"

"It's better if you see it for yourself. Along with

securing security clearance to share our latest intel on Nero with you, I have permission to share the live map. You'll find login information and a link in your email. We expect to have an app ready to download within the week where it will be easier to watch the progress."

"That's... amazing," I said, impressed at this nimble reaction the agency was able to muster in the middle of such chaos.

"It is, but I fear the heroic efforts being made by our mages and ex-mages is not enough. We still don't know why the fires are going out, and if we don't know why then we can't stop it. There's a feeling like the ground is crumbling beneath us."

"Does it have something to do with the orb Ryan gave Nero? It must."

"I believe so but I am having a difficult time convincing my superiors. The old legends don't hold much credibility."

"I didn't know you had superiors. Didn't you start the Agency?"

"I got it off the ground, yes, but I don't run it. I'm just a member of the board. I don't have authority when it comes to operations. If I can't convince them that the relic has something to do with what's happening, then they'll never redirect resources, especially with our ranks running so thin."

My mind spun like a carousel and I felt like I was trying to breathe in hot soup. Pressing my back against the cool stone wall behind me, I slid down to sit on the paving stones in the alley.

"Tell me what to do, Basil," I breathed. If I didn't have an order, I wouldn't move from this spot. I felt paralyzed and overwhelmed.

"When you're finished with the police, go straight to your villa. I would suggest you move out right away, but there's a chance Gage could free himself and if you move and they've taken his phone, he won't be able to find you. Sit tight for now. Do you have a WiFi connection there?"

"Yes."

"Good. Go into your email first thing and look at the map I'll send you access to. It will help you understand the scope of what we're dealing with. Make note of any patterns. It will be difficult, but try not to let it upset you. You'll want to contact some of your friends. Keep it to a minimum. The agency's hotline is being bombarded already so try not to alarm anyone unnecessarily."

I sucked in a breath and began to squeeze my temples with my fingers. It felt like my heart had taken up residence in my forehead. Why was Basil talking about my friends? Who had lost their fire? "What about Gage?"

"I'll send you the intel on Nero I have permission to send, but you'll have to wait for a login for an encrypted site. An agent will call you through that site. I believe our best chance of recovering Gage is to find Nero."

I pressed my back against the wall and got to my feet. Looking both ways as I stepped into the street. The police were standing beside their smart-car drinking coffee. I resisted the urge to make a face at them as I headed for the villa, happy at least for a task to focus on. "Okay. Thanks, Basil."

"Things are moving fast. I'll be in touch again soon."

RETURNING TO THE VILLA, the first thing I did was check my email for the link from Basil. When it hadn't yet come in, I turned on an audible notification, stripped off my clothes and stepped into the bathroom for my second shower of the day, more from a desire to wash off the horrific events than from any need to be clean. With hot spray pounding the back of my neck, I dropped my head and closed my eyes.

Wherever Gage might be I hoped he had water. The longer we went without contact, the more likely it was that Gage had been taken for his fire, not for his money.

I turned off the shower and got out, wrapping myself in a robe. As I was drying my hair, my inbox chime sounded from the kitchen. Not bothering to dry properly or dress, I scampered across the cool tile floor. Clicking on Basil's email, I opened his link and followed the prompts to download the Agency's proprietary software. While it downloaded, I hurriedly scrubbed my skin dry, pulled on a pair of shorts and a tank top, and spiraled my wet curls up into a topknot. I slid into the chair as the software finished downloading.

I installed it and input the username and password Basil had provided. A map of the world against a black background blinked into existence, borders and coastlines marked with a thin, pale gray line. Tiny individual lights scattered across the land masses in clusters, the way city lights looked from an airplane window at thirty-thousand feet on a clear night. My jaw went slack as I studied the backlit speckles. There had to be fifty-thousand of them. More lit up as I watched, concentrated around urban areas but occasionally in the middle of black, rural zones. I staggered under the realization that all of these individual lights represented magi whose fires had been snuffed. The sheer number of them made my vision blur as blood drained from my head. My hand drifted to cover my mouth and I stared, horrified, as tiny lights were added to the map with every second that passed. This was the intel trickling in from the agencies that were partnering with Arcturus.

When the shock wore off enough to think, I used the mouse to hover over a cluster of lights. Small boxes popped up in a menu down the right-hand side containing information connected to the lights I was rolling over. Some lights had full names and nothing else, some had names and a date. I noticed after some moments that the majority of dates were either March of this year or December of last year. A few were listed as July, from the snuffing that had just taken place. Some boxes had a birth date marked. Some lights had no helpful information attached at all, just three little flashing dots, indicating that intel was yet to arrive.

My eye was drawn to the island of the UK where clusters were concentrated in London, Edinburgh, Manchester, and other large cities. A few lights were scattered throughout the rest of the country. Rolling my mouse over these, I froze as Liu Xiaotian's name popped up.

Liu had lost her fire. Liu was Burned. So Burned magi were not immune to what was happening. I shivered as I continued to roll the mouse. Any hopes I had been resting on immunity to the snuffing thanks to my Burned status went up in smoke.

Names flashed before my eyes, and I began to pick

up on the pattern Basil mentioned. Not all, but a majority of the names looked to be of Asian descent. Noticing this in the UK prompted me to take the mouse across the world to the Asian countries, where clusters of lights congealed around urban centers. Rolling over these revealed a majority of Asian names with a few non-Asian names mixed in. Impatient to understand, I drew the mouse to the other side of the world where clusters of lights were gathered throughout the Americas. Rolling over these names revealed more information.

A higher concentration of December dates appeared when I rolled over the magi in South America, and there was a correlation between the Asian names and the July snuffing. It was a loose pattern, not completely consistent.

My eye was drawn to the little island of Japan, and the groups there. My stomach dropped as I thought of Tomio. Hand shaking a little, I rolled over the clusters there, dreading the appearance of Tomio's name. It didn't pop up, but there might be too many listed for me to stumble over his entry by chance.

Noticing a search bar in the upper left-hand corner, I clicked on it and typed 'Tomio'.

A long list of Tomios appeared, eliciting a squeak from me. But my heart calmed as I scrolled down the names and did not find any combination of 'Tomio' and 'Nakano'.

Still. Basil had mentioned I might want to call friends for a reason.

I liberated my phone from my bag and dialed Tomio as I checked the time and made a quick calculation. It would be almost seven pm in Tokyo. It rang twice and then clicked as Tomio picked up. From the light sound of his voice, I knew his fire had not gone out.

"Saxony? Hey!" He sounded delighted to hear from me.

"Hi." I let out a long breath as some of the tension eased out of my neck and shoulders. "You sound well."

"I am. Even better when I saw your name come up on my caller ID. After you updated me about Eira and the games, I wasn't sure you wanted to have anything to do with me until the school year started again. How are you? Man, I'm happy to hear from you."

He was grinning. I could hear it in his tone. I closed my eyes, dreading that I was about to wipe that grin away.

"You've still got your fire, I guess," I said, clearing my throat.

Tomio paused. "Yes. Why? What's happened? Are you okay?"

"I still have mine too, but lots of magi don't."

His voice turned breathy. "More fires have gone out?"

"Yes. I'm surprised you haven't heard anything about it over there. I'm looking at a map Basil shared with me. The agency is documenting who has lost their fire and where they are. A lot of them are Asian, Tomio. More than half. That's why I called you. I was worried —" I gulped and forced myself to slow down.

"Basil shared Agency intel with you?"

"Because Gage has been kidnapped. I'm in Naples, by the way."

Dead air. Then, incredulously: "Back up. What?"

"I'm sorry, Tomio. I'm doing a terrible job communicating. Are you sitting down?"

"Well, I am now. Holy shit-balls, Saxony. What is going on over there?"

Tomio listened while I caught him up. When I got to how Gage was taken around the same time Basil learned about more fires being snuffed, he interrupted me.

"I'm coming. Sit tight. I'll be there as soon as I can."

I stuttered in shock. "What? No. Th-that's not why I called."

Impatiently, and with a grunt of annoyance: "I know that, Saxony. But first of all, Gage—one of my best friends, or at least he was before I snogged his girl—has disappeared. Second of all, you're all alone there without any help from Basil, while I'm hanging out in the sun playing chess with my auntie. I'm wasted here, so I'm coming. I'm already looking up tickets."

I could hear his fingers flying over a keyboard in the background. "Are you sure?"

"Don't be stupid. This is an emergency. If I were you, I'd be getting on the phone to some of those elemental friends of yours and looping them in."

"They know I'm here."

"Do they know Gage is missing?"

"No, it just happened. I've barely had time to wrap my own mind around it."

"Do Gage's parents know?"

"Yes. Basil told them. I don't know how long they'll wait to come, it might depend on what the police suggest."

Tap, tap, tap on the keyboard in the background. Tomio sounded almost gleeful that he had something exciting to do. "Right. How about Ryan?"

"I tried calling him but couldn't get through so I

sent him a voice text. He hasn't responded. I can't tell if he's received it or not, but Gage said he was trying to get a rushed visa to visit Iran."

The tapping paused. "That's interesting. Why?"

"I have no idea but it has to have something to do with Nero."

Something thumped in the background, followed by a zipping sound. Tomio let out a long growl of frustration.

"You okay? What are you doing?"

"I just broke the zipper on my luggage. I have to go. I'm having butterfingers. I'll call you back as soon as I've booked my ticket."

We said goodbye but I kept the phone against my ear and didn't hang up until Tomio did. Hearing the sound of him on the other end gave me comfort. When the line went dead a feeling of abject loneliness washed over me, but incredibly, Tomio was coming, and the knowledge that I wouldn't be alone for long would tide me over until he arrived.

As I studied the map further, my thoughts turned to my mom. She'd never been happy about what had happened to me, even after I'd told her that I felt it was destiny that I had become a mage. I wondered if she'd be happy if my fire was snuffed. And how would I feel to return to the ranks of the natural? It would be weird, having become accustomed to having such power at my fingertips, only to have it disappear overnight. Maybe it wouldn't be so bad to go back to regular life, except that Akiko, Georjie and Targa had—in their own way—gone through this with me. I'd feel left out if I returned to normal.

Closing my eyes, I tuned in to my fire. It was quiet,

banked and waiting to be of service, my ever-present companion, my battery of heat and energy. Shivering, I opened my eyes, not wanting to think about it too hard. I didn't have the emotional stamina to explain everything all over again, especially to my mom. Better to leave them out of things for a little while. I'd rather call them when I had a resolution to share, not while trouble was mounting. All it would do was stress them out, they might even get the crazy notion that they could be helpful and get on a plane the way Gage had, the way Tomio was doing. I couldn't have that.

I also didn't have the fortitude to bring Georjie and Targa up to speed just yet. We'd shared a long video call before I'd left England, each of them taking a turn explaining adventures they'd recently been on, trouble they'd recently been in. Targa had been to Atlantis and Georjie had visited a fae-dimension she'd called Stavar-jak. They'd each faced life-threatening circumstances on their own and had prevailed. Not that I'd have been able to help them immediately even if they had asked for help, I'd been engaged in finals at the academy, and then the Fire Games.

I was one of a trio of powerful elementals. They'd been strong, even when mostly—or in the case of Georjie, completely—on her own. Targa had broken a curse and Georjie faced down that hellish sounding witch. No one had come to their aid, even when they'd promised to. I could be strong, too. It was my turn to buck up and use my powers for what they were meant for: taking on bad guys, and winning.

SEVEN

NO ANSWER IS AN ANSWER

The next time I found myself at the Naples International Airport it was mid-afternoon instead of dawn, and I was sick of the place. I couldn't shake the feeling of being watched. It seemed a suspicious character stood at every corner, looked down from the upper-floor railings, and lurked at the exits like haunted spooks. I moved away from small crowds to stand out in the open where no one was at my elbow, a tricky thing to pull off in such a busy place.

When Tomio emerged from the arrivals gate carrying a backpack and pulling a medium-sized rolling duffle-bag, I hardly recognized the look on his face as pleasure. I flew at him. He wrapped his arms around me and I squeezed back as I scoped out the faces of those behind him.

"Come on." Releasing him, I grabbed his hand and pulled him toward the parking lot on the south side of the terminal, elbowing my way through the crowd in a decidedly un-Canadian way.

"Nice to see you too, my flight was fine thanks,"

Tomio said as I dragged him along. "Don't you just love those new Dreamliner models with the tinted windows? Man, they are so cool, so roomy. And they say the upgraded ventilation system helps a lot with jetlag, though I've never had a problem with that myself. Would have been nice if they'd asked me ahead of time if lentils give me gas, though. I would have been able to warn the nice lady beside me—" Tomio prattled on until I stopped beside a small, red Fiat and popped the trunk. He finally stopped rambling when he saw my wheels.

"You rented a car?" Tomio lifted his bags into the tiny trunk.

"The Agency arranged it. Don't trust the cabbies anymore. Get in and buckle up." I commanded, sliding behind the wheel. He slammed the trunk and got in.

I piloted the Fiat out of the parking space before Tomio even had the door closed. Ignoring his side-long glances, which said he was wondering if I'd lost my mind, I guided the car onto the autostrada, noticing he hadn't fastened his belt yet.

"Seatbelt, please," I said with a glance at the rear-view mirror.

Tomio looked over his shoulder at the road behind us as he pulled at his shoulder-strap and fixed the belt into place. "Are you okay? Whoa!"

Dodging a semi-truck and slipping between two vans and into the fast lane, I dropped into third gear, angling for the Vespucci exit.

He twisted in his seat. "That was a sixteen-wheeler back there, not a dog-sled!"

I changed lanes to pass a laboring Mercedes spewing fumes. Tomio grabbed the handle above the door and shrank down like a dog about to get smacked as I took a roundabout a little too fast, eyeballing a black SUV with tinted windows as it swung across my rear-view mirror. More than one horn blasted as we exited the rotunda.

"I think you've spent too much time in Italy," Tomio muttered, cringing as I swerved too late to miss a pothole. There was a crunch beneath the car. Someone beeped.

"Italians use their horns just to tell you they're there," I said as we zipped along Via Nuovo Marina, the Bay of Naples looming large on the left.

Tomio watched the window as we flew by a white Audi with a disgruntled driver. "Are they also telling you to have a nice day when they flip you the bird?"

"Ha ha."

"Seriously, Saxony. This is a side of you I've never seen. Sam Hornish Jr. called. He wants his driving back."

"Who is that?" I geared down as the back of a yellow van with its brake lights on loomed in front of us.

"One of the most dangerous NASCAR spring cup drivers of the decade. His career is peppered with crashes and exactly zero trips down victory lane."

"You like NASCAR?" With another glance at the rear-view, I guided the Fiat onto the narrow Via Ernesto Capocci. Finally convinced we were not being tailed, I slowed down to thirty and swerved to avoid a trio of pastel colored Vespas carrying tanned, laughing tourists.

"Not particularly, but my dad's brother was a mechanic so I grew up around it." Tomio relaxed and gaped out the window at the old buildings as we entered the historical center of Naples. "Wow. If you ignore the little piles of dog shit on the sidewalks, Naples is really pretty."

I nodded. "Parts of it are. Especially the bay."

Tomio lowered his window and rested his elbow there as I took another turn, closing the distance to the villa. His head turned back and forth as he took in the highlights of Neapolitan life. "You're allowed to park on the sidewalks?"

"And facing the wrong way."

"Viva l'Italiano."

The villa had a small underground parking lot whose entrance gave the Fiat about two inches of clearance on either side. I parked the Fiat and turned off the engine. Tomio scraped the back of his hand across his upper lip, wiping off a bead of sweat.

"You okay?" I unsnapped my seatbelt.

"Just dandy." He forced a toothy grin and two thumbs up, asking a question in a voice higher pitched than his usual. "Where did you learn to drive like that?"

"Go-kart racing with my brother, RJ."

Getting out, we retrieved Tomio's luggage, locked the Fiat and took the narrow set of steps up to the villa's rear entrance.

"Makes sense," Tomio said as I took out the house keys and unlocked the heavy bolts. "I'm glad driving here doesn't seem to be a problem for you but I might need to change my shorts."

I laughed, stepping through onto the tiled landing and holding the door open for Tomio. Closing it behind him, I bolted it. I set my purse on the table near the door along with the Fiat's key fob. The sound of someone cutting grass began in the distance outside. It was a sound that reminded me that even though my world was in tatters, normal life was going on all around us.

"What *is* a problem, is that Gage has been taken, the police are useless, the Agency is in an uproar, and I've failed to convince Dante to abandon his maniacal plan." I blew out a long, shaky breath. "Thank you for coming."

Pressing my back against the door, I looked Tomio in the eyes, finally taking the time to really look at him. My heart began to slow now that we were safely home, but then tripped for a different reason as his dark eyes locked on mine.

"You don't have to thank me, Saxony. I'd never be able to look myself in the mirror again if I hadn't come. Gage is... was my best friend, and you—" He trailed off, raking a hand through his thick black hair, which he'd finally had cut.

I didn't ask him to finish whatever it was he was going to say about me. I wasn't sure I was ready to hear it. Kicking off my flip-flops, I moved toward the kitchen where my laptop sat open on the small round table.

Leaving his luggage at the door to deal with later, Tomio followed me into the joint kitchen, dining and living room. Making himself at home, he opened and closed cupboards until he found the glasses. Taking out two, he went to the sink, but paused. "Is the tap water safe to drink?"

I nodded, sinking onto one of the wooden chairs.

He filled two glasses and sat across from me, sliding one toward me. Tomio took a sip of his water, looking at me from over the rim. "So. How are you?"

The question was loaded with inquiry, filled with innuendo suggesting Tomio wasn't just interested in my state of being and frame of mind, but my thoughts about our relationship.

I wanted to tell Tomio what I'd learned from the kiss that we shared, but it felt wrong to be talking about it when Gage was missing. I was saved from having to answer when my cell phone chimed that a text had come in. Digging my phone from my pocket, I stared at the screen. It took me several moments to understand the meaning of it.

"It's Ryan," I murmured, showing the screen to Tomio.

He squinted at it and read the message aloud. "Nice try." He looked at me. "What does that mean?"

"It means he thinks I'm lying about Gage going missing, that I'm trying to trap him, I guess."

Tomio shook his head. "What an idiot."

"Yep." I set my phone down. "I should be thankful he even got back to me, I guess."

"So what's next?"

"Basil said he'd call me this evening, so I guess we're waiting for that."

"Does he know I'm here?"

I nodded. "I told him you were coming. He was happy."

"You know things must be crazy at the Agency when the best they can have at ground zero is a couple of teenagers who don't know what the hell they're doing." Tomio downed the rest of his water.

It was only now that I noticed the puffy skin under his eyes. "Are you tired? There's a freshly made bed in the room on the right." I didn't need to tell Tomio that Gage had occupied that room, slept in that bed.

He nodded and moved to leave the table. "You'll wake me when Basil calls?"

I agreed, and watched him disappear into the bedroom. I checked the time on my phone and re-read Ryan's two word text.

Nice try.

Did he really think I'd fake a kidnapping to get back in touch with him? It really showed that Ryan had no idea who I was and how I thought. He was projecting himself onto me, and wasn't that what narcissists did? They think everyone is as capable of deceit and manipulation as they themselves are. What a world Ryan must inhabit, one where no one can be trusted and everyone is most likely lying.

I typed out a response.

This is not a joke. Your brother needs you. By the time you pull your head out of your ass and take me seriously, it may be too late. It may already be too late. The police are useless and the agency can't send anyone to help. It's just me and Tomio. That's all Gage has. I know we have never seen eye to eye, but if you really love your brother, then you'll drop whatever it is you're doing and help us.

I hit send before I analyzed it any further, watching as it was delivered and read a few moments later. Wherever Ryan was, he had proper cell service now.

Three dots flashed on my screen. He was typing a response.

I watched and waited, holding my breath to see if I'd convinced him. We desperately needed Ryan to be on our side. But did he believe me? He didn't know what I knew. That more fires had gone out and the agency was crippled. Would he think I made that up, too?

The three dots stopped flashing but no message came through. Ten minutes later, when there was still no reply, I figured I had my answer.

EIGHT
CLEARANCE ACQUIRED

Less than one hour after Tomio went for his nap I received a text from Basil telling me to check my email. Waking my laptop, I found a fresh link to the map with the simple explanation: *Security clearance raised to level 4. Logout and login with updated information.*

Using the new username and password, I logged in to the map application. The updated map had three noticeable differences: There were many more illuminated dots concentrated mainly in urban areas, there was a small box in the upper right-hand corner containing a keypad. And on the left side of the screen sat a file folder entitled *Surveillance.*

A red dot surfaced above the keypad, flashing with the words 'incoming call'. Figuring it was Basil to explain the Surveillance folder, I rolled the mouse over the dot and clicked on it.

A man's voice I didn't recognize came through the computer's speakers delivering accented English.

"Hello? Saxony Cagney? This is a secure line, you can speak freely."

"Hello, this is Saxony," I replied, leaning toward the computer. "Who is this?"

"My name is Mehmet, I've been assigned to debrief you and aid you in helping recover your friend. Let me say first how sorry I am that this happened. The timing of it is especially terrible. If this had occurred last year, I would be at liberty to serve better."

Movement in my periphery drew my eyes to Tomio, who'd emerged from the bedroom, probably woken by the voice. He sat on the chair beside mine, studying the computer screen. His hair stuck up at the back. I couldn't resist patting it down.

"Nice to meet you Mehmet. I'm here with my friend Tomio. He came to help us rescue Gage."

"Yes. Basil told me you had a friend there and he has also been given clearance."

"Hello, Mehmet," Tomio said. "You're from the Agency?"

"Yes. My role for the last six months has been to collate and study surveillance footage of one Nero Palumbo, living in Naples. Mr. Chaplin told me that you're aware of the current crisis among the magi—"

I smiled. Someone who said 'magi' the same way I did.

"—that fires started going out in batches, starting last year. At first the agencies treated it as a one off, a phenomenon affecting a group of magi we are still determining the size of. When it happened, the initial reports led us to believe it had affected one percent of our population worldwide. A tragedy for some, to be sure, but not one of epidemic proportions. By the time the second incident of permanent quenching occurred, we had reached four percent with the first group. It became clear to us then that we were dealing with something much more serious than was at first understood. We directed more resources to its study, hence the map. The second incident sent us into code-red, and the third... well, you may be able to imagine something of its effects. We've lost half our new recruits, a third of our assets, and all of our projects have been disrupted. Those who can still focus well enough to work are clinging to self-control, in spite of psychiatric recommendations to retreat and convalesce."

Tomio and I shared horrified looks throughout this speech, though it was delivered in the calm and reasonable tone of someone who'd been trained to deal with a crisis.

"But I don't want to draw focus to this issue with your friend missing, I only wanted you to understand the broad strokes of why the Agency cannot better aid you. Let's move on."

"Thanks for the update, Mehmet. One thing before we move on, I was just wondering if you've been personally affected by the... quenching?" I asked.

He answered baldly and bluntly, without emotion. "I have. My fire went out with the most recent batch."

"I'm sorry," Tomio said before I could form the words myself.

We exchanged another glance. It was unreal how calm he sounded, and that he'd been assigned to help us over someone who had not been affected.

"Thank you," Mehmet said. "It's an interesting thing. Though our world is in chaos and there is a lot of fear running amok, those who have been personally affected by the snuffings seem to fall firmly into one of two camps. They either succumb to a mental and emotional breakdown, or they find they are not as adversely affected emotionally as they might have guessed they would be. I fall into the second camp, perhaps because for the first time in my life, I am learning what it is to live without pain. I'm not without grief, but it's not at a level where I must be dismissed from my work. Surveillance does not require the use of our fire, so I'm happy that my supervisor has allowed me to continue, though I have to check in with agency doctors twice daily and I'm not allowed to leave a designated area until they are convinced the risk of a breakdown has passed."

"How long before you're allowed to travel?" I asked.

"I couldn't say, but I can tell you that I'm on the clock for this call and have yet to give you the pertinent information. Shall we move to the matter at hand?"

Tomio and I agreed.

"For the purpose of this call, I have remotely taken control of your screen," Mehmet said as the map disappeared and the folder expanded and opened, the pointer moving of its own accord.

A series of files appeared, laid out neatly on the screen and captioned with a date and a short descriptor.

"With the lack of contact from any supposed kidnapper there in Naples, we can safely move the case into a different category. The intelligence you provided to Basil, including the meeting that you've had recently with Enzo Barberini first, and then his son Dante, together with the improbable timing of events and the transition of an artifact from the Wendig family to Nero Palumbo, we have reason to suspect your friend's disappearance may have been orchestrated by either the Barberini family or Nero himself. Even more likely,

Gage was disappeared by conspiracy of the two families working together. Do we have a similarity of under-standing?"

"Yes," I said.

Tomio got up and began to pace, listening with his brow wrinkled. "But when you say 'families' are you suggesting that we're dealing with a family of Palumbos and not just Nero?"

"I'm using the term family loosely here," Mehmet explained as he scrolled through the files on the screen. "We don't know who he might have helping him, whether they might be of blood relation or merely hired hands. It's safe to assume he is not acting alone however, because we understand Nero travels frequently and for long stretches of time, anywhere from three weeks to six months before he returns home. And with the mention of 'home', I have struck upon the biggest challenge you face. We have one known address in Naples for Nero Palumbo, a flat in Portici, but this flat serves mainly as his place to receive mail, sometimes as a bedroom and storage facility. We already know that your friend Gage has not been taken to this flat as we monitor all comings and goings and have already exam-ined the location with a heat camera. There has been no movement at this location since last month."

As Mehmet spoke, he opened files of photographs and a few video clips of an apartment building, first from overhead, then from street level. The building was only a block from the Bay of Naples, but the coastline was unlovely, with docks and industrial buildings breaking up stretches of otherwise pebbly beach. I would have described the neighborhood as one step above a slum, with very little green space and no personal gardens at all. Outdoor terraces were cluttered with clothes racks and laundry, tattered patio furniture, and litter boxes. Every door and window had robust iron bars protecting the glass. Many had rusted looking old-fashioned air conditioning units perched on thick window ledges. The roads were narrow and clogged with parked cars, even on the sidewalks, leaving barely enough room for a pedestrian to pass. Naples had pretty areas but this wasn't one of them. Portici was particularly unattractive, in spite of its proximity to the bay.

"So this apartment is not somewhere we should look? Is that what you're telling us?" Tomio asked, pausing at my shoulder to study the photos of Nero's Portici flat.

"Yes, that's what I'm telling you."

"Sorry, can we back up for one second?" Tomio asked. "Why is it that the agency didn't arrest Nero for the murder of Bellamy Chaplin a few decades ago?"

"I had wondered the same thing," I said, "Basil said there was never enough evidence to convict him, and international law is protective of a supernatural's privacy."

"That's right," confirmed Mehmet. "We also maintain the 'innocent until proven guilty' tenet of our natural counterparts. We are permitted to observe Nero's behavior when he happens to pass within view of our cameras, but we don't have a warrant to actively surveil him."

"How about now, though? With fires going out and Gage missing, surely you can get the warrant we need?"

"I'm hoping we can, but until I get that warrant, you cannot make any move to approach him. You can tail him, but only because you're not an employee of the agency, and you didn't hear it from me. Your movements won't be restricted by the Agency, you can go where you wish and verify my claims for yourself, but I think it would be expedient for you, and of course for Gage, that you trust my words on the matter and not waste time looking where he's unlikely to be."

"If he's not at that location, you must have some idea where else he could be?" I asked.

"Ah, here is the rub. We believe Nero has a secret location underground. You might not know that forty meters beneath the historical center of Napoli and beyond lies at least one hundred and seventy kilometers or more of subterranean throughways. Included are air-raid shelters, cisterns, an aqueduct, caverns, and even an ancient theater and museum. Tourists can visit a small portion of the Napoli Sotterrenea, but most of it is off-limits. Some is privately owned. One hundred seventy kilometers is the official and public number, but we are aware of an additional twelve kilometers that is not accessible and appears in fact to be walled up from the rest. We have not been given permission by Italian authorities to go down there, so officially, we can't."

Silence hung heavy in the air as his implication became clear.

"But we can?" Tomio put a hand on my shoulder. I lay my palm over it, heart beating rapidly.

"Officially, you can't either; however, a couple of high school tourists straying off the approved path in search of artifacts or rare photographs, not knowing any better, might achieve something that the Agency cannot. Individuals not employed by the Agency need not be fettered by the same red tape and bureaucrazy that usually complicates relations."

"Did he say bureaucrazy?" Tomio whispered.

Mehmet chuckled. "A word of my own invention, pardon. When you work in the intelligence business you quickly become frustrated by the number of permissions and restrictions one is forced to navigate. There is a perception in the outside world that agencies like ours can move through the world with impunity. I can tell you that the opposite is true. We are more constrained and monitored than the average organization, and intelligence is also an industry." He cleared his throat and opened more photographs.

"So, how do we get down there?" I asked.

"There are a few ways. You could join a tour group and wait for an opportunity to become lost, but this strategy is higher risk since you'd be involved with a tour operator. You'd have to rely in part on an operator who was slack enough not to keep a head count throughout the tour, a rare thing, given that these operators are very competitive and need positive reviews for their businesses to thrive. An operator who loses two patrons would not only lose good faith, they would be open to having their license revoked."

Tomio sat down in the chair beside me. I thought I could feel excitement radiating from him. "Do you think we could bribe the operator to turn a blind eye?"

"This is Italy. You can bribe anyone to do almost anything you want, but again you'd be involving at least one other person, and the more people aware of what you're doing, the more risky the operation becomes."

"What's the other option?" I asked.

Mehmet opened a photograph of a very old looking chapel squashed between hulking buildings. It had a tall black-lacquered door with a thick lintel, and an inscription over the door in ancient Latin. "This is the Cappella Sansevero. It contains priceless artwork and is a hot-spot for tourists. In the basement, among other articles of interest, is a section that has been under construction for many years. Progress there has been extremely slow. One might almost conclude that there is a force who does not want to finish the reconstruction at all."

A new photograph opened, this one showed a line-up of tourists waiting to get in to the chapel. Approximately central to the photograph was a man in a leather bomber jacket. His face was directed down, so we could not see the details of his features, but a sharp widow's peak made him stand out from the crowd. A plume of smoke drifted from his mouth and clouded his ear. The tourists around him also had plumes of exhaled condensation and were engaged in conversation ahead of and behind the loner.

The skin on my forearms prickled and I knew without having to be told that I had just laid eyes on Nero Palumbo.

"This photograph was taken in January on a particularly cold day, as you can see. There was even some frost reported on the top of Vesuvius that morning," Mehmet explained.

A new photograph opened, also of a line-up in front of the chapel, with an entirely different set of tourists, but with the same Nero Palumbo as the lone figure. This time he was looking at something off to his right and we could make out a strong Romanesque profile with generous lips and a hooked nose. Dark curls were tied into a short pouf at the back of his head while sunlight glinted off nearly black hair. A cigarette balanced casually between a thumb and a forefinger was either journeying to or from his mouth.

"A mage who smokes," Tomio murmured in wonder. "That's a first."

"We suspect the smoking is less about an addiction to nicotine than it might be about a compulsive behavior that calms him. If I were to hazard a guess, I doubt he inhales. It may be a tactic to appear normal, the way a mimic might do."

"A... mimic?"

"Yes. Aliens that appear human on the outside in order to move about the world..." Mehmet trailed off as though he could see the looks of shock on our faces. "Never mind. That's outside the scope of this conversation."

Mehmet opened more photographs of the same location, taken at different times of the day and in different seasons. "As you can see, we've established a pattern here. At first it appeared to us as though he just had an affinity for the art in the chapel—it is spectacular. Then we began to notice that a little over half the time, we would fail to catch him leaving the chapel. This too became an established pattern, until we surmised that he was leaving, but not the way he went in. There is a rear exit, which we have only photographed him leaving through on eight occasions, but two of those occasions were not on the same day that he was photographed going in. That is why we have pinpointed this chapel as an access point. We have documented much of Nero's movements throughout the city and we believe this chapel is by no means his only access point, but it appears to be one of the most often used ones."

"You think he took Gage underground?"

"I am as sure of it as I can be without photographic or videographic evidence."

Tomio and I exchanged a chilled and determined look.

"Then I guess we're going underground," I said.

PART TWO

SUBTERRANEAN SUBTERFUGE

NINE

BENEATH NAPOLI

Mehmet directed us to an image of a franken-map of the subterranean city, which he'd compiled himself by patching together what was available to the public, bribing a city worker for a few private maps from the city, and overlaying the power grid and waterways both ancient and modern. All known entrances and exits were marked with tiny stars while dead-ends were marked with a tiny x.

When I asked him how exactly Tomio and I were supposed to find Nero's secret lair in a timely manner when there were millions of square meters of tunnels and more yet to be discovered, he gave a dry chuckle I didn't love the sound of.

"I can only give you my intelligence and where I would look based on what I know. Nero's above ground movements seem to revolve around a handful of locations. One is the chapel, another is Portici, another is the airport, and another is the Vallone San Rocco and other unnamed catacomb entrances. If I were you, I would search the tunnels that are marked with dead-ends. If you decide to go down at night, then the chapel will be closed." He pointed out a short alley not far from the chapel. "Use this entrance instead. It's the one the tour operators use. If you're good at reconstituting metals, then no one will know you were ever there. The gate is locked with a padlock and chain."

He used my mouse to mark what he thought were the best places to search once we got underground. When he circled an area with a small skull-and-cross-bones with the word *Pericoloso* beneath it, I asked what made the area dangerous.

"Gas, apparently."

"You've circled it, though."

"Yes. The gases would be sulfuric and you should be able to smell them long before they become dangerous to you. Plus, magi are able to cope with gases and fumes that humans can't, so don't let it worry you."

My anxiety levels had climbed anyway, although I cheered immensely when Mehmet showed me a photo of Nero boarding a small plane and told me that he wasn't in the country—and that he'd left alone.

I wasn't all that fond of going into the earth. It helped to go out and get supplies with Tomio as the sun was going down: a backpack, some sandwiches and water. Mehmet directed us to a trustworthy printer who produced the map in eight pieces of paper we had to tape together.

We decided going down at night was the best option since the sun was setting and we were eager to get moving. The underground was big, but with Mehmet's help, we were hoping to locate Nero's bunker, or whatever it was, by morning. We crawled into bed at 8:30 p.m., with Tomio setting his alarm clock for 11:30 p.m. My imagination decided to keep me awake, thinking up all the things that could go wrong. Who needs sleep before an all-night expedition? I tossed and turned until I heard Tomio's alarm then threw back the covers with a frustrated exhale. It was time to go.

Carrying backpacks and wearing black jeans, black ball-caps and black tank-tops, we stepped out into the hot, humid night. The historical centre after dark was a busy, vibrant place. Young men stood in groups on street corners, laughing and joking with each other, smoking cigarettes and whistling at girls in scanty summer dresses. The young women expressed a spectrum of emotion at this attention, from outright disgust to thinly veiled pleasure. Scooters buzzed along sidewalks, street dogs barked at one another, warning each other to stay out of territory that didn't belong to them. Street cats slunk between legs and narrowly dodged the wheels of passing cars and motorcycles. Late-night vendors bellowed about their offerings: sizzling, steaming panini or fresh-squeezed succo di frutta.

Weaving through the busy streets with Tomio at my back, I felt eyes linger on me, some friendly, others not so much. One dark-eyed youth barely old enough to grow a full beard stared baldly at me as we passed, dragging on a cigarette. He scanned me from the top of my red ponytail and baseball cap to the black sneakers I'd bought from a street vendor. After a quick squint-eyed glance at Tomio, he punched out a sound meant to get my attention.

"Eh!"

We ignored him and kept walking.

"Perché indossi i pantaloni? Eh! Bella ragazza?"

My Italian had rusted to near-useless in the year that had passed since I'd been in Venice, but I had enough to know that he wanted to know why I wasn't dressed in flimsy summer clothing, like the other girls.

Black clothes blended in at night, but I wondered if we should have worn something more weather appropriate until we arrived at our destination. Too late now. The wardrobe I'd chosen to keep attention away from us had done the opposite.

"What did he say about your underwear?" Tomio hissed into my ear, miffed.

"Pantaloni is pants, not panties. Don't worry about it, just keep walking."

Since we'd opted to use the tourist entrance and not the chapel (which was closed anyway) for the Napoli Sotterranea, it was a half-hour walk from our villa, hidden in a short dead-end street sandwiched between four major tourist attractions: the Royal Palace, the Galleria Umberto I, the Teatro San Carlo, and the Maschio Angioino. Mehmet had shown us other entrances, but we'd chosen this one not just because it was the closest to the villa and we could reach it on foot, but because attention would be diverted away from the Sotterranea's entrance.

The main attractions were illuminated and bristling with street vendors and buskers working hard for their euros. Traffic flowed past the shadowed dead-end as Tomio and I slipped unnoticed down the short passage to the entrance gate.

A stone face making a surprised expression, its lips forming a perfect 'o' shape, heralded that here was where intrepid souls could descend forty meters below the city streets to experience a world 2400 years old, isolated from but connected to the world above. According to the tourist information, sixty percent of the city sat above this hidden world, with thirty percent still unexplored.

It took me moments to melt through the heavy chain sealing the gate, while Tomio used his body to block my fire-light from passersby. Using a little fire-power to heave the crude, wrought iron gate open, I held it for Tomio and closed it behind him. I reformed the chain just enough so that it wasn't hanging open. Within a few seconds of descending into the pit of darkness, we lit fires in our hands: living hand-torches. The temperature dropped as steadily as the noise from the traffic and people above, leaving us insulated by the cool, stone womb of one of Italy's oldest cities.

Ahead, hanging in the gloom and reflecting my fire-light, hung a WWII era bomb, a prop. It made me shiver.

"Why do I always end up underground?" I mumbled.

Tomio was too far back—probably awed by the environment—to hear me, but he either saw or sensed my unease. He hurried to catch up, his sneakers soft on the stone floor. "You okay?"

A natural might have asked if I was cold after witnessing a shudder like the one I had but Tomio knew better. A powerful feeling of gratitude that he'd flown all the way to Italy on a moment's notice to help, gripped me. I'd already thanked him for coming, several times, but I wondered if he'd ever understand just how thankful I was not to be alone.

Keeping my hand-torch to the side so I could see, I

followed the tunnels leading through caverns. We talked quietly even though we were alone.

"The last time I was underground—"

"Right." Tomio was close enough to squeeze my arm. "Ryan."

Moving forward through the darkness, we passed a collection of staged props from WWII including a soldier's outfit complete with helmet, boots and trench-coat.

"Yeah. And the time before that—"

"Dante."

"Exactly. Good things don't happen underground, in my experience."

"Maybe the third time's the charm."

Tomio then waxed long on just how charming this third time underground could be as we moved through the aqueduct section of the tour, passing displays of dusty children's toys and even a collection of plants with hydroponic lights above them. The lights were off for the night, but the air was rich with moisture and the plants were obviously happy enough down here, their leaves brightly colored and springy with good health. A long row of unlit candles sat clustered together on a shelf. The room with the plants ended with a damp passage so narrow we had to turn sideways to go through it.

Tomio's chatter kept me from thinking too hard about just how many tons of rock loomed over our heads, and how the walls of this tunnel were so close I could hear the sound of my own breathing bouncing back at me.

After Tomio had painted a picture of us success-fully rescuing a perfectly healthy Gage and giving the

Agency the coveted exact location of Nero's secret hide-away, he launched into telling stories about his child-hood. Though many of them featured martial arts, the easy sound of his voice and his humorous storytelling style distracted me until we reached a cistern where we could break past the borders of the tour. To our right, the tour continued around the cistern and up a set of stairs. To our left, a narrow roped off exit led who knew where.

Tomio eyeballed the small exit dubiously. We'd have to duck our heads to pass through it. "Should we check the map?"

Nodding, I shrugged off my backpack and unzipped the small front pocket. Being taped together meant the map was fragile so we squatted and laid it open on a dry spot on the floor to study it with our fire-light.

"There's where we came in." Tomio pointed to the entrance marked on the map with a black bar. Following the tour's trail, which was marked in blue ink, we located the cistern we were currently standing beside on the map, then the exit leading to the stairs which delivered visitors back to the street. The little passage sat almost directly across from the stairs, but no markings on the map told us what we'd find after we entered it.

We drank water as we discussed the options. There were a series of the dead-ends Mehmet spoke about not far from the cistern on the map, but no clear way to reach them. We'd passed other potential exits on our way to the cistern, but they were even further from where we needed to get to, so heading back didn't feel right. We decided to give the narrow passage a try and hope for the best. If it failed to connect us, we'd have to come back.

Tucking the map back into its pocket and hooking my backpack into place, I ducked into the narrow passage, following Tomio's fire-light.

It was not a dead-end, but led us through more of the same types of caverns, aqueducts, and squeezy tunnels that were part of the tour. The difference with these though was that they were dirtier, wetter and creepier. No one had staged these spaces nicely for paying tourists. There were no lovely potted plants or battery powered candles for the taking. The ground was rough and uneven and dotted with puddles. My sneakers were soaked by the time we broke into a place that was so unexpectedly different it made Tomio and I look around in a kind of dazed amazement.

We'd been dumped out into a massive cavern with ceilings as high as a church. Beyond our torch-light was more gloom but it seemed like this broad, high-roofed way went on for a long time in both directions.

"Was it a road?" Tomio wondered as we roamed back and forth, staring up at the square columns arching overhead.

"It's big enough for two cars to pass, so maybe. I think this might be that thick part on the map from which all those dead-ends branch off."

With one knee in the dust, I laid out the map to inspect once again, trying not to let my imagination overwhelm me. This big gloomy expanse of darkness was almost worse than the narrow passageways. Something made a scratching sound in a distant corner and Tomio lifted his fire-light for a better look.

"Likely rodents."

"Probably." Did rodents come this deep underground? The crafty rat was more likely to make his home where there was plenty of garbage and discarded food scraps to feast on than in the deep, dark, uninhabited bowels of the city. But what did I know?

Tomio suspected we'd moved too far south and should continue up the 'road' to our right. I thought we were in the block Mehmet had marked as being a main artery for a spate of those juicy dead-ends he'd recommended we'd focus on, which meant we should move to the left. In the end, I convinced Tomio I was most likely to be correct because he'd been sleep-groggy when we had the meeting with Mehmet and I'd been clear-headed.

After a standing snack of cold panini and more swigs from our water bottles, we headed down the dusty road of darkness in the direction I'd chosen.

We were rewarded for this choice when we passed a collection of neatly lined up wrecks of vintage vehicles. Pre-1950s cars, trucks and motorbikes sat side by side in forgotten heaps of broken glass, rusty metal and moldering fabric. To see such current manmade items in such an ancient setting gave me a kind of cultural vertigo.

After the second batch of abandoned vehicles we found our first off-shoot. Exploring it together, we found it was a dead-end, confirming that I'd been right with my guess. If we kept moving along the big road, we should hit a lot more of these off-shoots.

We examined every square inch of the first off-shoot, discovering not so much as a crack in the wall or a loose stone that could be jostled out of place. Moving to the next and the next, we found more of the same. The off-shoots had their own clusters of dusty museum pieces, everything from piles of twisted children's bicycles, to old bed frames and the skeletons of springy mattresses, warped beyond recognizable shape.

One dead-end hosted a cistern very similar to the one near the end of the walking tour, but otherwise the dead-ends were just that. Solid walls. No exit, no entrance, no shirt, no shoes, no service, thank you for coming.

As the night wore on and our exploration remained fruitless, I felt weariness creeping in behind my eyes. When Tomio announced with a yawn that it was almost three a.m., I figured it was time to double our productivity.

We agreed to split up, but stay close. We would leapfrog one another and study the dead-ends alone. Though I dreaded going into the creepy blackness without Tomio, we'd never be out of shouting distance. So we continued in this manner, and as the time closed in on five a.m. I'd lost count of how many dusty dead-ends I'd run my eyes and hands along.

I paused to take a drink of water, but an excited shout from Tomio shot my heart into my throat and my legs into a sprint.

TEN

UNDERGROUND SWIM

Sliding around the corner of Tomio's dead-end, I saw him standing at the end, his hand-torch held high. His fire cast a glow toward the ceiling, revealing a series of cracks weaving between the broken bricks. Tomio was staring upward but when I followed his gaze I couldn't see anything special. Cracks might be interesting if we could reach them, but these were high up. Too high to be an access point for a person.

"What is it?" I gasped, panting from my run.

When Tomio turned his head to look at me, it was like a chilly breath blew across the back of my neck. He looked pale in the dark, and his eyes were wide with shock. He raised a finger to his lips, then put it in the air, pointing toward the cracks.

"C'è qualcuno?" asked a rusty sounding female voice.

I jumped like a freaked out cat and just barely kept in a shriek.

She sounded like she was coming from inside the wall. My heart began a steady gallop as I craned my neck to look for some opening through which the voice was drifting.

"Ciao?" She sounded like a young woman, albeit a tired one on the edge of tears. "Ho visto la tua luce," she said.

She was saying she could see our lights. This woman was afraid, she needed help. What the hell was she doing down here? I hadn't found my voice yet and Tomio hadn't spoken either, afraid to fully give ourselves away. But instinct and her tone told me that this woman was no enemy, she was not a trap.

She spoke louder this time. "Per favore aiuto!"

"Parle ingleze?" I forced a calm into my voice that I did not feel.

"You are American?" I heard a windy laugh of disbelief, followed by a dry cough. "Yes, of course I speak English. Who are you?"

Her sound changed, like she'd moved closer but had to go higher in the process. In the gloom it was difficult to see what were cracks and what were shadows.

"Keep your light on," I told Tomio. "I'll climb up to her."

I kicked off my shoes and raked off my socks, tucking them into the toes of my sneakers. Shucking the backpack, I dropped it on the dusty floor and took off my baseball cap so I could see better.

"We will come up to you," Tomio called. "Is there a hole near you? It sounds like it."

"Madonna, there are two of you." She gave another dry laugh. "Yes, there is a place here."

A scratching sound overhead was accompanied by a scattering of dust falling around us.

Tomio lifted his fire to send the light further up the

wall. Movement small enough to belong to a mouse drew our gazes to a crack between stones where something emerged and retreated.

"How did you find me?" she asked. "You cannot be polizia. Did my father hire you?"

Hooking my fingers into the shallow crack between stones, I sent my fire into my grip and used slow-burn to pull myself up the wall. Toes hot and hard, fire oozing into my limbs and digits in smooth and fluid motions, I ascended to the place I'd seen movement and brought my eye level with the crack.

At first, I saw nothing, then she shifted and a pale shaft of light illuminated an eyeball staring back at me.

"How long have you been down here?" I asked.

The eye blinked and she took a moment to respond. "Then my family did not send you. Otherwise you would know that I was taken from the university three years ago."

I almost fell off the wall. I stared at the shadowed eye and it stared back at me.

"We're looking for a secret place," I told her. "The place of a dangerous man."

"You've found what you were seeking," she replied. "I was taken by a dangerous man. I have been forced to work for him these last three years."

"Nero?"

The eye widened and bobbed up and down as she nodded. "What is your name?"

"I'm Saxony, and my friend below is Tomio. You?"

"My given name is Johanna but I've gone by Janet since I was a little girl. Janet Silvestri."

Heat fluctuated through my body as I clung to the

wall like a spider, holding myself steady enough that I didn't lose view of her eye.

"How do we get you out of there?"

She murmured, "I suppose it unlikely that you have a combination for the door, otherwise we would not be talking through the wall."

"Combination? No."

"Then you must go through the water."

"What water?" Then I thought of the cistern we'd passed and a lump formed in my throat. "The cistern?"

"Yes. It's the only other way."

My belly gave a sickly drop. "But it must be six hundred meters from here."

"I wouldn't know," she replied.

"Do you know how we can get through the water?"

"I can't tell you. I wasn't conscious when I was brought down here, but sometimes when he arrives, the door with the code does not open. I listen. I know all the sounds by now. I hear him walk across the room in wet shoes. I cannot tell you how the water leads here, but I know that it does."

"What is she saying?" Tomio said. "I can't hear."

My mouth felt pasty and I desperately needed another drink of water.

I looked down at Tomio. "Give us a second." I looked back at Janet's hopeful eye. "Do you know when he will return?"

"No. But it won't likely be soon. It could be in several weeks or even months."

"Okay. We will try to find a way through the cistern." I began to move away.

She gasped with a sudden cry of panic. "Please, don't give up. Don't leave me here. You're the first hope

I've had in three years that I might see my family again."

"We won't give up," I promised, suppressing the urge to hyperventilate myself. Just the sound of her fear was contagious. "Is there anyone else in there with you?"

"No. I am alone."

"Did Nero bring any other captives to this place recently? Maybe for a short time and then took them away again?"

"Captives? No. Not that I heard. Why?"

"We're looking for a friend of ours who was taken."

"Ah. I am sorry."

I nodded. "I'm going down now. It might take us some time to find you, but we won't give up."

"Good luck," she said, hesitantly, like she wanted to say a lot more but didn't want to hold us up. "Thank you."

Fire sliding across my back and down my legs, I retreated down the wall, dropping the last several feet to the floor. I eyed Tomio's shadowed features, the worry line between his brows made deeper by the fire-light.

"What did she say?"

"You're not going to like it."

TEN MINUTES later we stood on the edge of the cistern, looking into the large square pool of dark water. Cracked and broken mosaics on the pool's bottom mingled with rough scale and pebbled concrete. It wasn't particularly deep but neither was it inviting, in spite of the lazy current that kept it from stagnating. A longing for Targa squeezed at my heart as we looked around for diving equipment or places it might be stored. No dice.

The pool edge was lined on two sides by a crumbling edge of brick and stone. The rest of the pool vanished beneath uneven walls, broken by a set of stairs leading to an impassable doorway full of rubble. The sound of trickling water echoed through the cavernous room. Several yawning holes far overhead marked the places where, at one time, those living in the villas above would lower their water jugs to fill them.

Tomio and I kicked off our shoes and left our hats and backpacks on the floor. Our phones weren't waterproof so we zipped them into a pocket. Sitting on my butt on the edge of the cistern, I lifted my legs over and lowered my bare feet into the water.

"Cold?" Tomio tucked his wristwatch into a side pocket of his backpack.

"The temperature isn't what concerns me," I muttered, eyeballing where the water vanished beneath the wall as I waded in, chest deep, toward the right-hand corner. "You take the other side. Holler if you find a through way."

"How can I holler from underwater?"

"Come back and yell at me, obviously."

The water's surface rippled as Tomio got into the pool. It lapped at my torso. The smell of damp stones and minerals filled my nose as I approached the wall. Running my hands below the water's edge I discovered the wall ended at knee height. My fingers slipped around the edge and underneath.

"Here," I said, looking over at Tomio with my cheek pressed against the cold wall and my chin underwater.

At the other end, Tomio was running his own hands down the wall as he turned to look at me. "Here, too. The wall ends."

Feeling our way toward one another, we discovered that the entire bottom two feet of the wall did not exist. Tomio and I stopped when we came together and straightened, sharing a look of apprehension.

"Nero does it, so can we," I said. "Right?"

"Right." But Tomio cast his gaze doubtfully toward our feet. "What if he's boobytrapped it?"

I swallowed around the lump in my throat. "Why did you have to go and say that?"

His lips twisted into a wry, humorless smile. "Wouldn't you? If you were some psychotic mastermind bad guy trying to protect your secret lair?"

"I think you're giving him too much credit," I replied quickly.

"You're choosing to believe that."

"Yes, because otherwise I would never go cave-diving under a massive, ancient multi-ton wall with an end we can't see. What other option do we have?"

His eyes widened with hope. "The front door?"

"We don't know where it is and we don't have the code."

"Janet can tell us where it is. The door, I mean."

"We still don't have a code."

"But we have fire-power."

"But if we damage the door then we'll have given ourselves away and there's no coming back from that. Right now, Nero has no idea that we're here, that puts us at an advantage."

"Why?"

I spluttered. "What do you mean *why*? You're wasting time. You know why. You're the freaking battle strategist here, not me. Why do I have to explain—"

Tomio put a hand on my shoulder as an enlightened look appeared on his face. "Do you suppose he uses his fire to get through the water?"

"How do you mean?"

"I don't know. Like, boils it so it evaporates and lowers enough so he has an inch worth of air to breath to get through?"

"I don't know if you noticed, but the water here is chest deep."

"Yeah..."

"And the entrance is knee-deep."

"Yeah..."

"Where exactly is all this water supposed to go?"

He pointed a finger toward the hole in the ceiling. "Through there."

"You don't think all the steam emerging above us might attract attention? Plus it would take hours. We could have been out the other side by now if you weren't holding us up."

His expression went deadpan. "You're right."

"So we go?"

He nodded, taking a chest-expanding breath. "We go."

"Ok." I took a deep breath and was about to plunge under the wall when he grabbed my shoulder again. "For Pete's sake! What now?"

He templed his fingers together and tapped them a few times. "It'll be dark under there."

"Yes. And?"

"Can you keep a flame going underwater? Because I can't."

"You want me to make a torch?"

"If you don't mind. You lead, I'll follow."

"Fine. But I can't promise it won't go out." I had made fireballs underwater before but I'd never tried holding a flame steady.

"Just try."

"Fine." I took another breath and bent my knees.

"Wait!"

I let my air out on a groan.

"Should we go under with a rope? Tie it to something here so we can pull ourselves back if we get too far and there's still no air?"

"We don't have rope. We opted for sandwiches."

"There's rope up there." He pointed again to an old dangling jug.

"Will you quit stalling!"

He put up a hand, splashing water into my face and hair. "Ok, ok. Don't get your knickers in a bunch. Can you blame me? I'm fond of oxygen... and living. So..."

"So?"

He gestured to the submerged passage. "Ladies first."

I rolled my eyes but it was good-natured. Tomio's banter had actually worked to fortify my courage. I was just as nervous as he was but I believed that if Nero could make this swim, then we could make this swim.

I took a deep breath and held it. Just before water filled my ears I heard Tomio chanting, "Omigod, omigod, omigod," under his breath.

The cold closed over my head and soaked my hair. Hoping it would not sting, I opened my eyes as I sent fire down my arm and into my hand. Flames burst from my palm and fingertips, hissing and sizzling as they met with water. I quickly discovered that it took too much energy to keep a flame flickering underwater, but illuminating my hand to make a glowing appendage was enough to cast the shadows back and wasn't difficult to maintain.

Thrusting my hand under the wall, I pulled myself down and into the space. My ears made little popping sounds and I realized with a short moment of unpleasant panic as I pulled myself forward with my left hand, that the passage tilted on a slight downward angle.

My vision blurred but it was good enough to see the rough, algae-coated floor as it rolled past. Silt drifted along the stones with the current that brushed by my skin with a gentle caress. The splashes and trickles of Tomio entering behind me accompanied the audio of my knees brushing the floor. Tomio's hand wrapped around my ankle and clasped gently, letting me know he was following.

My glowing hand pushed the darkness back and back as we pulled ourselves forward and forward. I expected to see the stone surface above us disappear at any moment but instead two ghastly pale things emerged in the gloom to my right.

I paused, my lungs just starting to complain, to identify two human skulls. A low moan of horror rumbled in my throat. I felt Tomio's grip tighten on my ankle as he saw what I was seeing.

When the initial shock of seeing the skulls eased, I realized they'd been positioned to face one another. Beyond them, two more pale blobs hinted that another pair had been strategically placed. They were providing a grisly road through which we had to pass.

Tomio followed as I propelled myself between the two skulls, noting with no small amount of relief when I got close enough to make out the details, that they were Halloween props, not actual skulls. Still, what kind of weirdo were we dealing with?

The second set of skulls zoomed by as I picked up speed, feeling pressure build in my lungs and head. My chest was burning as we passed a third set of staring skulls. A black edge ahead told me the ceiling ended and relief rushed through me. Hooking my fingers over the edge I gave a fierce fire-enhanced pull, enough to speed myself and Tomio, who still gripped my ankle, toward the exit.

My head broke the surface as the light in my hand went out. Taking deep breaths, I turned toward Tomio spluttering in the dark.

"We're through," he panted. "I can't believe it, what kind of nutjob uses skulls for landmarks?"

"They're fake," I gasped, filling my lungs with air.

"Still."

When I'd recovered my breath enough to regroup with my fire, I lit a hand-torch and held it up.

I had to clamp my other hand over my mouth to suppress a scream.

We'd emerged into an arched catacomb lined with hundreds, maybe thousands, of grinning, staring skulls.

And these ones were not plastic.

Tomio and I gaped around, hair plastered to our heads and skin raised with goosebumps. I shuddered and waded toward the edge of the cistern, loosing a sound of disgust.

"They're old," Tomio said as he moved toward the stone lip and crawled out. "Too old for Nero to have put there."

"How do you know?" Getting out of the pool, I took my hair out of its pony and shook it out. It was too dark to inspect the skulls close enough to determine age, even if I'd wanted to, which I didn't.

"I don't, but it makes me feel better to think so."

Pushing heat into my skull and skin, clouds of steam lifted from my form as the water soaking my clothing and hair evaporated.

Tomio had to close his eyes and concentrate to do the same. His water steamed off in uneven clouds, starting in his torso and head, then moving down to his legs and feet. He opened his eyes and looked at me, starting to laugh.

"What?"

"Your hair."

I smiled and patted down the thick mass of frizz I'd created. Letting my hand-torch go out, I twisted my locks into a rough braid and fastened it with the elastic. Relighting, we discovered that the cavern of skulls transitioned into a large bricked room which ended with a set of dusty steps leading up to a doorless passage. A pretty herringbone pattern in the brick had been topped with horizontal bricks laid by some later civilization, the Greek style, followed by the Roman way of laying brick. They had each left their marks here.

Climbing the steps, we passed through the doorway and into a long, dark tunnel. Using hand-torches, we walked until the passage turned to the right, then continued on until it turned left. It went on in this zigzag way with no doors or windows or even holes in the walls.

Turning a corner for the umpteenth time revealed a source of low light and an end to the passage.

We emerged in a huge cavernous room with a vaulted ceiling that was a mashup between ancient and modern. A dusty desk and bookshelves occupied the wall to our left. But what was really curious was the way half the room had been divided from the rest by a thick wall of plexiglass. The plexiglass room had a clear door with a lock but no door handle.

Behind this glass was a doorway leading into another room. Also behind the barrier sat another desk, this one with a computer. There was also a bookshelf with volumes of texts both old looking and new, a table heaped with scrolls and other documents, and a rust colored office chair on wheels. A bare lightbulb hung over the desk but it wasn't lit, instead there were three other sources of light sitting on the desk, two kerosene lamps and one camp light that looked battery operated.

In the office chair sat a woman.

She stared expectantly at us with wide, haunted eyes. Her hair lay over her shoulder in a thick brown braid, the curl of its tail dangling at her waist. A red paisley kerchief covered her head, knotted underneath the braid, giving her a pseudo Rosie the Riveter kind of look. She was not very old, my guess was mid-thirties, but the dark eyes that stared back at us carried the weight of several lifetimes. She wore a thick, knit cardigan so worn at the edges that yarn dangled from the sleeves and the hem. A loose scarf looped around her throat almost covered the choker of wide amber stones she wore. She had neatly manicured eyebrows and finger nails, but no makeup.

Tomio and I approached the plexiglass and she stood up, nearing the glass on the other side.

"Janet." I put a hand on the glass.

She nodded and put her hand on her side of the glass, positioned exactly where mine was. She spoke in a voice that also sounded much older than her face looked, soft and accented. She was almost as pale as a porcelain doll, her naturally olive skin tone no doubt turned green from lack of sun.

"I can hardly believe you are real. I thought I hallucinated. Thank you for not giving up."

Tomio lifted his hands to the glass. "You might want to step back."

I was about to warn Tomio that there was a possibility that Janet didn't know about Nero's supernatural nature. But Tomio's fingers and palms were already glowing and she had not screamed or appeared surprised.

"Wait!" Janet patted both palms on the plexiglass, her expression urgent. "If you break through this glass, the security cameras will wake up and record everything."

We looked at where she pointed and saw two cameras had been fastened to the corners of the room, in the crooks where the walls and ceiling met.

Tomio lowered his hands. "They're not on right now?"

Janet shook her head. "He doesn't like to use the electricity unless absolutely necessary so he's set motion sensors that trigger the cameras if anything other than pre-mapped movements take place, like me moving around my rooms. Coming through the cistern doesn't trigger them because Nero believes no one would ever come in through the water."

Tomio's gaze darted back to her face. "Won't it alert the system if there are two of us?"

"Normally, yes. But he had someone down here with him before he left and changed the system not to go off at the presence of multiple people. He didn't reset it before he left. I can see how he sets his security system because he does it from there." She pointed at the desk which sat at the wall opposite her clear prison. She had a perfect view of the desk, but no way of ever reaching it.

"He doesn't care that you can see what he's doing?"

Janet shrugged. "Who can I tell? He knows it is cruel of him to hide the tools to my freedom where I can watch him put them away. But now, I can tell you that there is a key to my cell door in the drawer of his desk. Let him put that in his pipe and smoke it."

Tomio went to the desk and yanked open the drawer, snatching up the key with a sound of triumph. There was only one key on the keyring, a simple silver one.

As Tomio slid the key into the lock, Janet stared with the eyes of a woman who has seen the great gears of her destiny begin to turn in a direction she'd been powerless to incite herself. When the door swung open and Tomio stepped out of the way, she did not move.

"Come on, then. We won't bite," Tomio said.

Her chin wobbled with suppressed emotion. With a deep inhale, she stepped through the doorway. She looked at Tomio and extended a trembling hand. "Janet Silvestri. Nice to meet you."

Tomio shook her hand. "Tomio Nakano, nice to meet you too."

With shining eyes, she turned to me, holding out a hand. When I clasped her palm and felt her vibrating on the edge of tears, I gently pulled her into a hug.

Her skin touched mine and I was alarmed at how cool she felt. "Ohhhhhh," she sighed. "You are so warm."

She hiccupped as she melted against me. I held her until she signaled she was ready to let go. She stepped back, rubbing at her eyes.

"It's been a very long time since I've had human contact. It's incredible how much we humans need it." She caught herself and blinked up at me. "Does your kind need it too?"

I smiled. "Just as much as you do, yes."

"You must be desperate to get out into open air,"

Tomio said. "Is there anything you want to take with you?"

"Strangely enough, I am nervous to ascend. I've forgotten what life is like above. More importantly, since we are not in danger of being discovered, I would like to tell you how I came to be down here. Maybe my story will direct you to things useful in your search for your friend."

I was relieved, desperate myself to know everything, pick up any clue we could, understand who this man was and what he was up to.

"Who was the second person Nero had with him recently?" I asked, stomach tightening.

"A new partner. Nero never brings guests, only people he is working with. But recently there were two. Not at once. He brought one, then the other. The first one was a young man he introduced as Wendig."

"Ryan or Gage?" Tomio asked.

"I don't know, he never said his first name aloud."

"Did he have facial hair?" I asked, feeling my hands curl into fists. I forced them to relax, lest I alarm Janet.

"A little."

"That's Ryan. Who was the second?"

"Another young man, but he didn't introduce us. This one seemed about the same age as the first, only he was clean-shaven and had a ponytail."

"Dante. I know him." I looked at Janet, feeling an unpleasant sensation in my stomach. I put a hand over my tummy, hoping I didn't throw up my panini from earlier. "Did they discuss their plans in front of you?"

"Only partially. Nero and Wendig's plan involved me so they had to, but they also had conversations through there where I couldn't hear them." Janet pointed to a closed door opposite her plexiglass-enclosed office.

"Any idea where they are now?"

Janet gave a wry smile. "Based on the most recent discoveries in my work, I would guess that Ryan has gone to Iran and Nero is in Yangjiang, China. If things went well there, he may already be on his way to Australia. I can't speak to Dante's whereabouts."

Questions circled my head like a swarm of irritated ravens. As important as it was to us to rescue Gage, Janet was also in trouble and needed to be returned to her life and her family. But breaking her out of here might mean losing Gage forever, since she was the only connection we had to Nero, who had no idea we were here. Plus I still had to find a way to get Dante to go home. Before we left this place, we needed to understand more.

Stalking across the room, I grabbed the office chair from under the desk and rolled it over to the bench against the wall so we could sit facing one another. "I think you'd better take us back to the beginning."

"I WAS BORN Johanna Silvestri in 1991 in Salerno," she began. "My parents nurtured a love of history both modern and ancient, but came to love ancient history the most, specifically ancient languages. I attended the University of Rome's history program. My university schooling was heavily slanted toward classical Greek and Roman but I wanted more, I wanted to study the exotic, jeopardized, or unknown. When I graduated, I applied to attend a competitive post-graduate program run through a private school in Novilara that would feed my hunger. It was a dream come true when I was accepted. There, I was able to submerge myself fully in the study of ancient linguistics. I dreamed of working for a well-funded museum whose interest lay predominantly in deducing the origins of ancient languages and preserving endangered languages, if such a role could be found."

I tilted sideways to stretch my back. My exhaustion was gone thanks to the excitement of finding Janet, but my body was tired. "How many of these rare languages are there? One would think that by now we've discovered everything there is to discover."

Janet shook her head, eyes wide. "Not remotely so. The more we discover, the more we realize the huge gaps in our understanding of history. Artifacts are found on a daily basis that baffle historians, I've known some professionals who retired from pure overwhelm and frustration. Yes, there are many languages and cultures we can classify, we can say this belongs to such and such era, but there are just as many items who appear not to belong in any known family but must be classified in a group unto itself. This work is why I am here."

Tomio shifted to a cross-legged position on the floor, a posture I guessed he found comfortable thanks to all his years spent in a dojo. He was nodding. "I know what you mean. In Japan we have an indigenous group called the Ainu who were unlike any of our other ethnic groups."

"Exactly." Janet punctuated her words with a finger to emphasize. "The Ainu are both culturally and linguistically different from the Japanese and are said to have migrated to your country as far back as fourteen-thousand B.C. Ainu is very endangered. Only a handful of people in the world, including me, know the language because it has no written form."

"So you're an expert with a rare set of skills, but what are you helping Nero to do?" Tomio leaned forward and braced his elbows on his knees.

"Don't jump ahead, we don't know yet how she ended up down here," I said.

Janet shot me a grateful look. "Thank you. It's been so long since I've spoken to anyone but Nero, and I've never been able to speak my story out loud. I've written it down, of course, but this is the first time its coming out naturally."

I was amazed at the pure control over her emotions she was exhibiting. "You're doing perfectly."

She smiled wistfully. "I cried all my tears a long time ago. I made things very difficult for Nero in the beginning, but eventually accepted my fate. Nero has agreed to release me when his goals are met, but honestly, I don't know what would prevent him from just killing me, so sometimes I draw out the work longer than it needs to be. Isn't it funny how one can go from suicidal despair back to viewing life as precious. Even a life like this." She gestured to her clear cage.

I'd never been suicidal, but I'd had my own turn on the dancefloor with despair so I could relate in some small way.

Janet looked far away, lost in a distant memory. "I don't know how long he searched for the right candidate. I think he probably narrowed in on my school first and then chose a target, someone who excelled at language analysis, which I do. He even set up what I know now was a fake interview."

Tomio's jaw dropped. "What a snake!"

"I was excited because I thought he worked for the Louvre. He brought me three very interesting artifacts, all of which contained some form of ancient writing. He wanted me not only to decipher them, if I could, but to present any connections they made with other cultures. I was so absorbed in the task I did not think to ask him for credentials or grill him about his own studies."

My mind immediately jumped to the orbs Basil had been trying to recreate in the studio below his office. "What were these artifacts?"

"A stele, a small statue, and a scabbard overlaid with gold. They were beautiful, but it did not take me long to identify their sources as North Picene, Vinca, and Etruscan."

"You had seen the languages before?"

"Yes. All three of them had obscure and disputed origins. He told me he had work for someone like me, if I was interested. Of course, I was. When the interview was over, he told me he would call. He never called. Instead, he took me from the campus late at night the following week. I don't even remember being taken, which is why I suspect he used chloroform. It can cause amnesia. I woke up here. Not in this side of my cell, but through there." She turned and pointed to the door at the end of the narrow galley that functioned as her office.

"What's over there?"

"The rest of my space. I'll show you." Janet got up and led us through one of the doors. This room had been divided into two sets of living quarters. A plexi-glass box with a locked sliding door had been installed mid-way up the wall dividing the space. It was where he would have passed supplies through to Janet.

Instead of an office, here was a larger space that functioned as a kitchen: a hot-plate and a mini-fridge, as well as a small sink and cupboards. She twitched aside a red fabric curtain to reveal a pantry full of dried goods.

"I have all kinds of lentils, beans, dried fruits and nuts. I can sometimes make a guess for how long he will be away based on how much dried food he gives me. He always gives me too much, though. I never run out before he gets back. Not so far."

"Doesn't he give you anything fresh to eat?" I asked. Dried fruits and nuts were fine but after weeks or months of them? I would have major bathroom issues.

"Oh, yes. When he is in Naples, he brings me a lot of fresh fruits and vegetables. When he's not here I make spirulina and vitamin smoothies."

"How kind of him," Tomio said wryly. "And he even gives you a nice comfy bed to sleep on." He gestured to a dingy pallet with a thin mattress, a stained pillow, and a collection of small, square cushions that looked scratchy.

"I don't sleep there. Not anymore. I'll show you where I sleep now." She led us through another door opposite the one we'd just entered. Tomio followed Janet and I followed Tomio, which was why I crashed into the back of him when he came to an abrupt stop.

"No," Tomio breathed. "You sleep in a sarcophagus!?"

"What?" I peeked around Tomio to see another room divided by a plexiglass wall. There were two entrances for this room, the one we'd just used, and the one behind the clear barrier inside Janet's cell. Behind the plexiglass and against the far wall sat a large, thick-walled black box with a lid propped open and leaning against the stones.

Janet laughed. "It does look like that, doesn't it? It's a lead-lined box."

Upon a closer look we saw bedding inside. These linens looked much newer and cleaner than the ones on the pallet in the kitchen. Janet pointed out the slits along the sides. "Those allow air to come in if I put the lid down. That is how I saw your lights." She gestured to a hole in the wall above the lid. "He had it made for me after he returned from his second long trip abroad. After he came back... different." Janet's expression looked faraway as she remembered something.

My skin prickled at her expression. "Different how?"

Her gaze cleared. "When he went to Brazil, he was gone for five weeks. When he came back, I began to notice that if he came too near me, I would feel strange. I would get a mild headache and sometimes I would lose my appetite. Then he went away a second time in January. He was gone for even longer."

"Where did he go that time?" I asked, tearing my eyes from the crazy coffin-bed.

A place called Karunagappalli, in India."

"What is he doing when he travels?"

"I don't know exactly. I know he looks for things, artifacts of interest, because he always brings back more items for me to study. But when he came back from India, the sick feeling if I was too close to him for too long was worse. He began to bring me tinctures and more green vegetables to eat. He brought me ingredients to make the vitamin-rich smoothies. He gave me this to protect my thyroid." She put her hand up to her throat where a pretty choker made of amber snugly encircled her neck. "I'm not sure it actually does anything but I wear it because he seems to think it does. He brought in the lead-lined box for me to sleep in whenever he is home. It is actually much more comfortable than the pallet, so I sleep in it even when he is not here."

"He acts like he cares for you," Tomio observed.

"His motives are purely selfish, like someone else we know," I muttered.

Janet agreed. "She is right. He is nice to me, but only because I have the skills he needs. Without me, his work would take much longer. Maybe it would never get done. He is protecting my health because if I am not feeling well, I'm not productive."

"But, are you saying that when he comes back from these long trips, that he returns *radioactive?*"

"It appears so," Janet replied. "I'm a scientist of sorts, though I don't work in a lab and my specialty is ancient technologies, specifically languages. Without tests, I couldn't say for certain that he returns radioactive, but he seems to think he is dangerous to me, and I don't disagree. The lead-lined box and the tinctures, mushroom lattes and algae smoothies do make me feel better, as disgusting as they sound. He even provided me with a light to boost my vitamin D levels because it has been years since I've seen the sun. I am certainly not as healthy as I would be if I were a free woman living the way I please. I miss swimming in the Mediterranean more than I can say. But when I ask for something, Nero does his best to supply it for me, and I'm doing work that I love. I find reasons to be thankful."

Tomio blew out a long, slow breath at these words.

She nodded like she knew what he was thinking. "I have to keep positive any way that I can, otherwise I would commit suicide."

"You never thought of it?"

She waved a hand. "In the beginning I threatened it, though I had no easy way of doing it. I had only a bed and the toilet and shower that is through there." She pointed to a curtain similar to the one covering her pantry. "Nero made all of my meals because at that time, he lived down here permanently."

"You mean, he never went out?"

"No, no. I just mean he never took long trips. He went out for shopping and maybe to socialize, I don't know, but he slept and worked down here alongside me in my cell. In the early days, I don't think he knew exactly what he was looking for, he just wanted to understand the world's ancient cultures and stories. But as he found artifacts and made connections he seemed happier, until one day he brought me a sheet of scribbles and asked me to decipher it."

"A sheet of scribbles?" I blinked at her. Up until this point I had thought everything was about artifacts.

"Yes, something it looked like he wrote himself, on a regular sheet of note paper. I thought it was very strange too, but he's done it twice more since then."

"What did you decipher in the scribbles?"

"It was just a collection of words that had no meaning when strung together, but I eventually connected one of them to an endangered language of Brazil. Come on, I'll show you."

Janet led us back to the original room and went to a set of rickety looking wooden drawers. She opened one and rifled through it. "Nero made all this furniture himself, if you can believe it. He salvaged bits and pieces from the underground."

"How did he build your cage?"

"That, I don't know. It was here before me. Here we are." Janet pulled a crinkled piece of paper from the drawer and handed it to me.

I took the lined A4 sheet feeling incredulity mount. "Nero did this?"

"I assume so. I've never seen him do it. Strange, isn't it."

"Very." Tomio moved closer to look over my shoulder. "What does it mean?"

"It's meaningless, just a garble of words and phrases that when put together are nonsensical. The first time he gave me one like this to analyze, I thought he'd lost his mind, or that maybe it was a psychological experiment. When I did the second one, I realized that he didn't care about the content, he cared about the language."

"The others he did were different?"

"Completely. As different as French is from Korean. The only thing they had in common was that I didn't recognize them as anything I had come across in my studies before."

"He produced an extinct language and had no clue what he was scribbling?"

"Precisely. Then he needed me to make a connection with a language that either exists today or is documented well enough in our history to pinpoint a place of origin. It took me a while, but Nero provided me with a computer program that helps. This one I was able to link most closely to Kaiwa, in Brazil."

"That's why he went to Brazil?"

"That's right. Last November."

"And he came back different."

She nodded.

"How does he make these scribbles?"

"He never produces them in my presence," Janet said, but her eyes narrowed. "But I believe they have something to do with the orbs."

I felt my jaw go slack. "Orbs..."

Janet held out a cupped palm to indicate the size. "Yes, he has these strange old orbs, very ancient, I suspect, though he never allows me to handle them. I don't know where he finds them, but they are precious to him and he is always excited when he gets one. They were clearly made by the same artist. They are the same but also unique from one another, like a collection of paintings in the same series."

"How many of these orbs does he have?"

"After the one Wendig just gave him, he has three that I'm aware of."

Seeing the look on my face, Janet's own expression changed. "What do *you* know about these orbs?"

"Not enough. I wish now I'd grilled Basil for more details but there hasn't been time between the fiasco with Ryan, and the games."

Janet cocked her head. "Games?"

"Yes, never mind, they're not important. Do you know what Nero is?"

Her lips twisted. "You're not referring to his psychopathy, I presume. Yes. I know that he is a 'mago del fuoco'. I also know that his partners are crazy to trust him."

"What makes you say that?" Tomio asked.

Janet held up a finger. "First, he comes down here with Wendig, Ryan as you call him. Ryan has traded him an orb in exchange for mentorship and a piece of whatever wealth or power Nero is in pursuit of. He sends Ryan away and takes the orb in there, where I cannot see what he's doing." She leveled her finger at the closed door across from us. "He returned later with scribbles, which he gives to me to decipher. It takes me hours to learn that the scribbles are another unique language but is clearly the basis of two languages, an old form of Gilaki, and Tabari. Though I delayed sharing this information with him for a few days, which was as long as I could get away with before he grew angry with me."

"Galaki and, I've already forgotten the other..." Tomio murmured.

"Tabari. Caspian languages spoken only by people in a region of Iran called Ramsar. Nero's scribbles appear to be a root language that broke into at least two other languages, many centuries ago."

"And Nero sent Ryan there because..."

She raised her palms and lifted her shoulders. "My guess is that they suspect another orb can be found there. Following Ryan's departure, Nero brings the other boy here."

"Dante," I grumped.

"So it appears. Dante has a rubbing taken from a stele. Nero gives this to me for analysis. The language on the stele points vaguely to a language spoken in a province of China."

"Yangjiang."

"Correct. As soon as Nero had this information from me, he left for China."

"And do you know what Dante is getting in return?" I asked, bracing myself for the answer.

Janet bobbed her head. "Nero will help him acquire fire."

It was not news, it was exactly what I had suspected, but somehow hearing it from Janet's lips made my heart skip a beat. I looked at Tomio and could see the same horror reflected back at me.

"Whose?" he asked hoarsely.

It took me a second to find my tongue. "I think we both know the answer to that."

TWELVE
EMERGING

"Got everything you want to take?" I asked Janet as I bent to snap a photo of the locking mechanism on the front door. It was an antique combination lock, the kind you saw on old-fashioned safes in caper movies. Nero must have filched it from somewhere and installed it in a thick metal sheet to build a makeshift vault door. It was one detail of many that I'd photographed for Basil once Tomio and I had retrieved our gear from where we'd dropped it.

Tomio and I had left the hideaway through the front door, leaving Janet to go through her things, and then Nero's things, putting whatever she wanted to take with her into a pack. It took us an hour, but when we were able to identify our location on the map, it was a matter of retracing our steps to the cistern we'd swum through to retrieve our backpacks. We double-checked that we'd marked the map correctly as we returned to Nero's hideaway, where the door had been left propped open. The agency was going to want to know exactly where he'd been hiding all these years and if we couldn't give them good directions, Basil and Mehmet wouldn't be impressed.

We returned with an apology ready on our lips for taking so long to get back. I'd been worried Janet would get frightened we'd left her alone, but she was rummaging through Nero's desk and barely looked up.

"Is it weird that I want to take everything," she said, looking around like a woman who'd just stepped into a dream, "and nothing, at the same time?"

"I don't think it's weird at all," Tomio replied as he slid Nero's scribbled pages into a zippered freezer bag Janet had given him. He put them into his backpack along with a few smaller artefacts we'd found.

"You're bound to have mixed feelings," I said, standing by the door to signal I was ready to leave. "I would. You're proud of the work you did here, even if it was for a madman."

"That's part of it. I wish I knew what he's doing with the information that surfaces."

"Basil or someone at the Agency might be able to shed some light on it," I suggested. He's talked about ancient legends about the origins of the magi, but he's never gone into them in detail. It's high time he did."

Janet walked through the front door more slowly than I would have guessed someone who'd spent three years here as a captive might have moved. I let the door close and lock behind us and she jumped but didn't look back. Tomio lit his hand-torch and took up the lead as we headed into the narrow tunnel curving to the left.

"I'll never get used to seeing someone produce fire like that," Janet murmured.

"Does it freak you out?" Tomio asked over his shoulder.

"Not anymore, but I'm not sure my parents will believe me when I tell them that we share our world with fire magi."

It was on the tip of my tongue to tell her that fire magi were only one species in a plethora of supernaturals, but maybe now wasn't the best time for it. The mention of her parents had lifted an unsettling thought, one I hesitated to give voice to.

I noticed Tomio checking his watch. "What time is it?"

"Six forty-five," he muttered as he sped up. "Not good. Sun is coming up. We'll have to be extra careful when we leave."

It took us far less time now that we knew where we were, but we still had several kilometers to go and Janet needed to stop and rest a lot. Her legs weren't accustomed to so much walking. When she started asking for breaks every ten minutes, Tomio and I shared a look of dismay.

"Sorry, Janet," I said with an apologetic smile as I fired along my limbs to strengthen them. I put an arm behind her back and one behind her legs so that she knew that I was going to pick her up. The tunnel was wide here so there was room enough for me to pass without bashing her head or feet against the walls. I thought she might protest but instead she just gave a breathy laugh as I swept her off her feet.

"You can't," she said, even as she put an arm around my neck to hang on. "You'll tire too quickly."

"You don't have to worry about that," said Tomio, already heading down the tunnel at a near jog.

"I've carried much heavier than you for much

longer," I told her, trying not to jostle her too much as I kept up with Tomio.

"You're so warm." I felt her give a shudder in my arms.

"Too warm?" With fire sliding up and down my limbs and giving soft pops of power in my joints, I should have considered that my body temperature might actually be too hot to carry a natural very far.

"No, but you might put me to sleep. I'm not used to so much activity."

"If you can sleep, I'm all for it," I said as I recognized that we'd entered a section in the guided tour. "I'll wake you up when we get there."

Again, that uncomfortable thought about Janet's family niggled at the back of my mind, and again I squashed it down.

"What's that?" she asked with a wondering tone as we passed a neatly organized collection of props.

"They give tours down here." Tomio explained. I could hear the strain in his voice and caught him glancing at his watch for the umpteenth time. It was getting late. The city streets would be getting busy. Our window of opportunity to escape the underground unnoticed was shrinking.

"Seriously? People come down here for fun?" Janet sounded horrified.

"You didn't know? You're from Naples aren't you? They've been giving these tours for decades now. Look!" Tomio let out a breath as the stairway we'd taken to get down here came into view.

"No, I was never interested in the tourist attractions, I always had my nose in some book or computer program." Her grip around my neck tightened. "Are you sure you can carry me up these stairs?"

"No problem," I told her, "just tell me if you get too hot."

Janet felt like a loose collection of bones in my arms. I wondered what it had done to her health to be living on vitamin smoothies and getting vitamin D from a lamp. I felt torn between despising Nero for what he'd done to her, and grateful that he'd afforded her some way of maintaining her health, even if it had been purely selfish.

Directing the fire into my legs and back, I took the steps two at a time to keep up with Tomio. When we reached the top, Tomio put up a hand for silence as he peered out the front gate. After judging it safe, he melted apart the chain, pushed the gate open and slid through. Stepping into a shadow along the nearby wall, he beckoned for me to come out. A sign proclaimed that the first tour of the day started at eight-thirty, it seemed we'd squeak by before the tour employees arrived.

I slipped through with Janet, then put her on her feet so I could reconstitute the chain back to its original state. Tomio used his bulk to hide what I was doing from the rest of the alley, just in case someone happened to pass by and glance over.

"Can you make it another couple of kilometers?" I asked Janet once I'd finished with the chain. "I can carry you, but it'll attract attention."

She gave a wobbly smile and nodded. "You've given me a chance to catch my breath, thank you."

The characters moving about the morning streets of Naples didn't have much in common with the drinking, smoking, Vespa-riding teens and twenty-somethings we'd observed the night before. A street dog scampered by our legs, his toe-nails scraping along the sidewalk. Three merchants chattered loudly as they set up their kiosk to sell SSC Napoli football club memorabilia. One of them appeared to be exuberantly re-enacting a heroic goal from some past game. The smell of fresh-baked croissants, pastries, and fresh-ground espresso made me suppress a groan. The small, quaint tables in front of the cafés were already half full of patrons sipping cappuccino and reading the local rag. Someone laid on their car horn as pedestrians weaved into the road and didn't get out of the way fast enough. Two beefy men trundled in and out of a delivery van carrying boxes of sausages into a sandwich shop, passing beneath a woman perched on a ladder using colored chalk to write out the specials of the day in pretty script.

We received a few curious looks as we joined the flow of traffic on the street, but no one said anything to us. I was starving and tired, but I couldn't wait to get home and let Basil know what had transpired. I reached for my phone, intending to send him a text.

Janet made a little noise beside me and I looked at her at the same as Tomio did, from her other side. Her eyes were huge and round, her face deathly pale. Even as her legs and feet attempted to propel her forward, her eyes rolled up in her head.

"Tomio!" I gasped.

Together we caught Janet before she hit the pavement, though the back of her hand scraped along the sidewalk and I almost stepped on her braid. There were a few shouts from around us, and three strangers came over to help.

"Chiamare un'ambulanza?" someone shouted at me.

"Aspettare, per favore," I panted, asking him to wait as I lifted Janet into my arms.

A kind looking man retrieved the kerchief that had fallen from Janet's head. He tried to put it back on for her but put it on backward so the tie was at her forehead.

"Cosa c'è che non va in lei?" he asked, wondering what was wrong.

"She's ok," I said, feeling Janet's breathing against my chest. "She's very tired."

"Too much drink." Tomio mimed drinking from a bottle.

I shot him a half-amused half-exasperated glare, but the three people closest to us made sympathetic sounds of understanding, as if they themselves had frequently fainted from too much drinking the night before.

As they moved away, Tomio put his fingers under her jaw. "Her pulse is strong. I think she's just overwhelmed. We need to get her home and into bed."

He fell in step beside me as the sun began to light up the tops of the buildings and rectangular slashes of pavement on one side of the road.

"Of course she fainted," he murmured after a few moments. "She's been underground for years and we just brought her out into daylight and streets full of people and smells without any thought to how it would hit her."

I felt stupid for not having thought of it myself. How would it feel to live in a silent, isolated cell with only one other person for occasional company, to then be suddenly exposed to thousands of people, the sounds of traffic, street animals, food smells in the air, raw morning sunlight slicing into her retinas, and fresh oxygen pouring into her bloodstream?

We hurried toward our villa, more in a rush than ever to reach home. No wonder she'd fainted. I would have too, and probably thrown up in a gutter to boot.

THIRTEEN

DESPERATE MEASURES

Thankfully, as Tomio unlocked the villa's front door Janet's consciousness returned, in the form of a croaky stream of Italian that neither of us understood.

"Almost there," I murmured, turning her sideways so I didn't bash her head on the door's frame. "You can sleep for as long as you want."

"Does that go for us too?" Tomio replied as he lowered his backpack to the floor and moved to open his bedroom door for me.

I found a wan smile for him as I carried Janet to the bed and waited as Tomio pulled back the light blanket. As I relinquished her weight to the mattress, she murmured something in Italian about the room being too loud and bright. Without opening her eyes, she rolled over and buried her head under the pillow.

To us, the room was neither loud nor bright.

Tomio went to his luggage and rummaged through what looked like a toiletries bag. He pulled out a small plastic packet with something orange inside, then returned to where Janet lay on the bed. She peered out from under the pillow to look at him when he nudged her hand and he held up the packet so she could see the fresh set of earplugs inside.

She nodded and murmured thank you in Italian four times as he opened it for her and put the soft plugs into her hand. As Janet muffled her hearing, I closed the interior scrim just behind the drapes, shutting out more daylight. I suspected she was asleep before Tomio and I had even closed the door.

"Should we call the polizia?" he whispered as we retreated to the kitchen.

I pulled two glasses from the cupboard and filled them with water, passing one to Tomio. "I think we should call Basil first. He'll know what to do next. Because this is a crime by a supernatural against a natural, an agency will want to deal with it." I paused before swallowing more water, wondering how the Agency was coping. "If there's even someone available to take her case."

I finally sent the text I had been about to send when Janet collapsed, asking Basil how soon we could talk to him. It was an hour earlier in London but late enough that he'd be up. Even if he wasn't, I had a duty to wake him. He'd want to know about Janet as soon as possible. I took another gulp of water as we waited for his response. A glance at Tomio gave me pause. "What's wrong? You look like you swallowed some-thing nasty."

"It just occurred to me that Janet might not be able to see her family right away."

I watched his expression drop a foot as he came to the same conclusion I'd come to while still under-ground. "While Nero is free, she won't be safe, and neither will her family if she returns home to be with them."

Tomio put a hand over his stomach and set his water glass down. "Poor woman."

My phone buzzed as Basil replied that he could be online in three minutes. He told me he'd email me a link to a private video call hosted by the Agency's servers. I woke up my laptop, then clicked on the link when it came through. Basil's face fuzzed into view. An alarm bell rang in my head, high and intense as he came into focus. Basil had the same haggard look he'd had just before his father had died.

"We have news," I said. "I'd say it's nice to see you except that it looks like you have news too and it isn't good."

Tomio and I sank into chairs at the table, crowding together so Basil could see both of us at the same time. Tomio wrapped an arm around my back and let his hand dangle off my shoulder. I appreciated his solidity next to me.

"We're getting reports of another batch of fires having gone out," Basil replied, rubbing a cloth over the glass of his spectacles. He shook his head, his mouth a flat line as he placed his glasses on his face.

I was so shocked I couldn't speak. Tomio said nothing either, but I felt him stiffen.

"There's no protocol for a disaster of this magnitude. More than half the Agency is down and out. Our projections say that more than half the entire mage population has now lost its fire. We're getting reports coming through our network in multiples per minute. I don't want to alarm you but I don't think it serves you to keep it from you. Do both of you still have your fire?"

Tomio and I both nodded.

"How about you?" I croaked.

"Yes, I am fine, and so is everyone I share a bond with. The Agency has made an interesting correlation. Mage bonds are something that an agency in Istanbul has been tracking. It reports that the fires are not going out in random batches, but in groups clustered by bond. It doesn't have enough data to prove that it extrapolates out worldwide, but it has enough to show the relationship. That's enough for me. It's a theory, but a strong one."

I closed my eyes and went inward. The urge to scream was strong. It was too much all at once. My promise to Enzo. Gage missing. Fires going out. It all had to be connected. I took a deep breath and opened my eyes.

"It has to do with Nero. We found his underground hideaway and a woman he's been keeping there against her will for three years. If you didn't have enough evidence to arrest him before, you have it now."

Basil rubbed his face and looked at us with blood-shot eyes. "Now that we don't have a chain-of-command at the Agency equipped to go after him. How ironic. Before you tell me everything, I have to inform you that this call is being recorded. It's agency protocol. Are you okay with that?"

Tomio and I agreed, and then we began to talk. Basil listened quietly and made a few notes as we described finding Janet and the whole set-up underground. When we finished our story, he excused himself for a few minutes, leaving our connection open, to phone someone at the Agency. Sliding back in front of the screen several minutes later, he explained that he'd called the new acting director and she would contact an Italian authority who could be trusted with next steps in regards to Janet.

"What about Gage?" asked Tomio. "We still don't know where he is."

"I suspect that if you find Dante, you'll find Gage," replied Basil.

Unpleasant feelings collided like poorly aimed fireworks in my stomach. I disliked how Basil seemed to be putting this all on Tomio and me and implying that he wouldn't or couldn't do anything to help us. We might be capable, but we were still just teenagers. I understood that it was traumatizing to have one's fire go out permanently, but Mehmet had told us that some magi took it very well, even with some relief. Where were those adults? Couldn't they help us? Even if they no longer had supernatural powers, they were experienced. Weren't they?

Tomio voiced a similar opinion, his voice so weary and frustrated that he barely sounded like himself. "What do you mean if *we* find Dante? Even after finding Nero's underground place and all but solidly proving that he's connected to what's happening to mages all over the world, you *still* won't send help?"

Basil put up a hand. "I didn't say that. This situation is changing rapidly. Even now Ms. Shepherd, the acting director, is sharing your discoveries with three other agency heads. She will join us online here as soon as she can. She wants to hear from you directly."

I put a hand on Tomio's knee and immediately his fingers closed around mine and he dropped his head. He lifted it a moment later.

"We feel a little abandoned, here," I said, controlling my voice better than Tomio now that I realized he was further over the edge than I was. I had to be the calm one.

The screen flashed and split in two. Another face fuzzed into view, a woman who looked to be mid-forties with short auburn hair and intense gray eyes. She leaned close to her camera and her face loomed, then pulled back. "Hello?"

I lifted a hand in greeting. "Ms. Shepherd?"

"Yes. Nice to meet you, although I'm sorry for the circumstances," she replied. "Saxony and Tomio, yes?"

We nodded. Tomio's leg began to jiggle up and down under my hand and his fingers had not relaxed.

"I'm sorry we don't have time for ice-breakers." She looked down as though studying notes in front of her.

"That's alright," Tomio muttered, "we'd rather just get to the point."

She glanced up and nodded. "Good. To verify what you told Basil, and what the language expert told you—"

"Janet Silvestri," I said.

"Yes, Janet—" She spoke quickly and with sharp consonants. She sounded like someone who was accustomed to being in charge, and in spite of her assertive way of speaking, the way she oozed authority made me feel a little better. "Nero went to Brazil last November and didn't return until the new year. Stop me only if I am wrong about any of these points, please. He did this when she decoded an artifact that he gave her, linking it to a region by an ancient language. A couple of months later—" she bent her head to review her notes, searching for something.

"In March," Tomio supplied.

"He had her decode something similar, an artifact that pointed to a region in India via root language, and he went there. This time, he returned sooner, in late April. Following this, your school-mate Ryan met with Nero in Naples and fast-tracked a visa for Iran, while Nero himself went to China, and that's where Janet believes he is right now."

"She also said he plans to visit Australia before coming home, and he could be there already," I supplied. "All of these trips coincide with batches of fires going out, don't they?"

Ms. Shepherd nodded. "Yes, they do, and your finding Janet gives us the permission we need to pursue and arrest Nero as soon as possible. Thank you for your service thus far, our understanding of the situation has made leaps and bounds thanks to your discoveries."

"You're welcome. What's next?" Tomio's leg hadn't stopped jiggling. "We really need to find our friend."

"Yes, Gage was it? You believe he is in danger of having his fire taken?"

Tomio and I nodded.

"Is Gage of strong character?"

Her question took me off guard. "What do you mean?"

"Do you think he can withstand torture?"

Basil's expression changed noticeably for the first time since Ms. Shepherd had come on the call. He was unhappy about this line of questioning but he didn't stop her. Maybe he didn't have the authority to stop her.

"How are we supposed to know that?" Tomio snapped.

Unbothered by his tone, Ms. Shepherd went on. "You know him better than any of us, and it's not something we're prepared to ask his parents about. Do you think he can withstand being dehydrated? Because if he can, and like many mages, he would rather die than pass his fire on to someone else, then it's unlikely this Dante will succeed in his mission."

"We'd really like to find him before this torture takes place," I husked, barely recognizing my own voice.

"Of course, I'm merely trying to ascertain the likelihood of the transfer and how prepared you might be to do what must be done to prevent it from happening, if it hasn't happened already."

A cold spike of unease slid its way into my heart. I began to feel afraid of this woman and her icy, emotionless control, the way her soft face contrasted with hard resolve. "What must be done?"

"I'm sorry to say it, but these are desperate times." She didn't need to finish the sentence for my mind to call up the rest of it.

Desperate measures. A heavy dread descended over my shoulders and began to press down with stone hands.

"Just say it," Tomio husked, squeezing my fingers so hard I winced.

"You must return Janet to her underground prison, and quickly."

FOURTEEN

THE LEGENDS

I stared at Ms. Shepherd to confirm that she hadn't been making a terrible joke. Heat began to fill my cheeks. "Are you insane?"

"Saxony," Basil said reproachfully.

For the first time ever, I ignored my headmaster's chiding completely. My temper strained against control like an angry dog pulling against a chain. "Do you have any idea what that woman has been through? There's no way in hell you could ever convince me to take her back down there."

Tomio's voice was higher pitched than usual. "Why exactly, would we do that to her?"

Ms. Shepherd appeared unbothered by my indignation and answered Tomio instead. "It's the only chance we have to save Gage. If Nero comes home to find Janet missing, we've blown any advantage we might have. He'll pack up and move kit and caboodle somewhere else and the intel we have on his location will be useless. We'll have to start over and we'll be no closer to finding Gage."

"Ah." Tomio wiped a hand across his lips and shot me a sideways glance, his brow wrinkled. His look said that he saw the reason in her suggestion and he wondered if I did too.

"We should be facilitating contact with her family," I said, "not shoving her back underground to be used as bait."

"She won't be bait." Ms. Shepherd shifted as she pulled her chair closer to the screen. Her face loomed so close I could see the lipstick bleeding into the fine lines of her upper lip. "When Nero returns and sees his hideaway and his captive are just as he left them, he won't suspect anything. She'll be in no greater danger than the danger she's been in for the last three years. She can then use his trust in her and his knowing that she can't tell anyone anything to elicit the whereabouts of Gage."

I let go of Tomio's hand and crossed my arms to pin down my hands. I kept wanting to curl my fingers into fists. "What if he doesn't know? Isn't it Dante we should be looking for?"

"I understand Dante has already failed at least twice when it comes to mage rituals. Once with you and once with Nicodemo, who he killed. I doubt he will take such a chance again. He'll be relying on Nero's skill and knowledge as a mage who has facilitated Burnings, if not endowments, before. Everything points to this event having to happen after Nero returns, not in his absence." She blinked at us through the thick lenses of her square glasses, expression guileless even while she pitched us the unthinkable.

And, damn it, she was making sense.

"I'm sorry." I shook my head. "You are probably

right, but if you want to plant Janet back underground before Nero gets back you're going to have to send an agent to do it, because I can't. I won't."

"Isn't there another way we can locate Dante?" Tomio asked.

"Of course there are other ways. We always examine at least three options for every scenario. But the other options are less likely to be successful. We have powerful computers running highly sophisticated algorithms crunching all the data we can give them."

"Let's say we do it your way." I said, feeling Tomio's hand tighten over my knee. "I'm just asking the question. Say we take poor Janet underground again and she lies in wait for Nero. Say she gets the information out of him. How does Janet get that information to us in a timely manner? She'll be forty meters underground, it's not like she can send us a text."

But Ms. Shepherd looked happy that I had asked. "When you return her, she'll take something with her called a Miner Lifeline radio and stash it out of sight in her cell. These radios use ultra-low frequency to pass through rock and have a range of five kilometers. They support both text and voice communications."

Tomio and I were silent, absorbing this.

"What can't they do these days," Tomio finally murmured.

Ms. Shepherd didn't blink. "Actually, it's been around since the sixties. They improve the technology every time there's a mining disaster. Since we can't employ a telepath, we have to fall back on natural inventions. The first opportunity Janet has once Nero has left her alone, she can send communication to you. You can then decide whether one of you goes after

Gage and one of you retrieves Janet, or if you both go after your friend—assuming we understand that Janet is safe enough to wait."

Tomio and I sat in dubious silence. Her plan had merit, and we weren't coming up with anything better.

"What about Janet's family?" I asked. "What do you think they'll say about us using their daughter this way?"

"If it helps to find Gage before Nero and Dante do something horrible to him, they'll understand," said a voice from the door.

Tomio and I turned. Janet stood at the bottom of the stairs, wrapped in a blanket she'd taken from the bed. She was pale, but actually looked better than she'd looked on the street.

"How long have you been there?" Tomio asked.

Ms. Shepherd and Basil greeted Janet, though they couldn't yet see her on the screen.

"Long enough. My hearing seems to have sharpened considerably during my time underground. I couldn't *not* hear you, even with plugs in my ears." Janet indicated that the plugs were still in as she came into the kitchen and looked at the laptop screen over our heads.

Tomio and I shared a guilty look. We hadn't been speaking very loudly and the volume on the laptop had been turned down. Fat lot of good it had done.

Janet saw our faces. "Don't feel badly. I'll do it. I'm happy to."

Ms. Shepherd grinned so widely her eyes almost disappeared. "Thank you, Janet. If we are successful, you won't just be saving Gage but putting a stop to a kind of genocide that is sweeping through our species."

Janet nodded. "I don't want my family to know anything until it's all over. It will be too difficult for them."

"You're made of stern stuff, Ms. Silvestri. The agency and all fire elementals will forever be indebted to you, those of us who remain."

"A few more days or even weeks makes no difference to me. Knowing that you know where I am and that I have a way of communicating with the outside world will keep me sane until it's all over. Just promise me that you'll send a rescue party for me as soon as possible after Gage is found."

Ms. Shepherd gave a single nod. "Of course. Are you confident Nero will share his whereabouts with you?"

Janet lifted a hand to the amber choker at her neck. "I think he will. As long as we put his rooms back in the order we found them in, he has no reason to suspect me."

Basil said, "If you have the energy, can you tell us your story? We've heard from Saxony and Tomio, but we need as much detail as you can give. We understand if you need to rest further. They say you fainted on the street? Are you feeling better?"

"Yes, thanks. I was overstimulated. I am tired, but I can't sleep. I would be happy to talk."

Tomio vacated his chair for Janet and I slid the laptop over so it was her face Basil and Ms. Shepherd were seeing. Moving to lean against a kitchen counter by Tomio, we listened to Janet a second time as she relayed her story. By the time she was finished, she was drooping and yawning again. Ms. Shepherd had asked Janet (with our help as needed) to describe the rooms in detail including how much computer equipment was there, how old she thought it was, what programs Nero had her using, what kind of security he had including a detailed description of the lock on the front door, which I was able to provide. The questions went on and on until Janet could hardly keep her eyelids open, then Ms. Shepherd finally dismissed her.

As Janet returned to the bedroom and we slid in front of the screen, Ms. Shepherd told us she was needed elsewhere and would be back in touch with more details about the plan after we had some rest. It was time to pin Basil down.

"Wait, wait, wait," I said, putting up a hand when it seemed Basil was about to end the connection. "I won't sleep until I know everything that you know. I get that we're able to link Nero to these events. Every time he goes somewhere foreign, a group of magi lose their fires permanently. But what is he doing? How can these groups be so vulnerable?"

Tomio slid back into his chair, looking as tired as I felt but just as determined to wrap his mind around the threat. "Exactly. He went to Brazil in November, a bunch of fires went out in December. He comes back home, does more weird scribbles and then went to India in March. Another group of mages lose their fire, including our friend April."

"And Eira's dad, and Jade's ex-babysitter, Maggie."

Basil was listening patiently with the expression of a man who had been expecting to have to have this conversation.

"Then, while he's supposedly in China, two groups of mages lose their fire within days of one another. He's on his way to Australia next, we're bracing ourselves for another wave, but there has to be something we can do about it. We need to know whatever it is the Agency knows."

Basil took a deep breath and wrinkled his brow. "I don't disagree, but I'm afraid you think we have more information than we have. We've been monitoring Nero, yes, but we could only do so while he was above ground. He's aware that he's been surveilled, so he kept his interactions private. But what I can share with you is our understanding of the legends, because the old stories seem to have more relevance now than they ever did before."

"I thought you said they were bunk?" I sat back and crossed my arms, feeling a shiver of anticipation pass through my body. Would Basil admit that he'd been trying to make replicas of the orbs in his own private studio?

"Many versions are. That's the problem. Hundreds of cultures have versions of the same story. The great deluge, for example, has happened in every culture in the world, but the who, how, and why of the flood varies in every story."

"So how are we supposed to know what really happened?" Tomio murmured.

"Exactly. We have fragments of stories that involve our species in some way, taken from all the corners of the globe. We're only now getting a clearer look at our own origin story because Nero's movements are giving us clues about where to look. His foreign trips have not gone unnoticed. We know he boarded a plane to Australia."

"Could someone there arrest him?"

"Yes, but there's a new problem. They have the authority, but not the power."

Tomio's forehead creased. "I don't get it. Aren't authority and power the same thing?"

Basil shook his head. "Not remotely. If you drive a Lamborghini with three hundred horses under the hood and a cop in an intersection raises his hand, you have to stop. The Lamborghini has the power, but the cop has the authority. In this case, our mages have the authority to arrest Nero and bring him before our tribunal, but they've lost the powers they've had since birth thanks to the very man they wish greatly to detain."

He let that sink in before continuing.

"Nero's movements have actually helped your team to look in the right places? Is that what you're saying?" I prompted, skipping over the problem of powerless magi for the moment. It was too big and horrible to think about. I couldn't even allow my mind to fully form the idea that I might wake up at any moment without my own fire.

"Yes. We have archives and a database full of fractions of ancient stories. Nero's destinations directed us to pay more attention to the ancient cultures in those places and the legends we had that were connected to the lands and peoples there."

"So what have you learned?"

Basil pushed his spectacles up his nose, looking eager to impart what he knew but hesitant about how to do it. "Have either of you heard of a mysterious event called Tunguska?"

The name triggered a memory: when Ryan and I cleaned Basil's office as penance, the same day we discovered his secret studio. I'd almost forgotten about the black and white photographs of trees blown sideways in what looked like the aftermath of an enormous explosion.

I nodded. "You have pictures in your office from that event."

"Very good. Exactly. I was drawn to look at the event when it seemed to share similarities with our legends. The Tunguska event itself is not important, but it provides evidence that the earth can suffer an immense impact event without sustaining an impact crater. The Tunguska event is the largest ever recorded in history, but our legends suggest that in prehistoric times there was another event like it. The story goes that some immense and bright god crashed somewhere in Mesopotamia, in the cradle of civilization. The sky filled with fire and was rent in two. A streak of light disappeared over the horizon, followed by a terrific explosion as the god crashed and died."

"A meteorite?" Tomio asked.

"Naturally that's the first thing scientists attribute it to. The stories say the god was never found and there was no impact site, though the event flattened trees for hundreds of miles and destroyed the hearing of tribesmen hunting very far away. Possibly three generations later, settlers moved into this area to build homes and farm the region. The area had not been claimed as it had been considered dangerous for a long time, but as the new generations came up and young people wanted to build their own cities, this area was fought over. There were as many as twelve different tribes, each with their own languages, genetic heritage, culture and history who came from abroad to claim this space. Those with fewer numbers could not make a reasonable stand for land, but seven of these tribes were powerful, with great numbers of warriors who were prepared to fight for it. Alliances were being formed and things were shaping up for a slaughter when a young woman who was foraging came across a huge white fire burning in the middle of this land. It is written that this fire did not consume anything, nor did it grow or shrink, it did not even smoke, which was why it had not been discovered until this point.

"The story she told spread through the other tribes, who sent scouts to verify the truth of what she saw. They claimed it must have been either left behind by the great god who died in the explosion that shocked their grand-parents' generation, or it was the god itself."

Basil paused to take a sip of water. Tomio and I didn't make a sound and barely moved as we waited for him to continue.

"The elders of the most powerful seven tribes journeyed to see this phenomenon for themselves and while they stared at the fire, transfixed by its magic and beauty, it is said that they abandoned all thoughts of battle and of killing one another. Instead, they divided the lands into sections and distributed it among the tribes, keeping the fire at the central point. It became important to all of them and each tribe envisioned its own explanations about what the fire was, where it came from, how it came to be self-sufficient and benign."

I leaned forward and put my chin on my palm. "This is why you've been confused about our origins."

"Yes. You can find evidence of these stories all over the place, from Singapore to Chile. Further, the effects of time and the passing of these stories down through generations means no one really knows the truth of it anymore."

It was on the tip of my tongue to remind Basil that I knew an elemental who if taken to ground zero for these events could see the truth as easily as she could pick up a handful of soil from the earth there, but I didn't want to interrupt him. He'd surely had such a thought for himself. I wondered if he would bring up Georjayna's abilities now or later. If he didn't, I would.

"The legends suggest that these tribes lived in relative harmony with each other for hundreds of years before something happened to divide them. Famine. Change of the climate, or perhaps an ice age made life very difficult for them. When someone suggested that the white god was angry with them for being selfish, the idea quickly gained momentum. It was suggested that they should have been giving a portion of the earth's bounty to the fire every year because the prosperity they'd had was given by the white god and he or she was sick of being left out. They took what little food they had stored, divided a portion for the white god and threw it into the fire, but nothing changed. When someone suggested that food wouldn't be enough to make up for all the years they had not given anything to the god, they quickly jumped to the conclusion that they should have been doing something that foreigners did in strange lands that were rumored not to have been touched by the famine—sacrifice an individual from their tribe."

I shuddered. What was with all the human sacrifice in our history? It was difficult for a modern brain to comprehend that it had ever been an acceptable practice.

"The tribes agreed, but they had not been given to such bloody activity before and decided that the sacrifice had to be a volunteer, they would not murder someone to test their theory. At first, no one stepped forward."

"I'll bet," Tomio muttered, laying an arm across the back of my chair and rubbing a fist into one eye.

"But finally, when one brave young woman, a mother of three, stepped forward and volunteered to be sacrificed for a chance to save her children from further hunger, the other tribes were ashamed that it was not one of their own number who stepped forward so selflessly. This prompted a rush of volunteers and each tribe wanted to have what was now considered an honor to give for the good of everyone else. The elders decided that instead of taking a sacrifice from one tribe only, they would take one from *each* tribe. An equitable and fair contribution. Surely seven sacrifices would be enough for this god to bless them again with their previous good fortune. These sacrificial lambs would be forever lauded, the stories of their bravery would be put to songs and fables and passed through the ages. So, the elders selected one volunteer from each tribe and set a day for the sacrifice to take place.

"On the day of the sacrifice, the volunteers stood at a distance around the fire. Beyond them were members of their families and tribesmen and women dressed in their best ceremonial clothing and headdresses to represent their region. Moving together, the volunteers walked forward into the flames and were swallowed up."

Tomio recoiled. "They just strolled forward like

they were walking their dog? What person is capable of walking into such intense heat and pain?"

"Obviously this is not your average, garden-variety bonfire," I murmured, nudging Tomio to let Basil go on.

"The stories report that there was no pain, and that the silhouettes of the volunteers could actually be seen moving about inside the flames. There is a cave painting depicting this very event in Turkey. The tribespeople waited for the fire to respond, they watched the figures of their people inside the flames. They did not appear to burn, but instead appeared to be congregating inside the fire, perhaps even able to talk. The story goes that the volunteers remained this way inside the fire, without ever sitting or lying down, in some kind of communion with one another. After three days, they emerged from the fire."

"But different from how they went in, obviously." The hair on my neck lifted at the scene that rose in my mind's eye.

"That's right. The seven emerged from the flame with the powers we three currently possess—for the time being. They became the progenitors of our kind."

"Wow." I could see goosebumps on Tomio's fore-arms and knew he was feeling the same awe. "What then?"

"That was the beginning of a whole new era. The mages returned to their respective tribes as gods. It's not written or told how much time later the crisis ended, but it was clear the age had ended and new one had begun, one where naturals and supernaturals lived together."

"There must have been jealousy among the people," I said, taking a sip from my water glass. The fatigue and my curiosity were waging war and curiosity could not hold exhaustion at bay for much longer. I hadn't slept in over 24 hours. "Did anyone else try to step into the fire to gain the same powers?"

"Of course. For a while, the people listened to and respected the mages with a religious fervor. The mages warned the people to stay away from the fire, that no others would be permitted to go in and come out alive again. But as the years passed and the mages were seen to still have the same errors in judgment, the same vices that any natural had, some tribespeople began to murmur against them. In dark corners it was whispered that the mages were lying to the people in order to keep their spectacular gifts to themselves. At first it was only a rebellious few who questioned the authenticity of the mages' claims, including the one where the mages told the people that they had to live with a constant pain in their chests and stomachs thanks to the fire now residing inside them."

"Well they weren't lying about that," Tomio muttered, now pinching his hair between his fingers and yanking it upward. It seemed like his fidgetiness was an attempt to keep himself alert.

"No. But how could the tribespeople verify it? Eventually those who doubted the mages' claims became a majority, and the fear of disobeying the mages had dwindled enough for someone to test it. Two tribespeople tried to enter the fire."

"And they... burned?"

Basil, nodded. "It is said they entered but could not leave, the fire held them captive and they were burned to death. After that the people believed everything the mages said and reinstated them to the positions of gods.

The mages took partners and had children. Three of the tribes were polygamists and so some had multiple partners. Young mages were born. As the centuries passed, the mage population exploded and we spread to all the corners of the Earth, mixing with all ethnicities and cultures. The stories were passed down, immortalized, bastardized, changed, and misremembered. But thanks to this new evidence Janet has brought forward, we now understand more about how the original progenitors of the mages came about."

Tomio and I shared a slightly dazed look.

I looked to Basil again. "And what about the orbs?"

"Ah." He scratched the back of his head as if trying to release the answer from some rear corner of his skull. "The orbs appear to have their own separate legend, and the origins of them is less clear. There are tales that suggest they were all made by one artist, and there are tales that suggest that each progenitor made their own. Why? We don't know, but many contemporary mages believe that if you are in possession of one of these orbs, they provide some connection or conduit to the power of the forefathers, and mothers, of our kind."

"Do you believe that?" I asked.

"You know I don't," Basil looked over his glasses at me.

"Then why did you paint pictures of them when you were young?"

"That's like asking why kids draw pictures of Superman," Basil replied. "Some kids go through an obsession phase with dinosaurs, others with rocketships, still others with cowboys. My obsession was these orbs. I felt destined to find one."

"And when that never happened, you grew out of your fixation?"

Basil tilted his head back to study me through the screen. "Not at all. I am currently in possession—technically the Agency is—of two of these orbs, and I can tell you that there is nothing whatsoever magical or power-endowing about them."

FIFTEEN

THE SET-UP

By the time we said goodbye to Basil, agreeing to let him know the moment we woke up, it was after eleven in the morning. The headmaster had suggested we not sleep too long because it would make it much more difficult to keep our body-clocks in order.

Peeking in on Janet as I brushed my teeth, she was a small lump under the bedsheet and snoring softly. Returning to the bathroom to spit, I glanced over the bannister to see Tomio standing in the living room. He was eyeing the too-short couch dubiously.

The skin under my eyelids felt coated with sand and almost too heavy to lift. If I were Tomio, I wouldn't be savoring the prospect of napping on a noisy, fake-leather sofa with my feet hanging off the end either.

The room I occupied had a king-sized bed. Not much else could fit in the room, but the bed was ridiculous. Letting Tomio crash on the couch when I had acres of fluffy mattress to myself was just wrong. I slipped down the stairs.

"Do you snore?" I asked.

He looked up. "Not that I know of. Why?"

"You can share my bed," I said, rubbing at one eye in the hopes that the lid would stop twitching. It didn't work.

Tomio's face split with a sleepy but delighted smile as he moved for the stairs.

He slid around the bed and squeezed between the mattress and the wall before sitting down and peeling off his socks and t-shirt.

I dug my pajama shorts and tank out of my luggage and went to the bathroom to change. When I came back, Tomio was already facing the wall, his breathing even and deep. I smiled as I lay on top of the sheet and closed my eyes. You know you're exhausted when you can share a bed with someone you're as drawn to as paperclips are to a magnet, and actually fall asleep.

I FELT Tomio move before I opened my eyes. The light had changed in the room, even with the curtains drawn. The sound of the kitchen tap running signaled that Janet was also awake.

Tomio lay facing me, his dark lashes long and straight against his skin. With most of my fatigue gone, I became aware of how close we were and how much I wanted to lean forward and kiss him, to see if it was as nice as the first one we'd shared. I was just about to get out of bed when he opened his eyes and found me staring at him. A slow smile spread across his face.

"Sleep well?"

I nodded. "You?"

"Like I was getting paid." He yawned and blinked,

peering over his shoulder at the window. "What time is it?"

I checked my cell. "Five-forty. I'll send a text to Basil."

He nodded and rubbed at his eyes, sitting up.

The sound of a glass being set down on the counter in the kitchen made Tomio raise his head and swear under his breath.

"What?" I got out of bed and stretched my arms over my head.

He cocked a thumb toward the door. "Did she really agree to go back underground, or did I dream that?"

"It wasn't a dream. Brave woman."

He nodded. "Yeah, if this works and we get Gage back in one piece with his fire intact, we'll owe her a debt we can never repay."

"Well, we did spring her from prison."

"True."

"And if you were in her shoes would you not do the same?" I asked.

"I've never spent three years underground. I don't know how I'd feel."

"Me either," I agreed.

"Yeah, you do. You wouldn't think twice about it." Tomio's utter confidence in this statement made me feel even more conflicted.

"What makes you think that?"

"Because it's the right thing to do and the risk is minimal. And..." he paused, hesitant.

"And what?"

"You're... Saxony."

I blinked at him in astonishment. It was the first

time Tomio had said such a thing in such a way. He sounded so admiring. As my coach, he'd never been gushy. I was about to ask him what he meant by that when he changed the subject.

"Anyway, let's not think too hard about the fact that we're putting her back in."

I shuddered and felt the cool rat's paws of anxiety run up my spine. What if something happened to Janet? What if Nero knew somehow, that she was part of a trap we'd laid for him? If he hurt her—

I mentally stomped on that line of thinking. I had enough to worry about.

As if Tomio was thinking something similar, he mumbled, "Man, I hope we know what we're doing."

There came a soft tap on the door. Janet stood on the other side looking apprehensive. "Your laptop woke up. I think someone wants to talk to you?"

The laptop's screen was a gray veil covering the map, showing at least double the number of specks of light. A text message from 'Kate Shepherd' blinked in the corner. The yellow text proclaimed: *URGENT: Updated directive. Click to open.*

When I clicked on it, a video screen opened showing Ms. Shepherd in the background talking to someone. She wore a headset and must have been notified we were online because she looked over at us, excused herself from her conversation and slid into the seat in front of her camera.

"Did you sleep well?"

We said we had as we arranged ourselves so that she could see all of us at the same time. Tomio pressed against my left side, and Janet on my right.

She got straight to the point. "We now have photographic and video evidence that Nero has landed in Australia. Every trip he takes has been shorter in duration than the one before it, which means this operation cannot be delayed. Janet, you must return to the subterranean location as soon as possible."

A glance at Janet inspired me to put an arm around her. She nodded without hesitation, but looked deeply unhappy that she had had so little time to enjoy her short-lived freedom.

"One question, though," she said in her soft voice. "How is Nero getting through security? If he's as radioactive as he thinks himself to be, wouldn't the machines detect him?"

Ms. Shepherd looked impressed that Janet knew this. "Yes, they would. He flies under an alias that has a membership to a private airline. He can fly alone and bypass much of the security routine, so he is not delayed by the protocols that affect those who fly publicly. He has been using this alias since Christmas when he returned to Italy from Brazil. It was the intel you provided that led us to uncover this alias after we examined all flights between Rio and Naples. There are zero direct public flights and very few private ones, which made it easier for us. We never would have known where to look without your direction, so for that we thank you."

"You're welcome."

"Moving straight into the project. We've arranged for meetings with two individuals, the first will take place the moment you arrive at the location we will share with you at the conclusion of this call. In the interests of brevity, I won't go in to the details of these meetings, you'll understand their purpose the moment they commence. I will show you photographs of these individuals so you'll know them on sight. Please follow their instructions and trust that they know what they're doing. I realize you'd much prefer to know all the details ahead of time, but this is how agency work is executed."

This nettled me and I suspected Ms. Shepherd saw it in my expression. Her gaze shifted on the screen.

"I understand you have an interest in agency work in the future, Ms. Cagney?"

I was taken off guard and wasn't sure how to feel about her knowing this. Most likely it was Basil who had told her I might be interested, but it still felt weird to have a complete stranger ask me about my future plans. "Maybe," I said. "If an agent has to go into a situation blindly trusting allies the agency says they should trust, I'm not sure if that's work I'm up for."

I felt Tomio shoot a surprised look my way.

As was her way, Ms. Shepherd showed no emotion at my displeasure. "At times, that is precisely what is required. Agents do not always have the luxury of analyzing all of the intelligence that leads to decisions being made. In the field, you are given orders and you follow them knowing that you're in the best hands possible and all outcomes have been analyzed."

I pressed my lips together against another retort. In my opinion, Ms. Shepherd could have used the time she'd taken to explain this to us to explain who we were meeting with and why.

She continued, "After Janet is reinstalled, we'd like you not to return to your current location. We've arranged a safe-house for you. We do not believe you to be in danger where you are at this point in time, but when Nero returns to Naples, we'd rather you weren't staying at a property owned by Enzo Barberini."

This made sense, but the mention of Enzo, whom I had not reported to since Gage disappeared, made my mouth feel dry. I also hated the agency lingo Ms. Shepherd was using, and realized that was protocol too. Referring to Janet's re-incarceration underground as an 'installation' grated against my sensibilities.

"That will be all. I know you have questions. Our contacts will make all things clear," Ms. Shepherd said. "Remember to vacate the flat, take all of your belongings with you when you leave for the first meeting. Good bye, and good luck."

The screen flashed dark as she cut off the video call without asking us for opinions or thoughts. It had been on the tip of my tongue to ask if Basil was there.

A new text message opened on the right-hand side of the screen, in the chat-flow. A list of three addresses in Naples. A photograph of a face was beside each of the first two addresses. The third address was that of our new safe-house.

Tomio, Janet and I leaned forward in unison to squint at the faces. The first contact was a dark-skinned man, expressionless but with lively, dark eyes and a glimmer of white teeth between partly-open lips. The second address accompanied the face of a young blond woman, smiling widely. She didn't look much older than me.

Snatching his phone from the table, Tomio took a photograph of all three addresses and faces. Then he looked at Janet and me, bemused but eager. "Guess we better pack up."

WITH TOMIO NAVIGATING and Janet in the back seat making noises of delight over the croissant and cappuccino we'd picked up from a corner bakery that was about to close, I piloted the tiny Fiat through the narrow streets. At another moan of delight from Janet, Tomio and I exchanged a look of amusement. It was late afternoon, the croissant wasn't even fresh.

"Just up ahead." Tomio pointed to the left side of the street where a narrow garage door painted a bright, lime-green stood partially open.

In front of the door, furiously chewing gum and grinning as I parked half on the sidewalk, was our first contact.

When he saw us coming, he ducked inside. We followed him under the open garage door, Janet still chewing the last of her pastry and starting on mine. I'd given her my croissant when it became apparent how much she'd enjoyed hers. Tomio and I shared a pizza instead.

The first thing to greet us was an antique Peugeot car, which we had to turn sideways to get past. After that the garage opened up into a much larger room with much taller ceilings. It was as though a villa had at one time been attached to the garage, but had been gutted and set up as a mechanic's paradise. Oil stained the concrete floors which otherwise gleamed, reflecting overhead fluorescent lights. Rows of floor to ceiling shelves lined the walls, loaded with mechanical and electronic equipment of all kinds, and from all eras—all neatly tucked away and labeled. Everything from radios to toasters, record-players to sewing machines large and small, and countless items I couldn't identify on sight filled row upon row of fourteen-foot shelves.

Our host had disappeared down an aisle, muttering to himself in Italian. He hadn't bothered to introduce himself or tell us what we were doing here, but the contents of the shelves made it obvious. This would be the man to set us up with the Miner Lifeline radios Ms. Shepherd had mentioned.

As we looked down the aisle where the grinning, gum-chewing contact had disappeared, we saw him perched on the aluminum platform of a rolling staircase. He pulled what looked like a large dress-box off the shelf. He carried it down the stairs—that's when I noticed he was wearing a nametag with the word 'Relay' scribbled on it in black magic marker. He passed us and continued further back to a space with a galley kitchen across the back and several large work-tables with the guts of some mechanical thing strewn about. He set the box down on a table beside a smaller slanted shelving unit containing what looked like an upgraded telephone system from when the world still used human operators. Loops of wires connected with inputs on a dashboard with flashing green lights and backlit green panel across the top displayed a continuously changing list of frequencies.

He took the lid off the box to reveal a collection of identical walkie-talkies. Picking one up, he turned it on and its screen lit up with a matching bright green shade. It also had a backlit keypad, handy for finding numbers in the dark.

"Janet?" He bobbed his head indicating she should come closer, still chomping vigorously on his gum.

As she swallowed the last of my croissant, she

listened attentively as he showed her how to turn on and operate the walkie-talkie. Tomio and I crowded in to listen. Once he got talking, it was apparent Relay was not Italian. He spoke with a musical Sri Lankan accent.

"These work without an established infrastructure, like most radio systems. Your communications will be received by them"—he pointed to me and Tomio—"and myself also. With underground comms, range is greatly reduced and requires a relay technique to get very far. Not this, but you still can't go beyond five kilometers or you'll lose the signal. The battery will keep charge for one week if you don't use it too much. This is your replacement battery." He grabbed a small black sack from a pile of them at the base of the box and handed it to Janet. "I'm told this operation should be concluded within ten days."

"What if it takes longer than that?" Janet asked.

He gave her a blank look that said he could tell she was a rookie to the whole sting thing. "We'll get new orders, in that case."

"What if something breaks?" Tomio asked.

"If anything goes wrong, I'll know it. Five times per second my routing algorithm is recalculating the best route through the strata for your communication packets to reach their destinations. If something goes amiss, I'll know within five seconds and can adjust accordingly. But nothing will go wrong. This system isn't pretty or fast but it's robust and near unbreakable. Just keep yours on you at all time, check your battery life in a week if the operation hasn't concluded yet, and if the agency doesn't instruct you to pass these babies off to another contact, make sure you return them to me when it's all over." He gave one charger and a walkie talkie each to Janet and me.

"Do you know what we're using them for?" I asked as I took the gear, wondering how much info he'd been given.

He paused chewing to look me full in the face for the first time. His brown eyes were wide and a little shocked. "No. Nor do I want to. I just want my tech back in one piece. Any questions?"

The radios were easy enough to operate, so we didn't have questions. Relay had us test them a couple of times to make sure we were comfortable with them, then he promptly and unceremoniously, kicked us out of his shop.

OUR NEXT STOP was two blocks from the underground entrance for the subterranean city tours. The young blond woman from the thumbnail stood just inside the open door of a ticket office sipping from a ceramic mug with a smiley sunshine painted on the side. She wore a blue jumpsuit with the arms tied around her waist. When she saw us approach she backed into the shadowy room behind her, beckoning us to enter.

Inside, she handed us blue jumpsuits like the one she wore. Just like Relay, she didn't introduce herself but wore a tag with a hand-written name scrawled across it. Hers spelled Campano in a loopy script. This made more sense when the jumpsuits were on—it was easy to see the slogan on the back and chest for a company called Campano Gas. She gave Tomio a tool belt equipped with screwdrivers, meters and other items a gas technician might need, handed Janet a bag for her radio and battery and me a larger bag for the backpack containing the stuff we needed to return to the lair.

"We're going in disguised as gas techs?" Tomio asked as he zipped the jumpsuit up to his neck.

Janet tucked her long coil of a braid underneath a matching blue baseball hat, which Campano had handed each of us. I twisted my curls into a bun and did the same.

"Is it really believable that we work for a gas company?" I asked doubtfully as I looked down at my slightly too-big jumpsuit and black sneakers poking out the bottom. I thought the only ones who looked somewhat convincing were Tomio and Campano. Campano's disguise included work boots and safety glasses. Tomio filled out his jumpsuit and looked like someone you could rely upon to fix a gas problem. I looked like someone playing in my dad's work coveralls, and Janet looked like a hippy in a Burning Man costume.

"It will serve its function," Campano said in a heavy Italian accent as she fiddled with some complex looking piece of equipment sitting on the desk in the corner.

She snatched up a pair of keys and a small hand-held device with a red backlit screen then ushered us out the door. We followed her on foot the block and a half to the subterranean entrance in the early evening light, acting like we had every right to be doing what we were doing. My heart was in my throat as we approached the gated entrance for the underground tours.

Caution tape had been looped across the street and

official looking sandwich-board signs that screamed *Attenzione. Perdita di Gas* had been set up. Campano led us to the gate, opened it, and stood aside for us to enter.

I wondered how Janet was feeling about having to sacrifice her long-sought freedom so quickly after having gotten it, but to her credit she didn't pause or complain. In fact she was the first to descend. I followed her and Tomio followed me.

"Lead the way," Campano said as she followed Tomio down the steps. "I'll be mapping for the Agency as we go," she explained as her hand-held monitor began to make a soft beeping sound. "Try not to take any wrong turns, it makes for a messy map afterwards."

Janet paused on the steps and I almost walked into her. She turned. "You'd better go ahead of me. I have no idea how to get back."

Tomio nodded and squeezed past me and Janet as he took out the rough map he had marked. He took the steps confidently and we followed like ducklings after a mama-duck.

WHEN WE REACHED Nero's front door, Campano produced another piece of equipment. It looked a bit like a high-tech stethoscope. One end—the bit that looked like a suction cup—fastened to the metal door beside the old combination lock, sticking like a magnet. The other end broke in two and had small nodes that she slipped into her ears. Putting a finger to her lips, Campano turned the dial slowly, listening to the lock's inner mechanism. It took her a little less than five minutes to open the door. We stepped through into the rooms.

"Madonna," she muttered under her breath, looking around, her gaze flitting from the dusty shelves and office furniture to the plexiglass wall and the prison behind it. "Che monstro."

Campano took a slow, panoramic video of the rooms with a cell phone while Tomio, Janet and I put things back the way they'd been when we'd first arrived, referring to the photographs I'd taken when we weren't quite sure where something had been. Tomio put the scribbles we'd taken back in their drawers, and replaced the small artifacts we'd removed from shelves, using the layer of dust to make sure they were precisely where they should be. I followed Campano's example and took some of my own footage of the rooms and of Janet's space and of Janet herself. I knew Campano was taking footage for the Agency, but I wanted Ms. Shepherd to see Janet as a human against the backdrop of her prison. While I knew this was the best plan we had, I felt a secret resentment against Ms. Shepherd for requiring it of Janet so blithely, without showing much empathy for what the woman must be feeling.

When the rooms were back in their original, un-rifled-through-looking state, the only thing left to do was to lock Janet into her cell and clean the glass of finger-prints. She threw her arms around Tomio's neck, then hugged me. I could feel her muscles trembling as she squeezed me. Her cool exterior was just a show. I admired her resiliency and fortitude. I swallowed around the lump in my throat as she let go and stepped back, giving me a wan smile. That smile was the most painful thing I'd seen since I'd watched Eira's body jump under the paddles.

We watched as Janet secreted her radio under some hanging folders in the bottom drawer of her desk. She turned to us. "You'd better go before I lose my nerve."

"We'll be back for you," I said, my voice breaking as Campano closed Janet in. Neither Tomio nor I had the resolve to lock the door.

"I know." She moved forward and put her hand on the glass.

I reached up to press my hand on the plexiglass over hers. When I removed it, Tomio cleaned the glass of prints with his sleeve.

As we left, I reminded Janet to give us two hours to get to the safe-house then test the Lifeline radio so we knew it worked. She nodded. The last thing I saw before the metal door swung shut was her large, haunted eyes.

PART THREE
THE STING

SIXTEEN

HOT PURSUIT

Tomio and I didn't exchange a single word as we drove to the new safe-house and unloaded our luggage. Lost in our own thoughts and feeling weighed down by memories of leaving Janet in her cell, and Gage—wherever he was—pressed us into a morose kind of lethargy.

Pulling our luggage over the crooked stones and up to a large metal gate, I found the key on the ring Campano had given us that matched the huge keyhole and unlocked it. We entered a small rectangular courtyard with an orange tree and a small garden in the center. Two stories of stone balconies with thick curvy spindles ran around the perimeter.

Our flat turned out to be a quaint two-bedroom affair with high ceilings and a window overlooking the street below. Thick storm shutters painted bright red unlocked from the inside and latched to the outer walls. Tomio took the bedroom with the two single beds and left me the four-poster double.

Between the two bedrooms was a bathroom with a claw-foot tub and a line of rust leading into the drain.

But the shower tiles were a bright cheery blue with a line of hand-painted lemons frolicking around the top edge, and there were a lot of clean towels in the cupboard. The fridge however was a disappointment of expired condiments and a half-eaten jar of pickles.

"We need to get groceries." Tomio shut the fridge door and pulled a crumpled menu for a local restaurant from under a magnet which had been fastened to the fridge door. He perused the offerings. "How about some buffalo mozzarella with salad, and a calzone?"

After we'd eaten, still mostly in silence, I leaned against the arch between the kitchen and the living room, rubbing a hand across my brow where I felt the start of a headache.

Tomio considered me. "You okay?"

"Yes. Just..." I couldn't finish, and it was obvious anyway. This whole situation sucked, except for the presence of Tomio himself. I just spread my palms out to indicate the circumstances in general.

The look on his face said, *I know*. He pulled me into a hug.

I lay my head against his chest and wrapped my arms around his waist. "How did everything get so messed up?"

Tomio's heartbeat sounded strong and steady against my ear. He propped his chin on the top of my head. "At the risk of sounding like a moron who hasn't been paying attention, which mess, exactly, are you referring to?"

"All of it. Ryan. Nero. Gage. Janet." I paused and Tomio's body grew still.

"You and me?" he murmured.

I nodded under his chin, then pulled back to look up at him.

His dark eyes roved my face, skimming across my lips in a way that made my heart beat faster.

"Where did you leave things with him?" I asked, knowing he would understand that I meant Gage.

He shoved his hands into his pockets. "You know Gage. He's all class. He forgave me when I told him what happened. But something like that, it breaks trust. I don't think we'll ever be the same. I told him I was sorry and admitted that I've been attracted to you ever since I met you. Where did *you* leave things with him?"

I shivered at the horrible memory, turning away from Tomio so he didn't see the stricken expression that took over my face like a cramp. "We broke up. He's hurt and angry and says I don't know what I want."

"Do you?" Tomio pulled his hands out of his pockets and crossed his arms over his chest, maybe to keep himself from touching me, maybe to protect himself from my answer.

"I think I do." I faced him, leaning against the archway dividing the kitchen from the living room. "I just don't feel right prioritizing what I want until he's safe."

A stillness passed through Tomio at my words. I could feel him processing. "You said before that you didn't think it was a mistake, what we did. I've replayed your words countless times since that day. Did you mean it?"

Tomio leaned against the arch opposite me. I slid down the wall to sit on the floor and he mimicked me, holding my gaze as we sank to the marble.

"I did mean it." I took a deep breath in an effort to

calm my racing heart. "It was a mistake in the sense that we shouldn't have kissed while Gage and I were dating. But it wasn't a mistake in the sense that I learned something important from it."

He waited, expression calm and patient.

"What a kiss is supposed to feel like," I told him, "when a mage-bond isn't ruining it."

The corners of his mouth turned up as the softest of smiles stole across his face. His coal-black eyes took me in with the surprised pleasure of a man discovering one of life's great precepts. He let his legs stretch out in front of him. "But you are hesitant to kiss me again because Gage is missing and you feel like it's another betrayal. You can't let yourself enjoy anything until he's found safe and sound."

"Would you?"

His brows arched. "What? Enjoy kissing you again, even while Gage is missing? Damn right I would, Saxony."

Though his admission hurried my heartbeat in a pleasant way, I shot him a look of surprise.

He lifted his shoulders in an apologetic gesture. "Listen, I do feel bad about what happened. You know I do. I should have been straight with both of you about my feelings earlier, and I should have controlled myself better that day, but we all make mistakes. I've apologized and Gage knows I meant it. He took it like a grown man. Plus, it's not our fault Gage is missing. Yes, I want to do everything possible to rescue him. We *are* doing everything possible to rescue him, more than anyone else is, including his parents, but this situation is not of our making."

I hadn't thought about Chad and Angelica since the

day Gage had been kidnapped. I made a mental note to ask Basil what—how—they were doing, if he even knew. If I really wanted to push it, I could send a text to my mom and ask her if she could find Angelica's number for me, but that would alert my mom and she'd ask a lot of questions I wasn't prepared to answer, and Basil had specifically told me to leave Gage's parents to him. Which led my thoughts to—

"Where the hell is Ryan?" I muttered, wrapping my arms around my knees and laying my forehead on my kneecaps.

Tomio didn't say anything for a long time, not until I looked up and read the open measurement in his expression. His look was not incriminating, but it still made me uncomfortable.

"What?"

"You can change the subject so easily." He sighed. "I'm tired. I should call my mom and let her know I'm okay."

He got up and disappeared into his room, leaving me feeling strangely bereft.

A day passed. Then three.

We got Basil on a video call only once and it was short-lived. In the background someone was crying. And though Basil tried to reassure us that the Agency was getting under control, the harried look on his face said otherwise. Arcturus Agency was in a state of shambles.

Tomio and I watched the map daily: the number of snuffed fires continued to climb as reports rolled in without ceasing.

"What do the shapes mean?" Tomio asked when a new metric appeared on the morning of our fourth day in the new flat. A smattering of squares, triangles, and star-shaped dots had joined the white circles. But even as we watched, the white dots became shapes and a legend appeared in the bottom left corner. Some of the shapes also had a diagonal slash through them.

"Look," I pointed to it. "The square ones are dated last December. The triangles are from this March, the stars and circles are from the two in July."

"Okay, but what are the slashes?" Tomio asked.

I sat back suddenly as the realization hit me like a bucket of ice-water. My hand covered my mouth. Tomio looked from me to the screen and back again, still not getting it.

And then he did.

"Suicides."

FOR THE FIRST couple of days after we'd locked Janet in her cell, Tomio and I couldn't stop talking about her. The outcome of these conversations meant we were too depressed to do much but sit by the radio and mope around the flat with the air conditioning on. When Tomio pointed out that there was nothing we could do but wait, and hammered into my mind that this situation was not of our making, we agreed to explore the areas of Naples we could, if anything just to pass the time more quickly. Waiting was killing us. Ms. Shepherd had told us to 'behave normally'. When one had to think hard about what normal behavior was, it wasn't normal anymore.

We got past our guilt-laden lethargy enough to venture out for a stroll and discovered that we both felt better. After that, we were gone from the villa for most of every day, spending hours under the sun walking miles around the historical centre, always keeping within range of the Miner's Lifeline radio.

Tomio seemed to grow browner by the minute and liked to make fun of me for spreading gobs of sunscreen on my freckly skin.

"The woman can produce enough heat to melt steel but she can't handle a thirty-six-degree day in Naples without a layer of zinc."

I smiled as I rubbed the thick white cream into my cheeks and forehead, standing in front of the mirror in the entrance way of our safe-house flat. "It's not the heat, it's the UV rays."

"But you tan eventually, right?" He leaned a shoulder against the door in a leisurely posture as he watched my ritual, coming close to rub it into my back where it was awkward for me to reach.

"If you want to call a darker shade of white, a tan"—I shrugged—"then sure."

Tomio laughed, and I almost felt normal, like a proper tourist, someone here to enjoy the quaint sights of an ancient city and taste the specialties. Pizza was invented in Naples, or so we'd been told, so we'd agreed to find the most famous pizzeria within our radius and judge it for ourselves. It was something we would do if we were here for fun, something that felt normal.

Well, almost normal.

Every experience was painted with a thin layer of anxiety and guilt. Forty meters below our feet, Janet waited for a psychopath's return.

Heat rippled off the paving stones as we entered Piazza Carità on day six after depositing Janet underground. Towering, well-manicured date palms heavy with yellow strings of fruit cast short fat shadows. A flock of pigeons coming in for a landing around a woman sitting on a stone bench made the familiar whistling sound that took me back to my summer in Venice. Specifically: hanging out in the Piazza san Marco. Crowds of people, some fanning themselves with tourist booklets and some carrying parasols to ward off the powerful summer sun, clustered around the entrances to the gelaterias and pizzerias. Sweat glistened on tanned brows and upper lips.

We walked the narrow stone streets, perusing the trinket shops, trying the famous rum-soaked Neapolitan pastry known as baba, drinking more than our fair share of cappuccinos (which always elicited a strange look if ordered in the afternoon), and taking photos of the picturesque bay.

"Let me take the bag." Tomio held out a hand for the small fabric shopping bag we kept the radio in. I passed it over then consulted the ratty tourist map we'd found on a table in the flat, left behind by a former occupant.

"The Santa Chiara Monastery, tombs and museum is only a ten-minute walk. Should we go there after pizza? I'm not necessarily jonesing to see another church, but the cloister is full of pretty, hand-painted tiles. It's supposed to be amazing."

"I don't feel like pizza anymore. Let's get gelato first, then visit the cloister. I'm in love with that bacio flavor." Tomio took off his sunglasses to clean them as he scoped out the ice cream shop options scattered throughout the piazza.

"Did you know that bacio means kiss?" I replied offhandedly as I tucked the map into the pocket of my shorts.

Tomio's dark eyes snapped to mine with an inquisitive look that asked if I meant to bring up a certain memory with that comment, or if it was an accident. He hadn't broached the subject of our kiss or our relationship since the first night in the flat when I'd changed the subject. Even sharing the flat over the last five nights, he'd been nothing but a gentleman. He'd averted his eyes when I came out of the bathroom dripping and in nothing but a towel. He'd moved back if I invaded his space in the kitchen while we were cooking together, and he'd taken the sofa opposite whichever one I was sitting on rather than sitting beside me, even if there was plenty of room. I'd gotten the message loud and clear. If we were going to talk about our kiss or our relationship again, he was going to leave it up to me to broach the subject.

"Just sharing my small Italian vocabulary."

Tomio selected a gelateria and walked toward it. I fell in step beside him. We joined the back of a line of sweating tourists. Air conditioning licked at my cheeks and the skin of my chest as we shuffled forward in line, promising more of the same once we made it over the threshold.

Through the corner window of the shop, I caught a flash of broad shoulders and a low ponytail lying against a powder-blue shirt. He passed out of sight before I had a chance to focus on him but my body tensed. I turned, wanting to peek around the corner and make sure my eyes were just playing tricks on me and it wasn't Dante.

"Where are you going?" Tomio asked.

"I'll be right back, I just want to double check something."

"What flavor do you want?"

"Stracciatella, please," I said over my shoulder.

Trying not to shove people out of my way, I rounded the corner of the shop and scoped the crowd milling through the narrow street. The street went downhill for several blocks before butting up against Via Nuovo Marina, which ran parallel to the bay. Beyond that the Bay of Naples sparkled almost painfully in the bright sunlight.

Squinting and stepping into the shadow of the street my gaze snagged on the powder-blue shirt and long hair. He wove his way through the busy crowd, disappearing and reappearing, walking alone. Without a better look, I couldn't be sure, but the way he moved suggested it was Dante. My legs moved of their own accord as my eyes gripped the back of his head and didn't let go. Muttering an apology as I bumped against a shoulder, I barely noticed when the person turned and asked me something in Italian.

It was impossible to run, but he was walking fast so I picked up the pace enough to close the gap between us. My heart began to bump heavily against my ribs as visibility of the man in the blue shirt improved. As he reached the end of the block and looked to the right at oncoming traffic, his profile gave him away. He crossed the road at a jog, and I picked up speed. It was Dante. I was sure of it now. I thought fleetingly of calling Tomio, but he was holding my bag with my cell phone, and this was an opportunity I couldn't pass up. If I turned back, I'd lose Dante.

My fire blazed to life, fueled by a sudden flare of

rage. What would I see when I looked into Dante's eyes. Would they have that telltale reflection? If they did, would I be able to stop myself from reacting?

Crossing the street, I followed him along a narrower block with less foot-traffic. He heard my flip-flops behind him before I reached him, and turned, lifting his eyes to mine. Recoiling, he staggered back a few steps as we both halted, glaring. Relief sent my anger into retreat when I saw that Dante was still only human. His eyes had not changed.

The initial look of startled shock at finding me behind him flickered away like he'd changed a channel inside his mind. His familiar and annoying self-assured smugness took its place. "Saxony. Fancy running into you—"

"Where is he?" I spat.

He froze for a fraction of a second before widening his eyes in a parody of confusion. "Who?"

His bad acting was enough to confirm what we'd suspected. I jammed a finger into the soft spot just under his collarbone, putting enough power behind it to bruise him. "My friend, Gage. What have you done with him?"

He swiped at my hand but missed, taking a step back as my blazing eyes and hard poke told him I meant business.

"You're insane," he sneered. "You've always been a little crazy, but now I know you're loco. Why would I know where your pretty boyfriend is? Maybe he finally realized his girlfriend was mentally ill and took off."

His words were harsh but he was backpedaling through the street as I strode forward, teeth clenched. I poked him under the other shoulder, harder this time.

He hissed, baring his teeth and snarling in Italian.

"Yes. It hurts, doesn't it? It will tickle compared to what I'll do if you don't tell me where you're keeping Gage. Right. Now." I poked him in the same place, sending fire into my finger to make it rock-hard and firing into my shoulder and elbow.

Dante yelled in pain and grabbed at his shoulder, his eyes filling with fear. "Cazzo fai?"

"I know you have him, you spineless, obscene little boy." I poked him again on the other side, using fire to make it hurt. "If you don't let him go, no number of rent-a-cops and no amount of money will save you. I know where you live. There will be nowhere to hide."

Even as the threats dripped from my lips I knew it was the wrong approach. I should be using my feminine wiles to get Dante to trust me before I resorted to threats of violence. But it felt too good to intimidate him, instead of being intimidated by him. I jabbed him again.

"Sei pazzo," Dante cried out, his voice breaking. Then he bolted toward the Bay of Naples.

Kicking off my flip-flops, I shot after him, firing down my legs and through my feet to put on speed and soften the blows of my tender soles against the hard pavement. Reaching out, I snagged the back of Dante's polo. He jerked away but I held the fabric fast.

Snarling, he twisted and bent at the waist as I yanked him toward me. The shirt ripped and then came off his body like a plastic casing pulled from a sausage. Vaulting away from me with a cry of genuine horror, he sprinted to the end of the street and turned the corner.

Dropping his shirt, I followed, pouring on speed only to have to pull back before I barreled into a family pushing a baby carriage. I skirted them, not worried that I couldn't catch Dante, there was no way he could outrun me.

He ran through the crowd ahead, dodging and weaving and sending terrified glances over his shoulder. I ran after him, feet light on the pavement, holding back but keeping close enough that I could grab him as soon as we cleared this crowd.

Dante ran with one hand jammed in his pocket, pulled something out and for a moment my heart went into my throat thinking he had a small gun. But though the sun glinted on metal in his hand, it was not a weapon but a fob with a silver key.

With a final venomous look, he turned another corner as I wove my way through a group of teenage girls taking selfies with the bay in the background. As I rounded the corner the sound of a scooter engine revving met my ears. The black Vespa jumped forward and its back tire screamed on the pavement as Dante took off up the street.

I clenched my teeth as fire surged down my legs and I took off after Dante like a sprinter off the starting block. My body surged forward, arms and legs pumping as I closed the gap to Dante's back wheel. My eyes felt hot and swollen and my vision sharpened and narrowed on my target. I stretched out a hand to grab the rail behind his seat.

With a glance over his shoulder, his face transformed and he shrieked, sounding more like a young girl than a grown man. His back tire screamed as the scooter surged forward. He lurched out of reach as he careened wildly, narrowly avoiding a dumpster.

Power detonated in my hips, knees and ankles as I

flew over the dumpster like a hurdler, front leg outstretched. Cushioning my landing as I reached for the swerving Vespa, my foot hit a divot in the pavement, throwing me off balance. Knowing I was going down, I tucked my head and rolled into a dive. The buzz of the scooter's engine grew loud in one ear as I came out of the roll and back to my feet. My tumble meant Dante gained another several feet. Cursing under my breath as he angled around a corner, I poured on more speed, this time heedless of the group of tourists who scattered before us, bleating like a flock of frightened lambs.

Someone screamed as I surged by, single-minded in my pursuit, someone else yelled in Italian, yet another uttered a stream of incredulous epithets. The group fell away behind and the street opened up. Dante pushed the scooter faster as my footfalls came closer and closer together. My breathing turned labored but my detonations did not cease, asking more and more from my system. I became aware of a vague wonderment belonging to the Saxony who was watching all of this with a type of dismayed amazement, even as my speed increased. How much of this could my heart and lungs take?

A one-word answer that was not an answer but meant I would not stop became a repeat in my mind.

Gage. Gage. Gage.

Ahead of me and trying to get away was the one person who knew where Gage was. If I didn't get him in my hands now and force him to tell me by any means necessary—and yes, I knew that in my current emotional state I would not hesitate to inflict fire and pain, even if it meant I'd be haunted by it later—I would not likely get another chance. Nero was not here to protect Dante, and even my promise to Enzo seemed distant and unimportant.

The black Vespa's rider bent low over the handlebars and the sound of the engine grew high-pitched and tinny as the machine complained that too much was being asked of it.

Sucking in breath but amazed at the continued power the fire was pouring into my muscles, I closed the gap.

Flashing another wide-eyed look back, Dante took the bend up ahead at a dangerous speed. The Vespa skidded and he almost lost control, scraping the front bumper along the brick wall of the narrow alley.

Lest I make the same misjudgement in my pursuit, I leapt for the wall and ran along it like a trick-biker rides a steeply banked turn. Another moment and I was back on the ground and in pursuit, but my laboring heart sank as I realized where this road led.

Straight onto Nuovo Marina, the busy, fast-flowing road running parallel to the bay. I could not continue into heavy traffic without risking many lives.

Dante knew it too and used the slight downhill ahead of him to add more speed. Recklessly, without any regard for oncoming traffic, Dante took the straightest path he could.

Straight through the patrons sitting at tables in front of a patisserie on the corner. Screams pierced the air as the buzzing scooter bore down upon them. Tables and chairs were overturned as people dove to get out of the way. Dante's Vespa plowed through the melee. He skidded and almost fell as he narrowly avoided a table rolling along its edge like an oversized, thin tire.

My legs and knees pumped like pistons, working

hard to bring my body to a halt. My bare feet slipped on grit and I landed on my butt and skidded, coming to a bruised stop in front of an overturned chair and a pile of broken ceramics.

Dante's scooter was already out of sight, swallowed by the flow of traffic.

Knees shaking and fire retreating, I got to my feet and helped a frightened old lady who'd half fallen and been shoved against the wall. A patisserie employee emerged from the open front door carrying a tray of pastries and drinks to stare wide-eyed at the wreckage.

Shame-faced, although no one seemed to realize that the chaos was partly my fault, I began to help the patrons and staff right the furniture and clean up the mess. Aside from a few scraped palms and bruised hips, no one was seriously hurt.

With a last sour look at the traffic, I began to jog back toward the piazza where Tomio would be losing his mind with worry, dreading the tongue-lashing I knew I was in for.

SEVENTEEN

DISSENTION IN THE RANKS

I found Tomio standing beside a garbage can in the piazza. He spotted me as soon as I entered the piazza. His shoulders dropped with relief, but he didn't call to me. I crossed the piazza, wearing my flip flops after finding them laying in the street where I'd left them, and stopped by him. He held no ice cream and was white around the mouth. I almost made a joke about the two untouched ice cream cups melting on top of the pile of rubbish to try and lighten him up, but I'd never seen Tomio's face so stiff nor his eyes snapping like this. He stared as I approached, the bag containing the radio and my cell dangled from one fisted hand. I waited for him to talk and when he didn't, a flicker of dread passed through me. I knew he'd be upset, but had underestimated just how upset.

"I am sorry," I murmured.

Tomio turned and stalked stiffly in the direction of our villa and I scampered to catch up.

"I thought I saw Dante," I explained, feeling my

tummy turn over. Why wasn't he saying anything? "I had to make sure and I was right, it was him."

Tomio shot me a glare that might have turned me to ash if I wasn't a mage. His bronzed complexion looked green, his generous mouth pulled down in an angry gash. He looked away like he couldn't stand the sight of me and turned up our street, picking up the pace. I almost had to run to keep up.

"I'm sorry, I wanted to come back for you, but if I had I would have lost him for sure."

Tomio didn't respond, just continued to stalk in the direction of our safe-house.

"Of course, I lost him anyway, but there was a chance I could have gotten information out of him about Gage."

Tomio sped up, the bag swinging wildly at his side.

"I'm sorry I frightened you, really. I am." I reached for his arm but pulled back. If he snatched his arm away, it might undo me. I scrambled to make him understand.

"What would you have done differently if you had seen him and there was no time to do anything but pursue? This is our friend Gage we're talking about. His life hangs in the balance."

Tomio rooted the villa's keys out of his pocket and jammed the oversized iron thing into the lock. The bolts clicked back and he heaved the heavy door open like it was made of parchment.

"Tomio. Talk to me." Following him to our front door, real dismay settled into my heart. I'd never seen him like this.

He unlocked our front door, strode into the entrance, set the bag on a side table, almost knocking over a glass statue of a woman carrying a basket on her hip in the process. Heading straight for the bathroom, he slammed the door shut. A moment later, I heard the sound of retching.

Horrified, I stood outside the door, not sure what to do. "Tomio? Are you okay?"

His answer was more retching, then the flush of the toilet.

"Was it me? Or something you ate? I'm really hoping it was the cheese toastie you had this morning."

The sink's tap came on and I heard the sound of Tomio swishing water and spitting. The sound of a vigorous brushing of teeth followed that, then another flush of the toilet, another rinse and spit.

"Tomio?" I tapped gingerly on the bathroom door with a fingernail. "I'm really sorry."

The door opened. Tomio stood there with wet hair standing up in spikes and two red circles flushing his cheeks. The glassy black orbs of his eyes settled on mine and he croaked, "I forgive you, you idiot."

I almost burst into tears. Instead I rushed at him, wrapping my arms around him. He made a surprised grunt but returned my hug, turning his head away so he didn't breathe into my face.

"Easy," he muttered.

I am an idiot, I thought. Gage had been yanked from the street like he was a little kid, leaving me all alone and feeling panicked and helpless. It didn't matter that I was Burned, I was not immortal and I could make mistakes. If something had happened to me, what would Tomio have done? He would have been left in the position that Gage's kidnapping had left me in.

We stood there hugging for several minutes, until Tomio began to hiccup and needed more water.

"Promise me you'll never do that to me again," he said when he'd taken three big swallows from a cup in the kitchen, a hand over his flat belly. "We have to stick together. You can't just go running off without telling me where you're going. We're partners."

I nodded, feeling dumber by the second, and still a little shocked at the violence of Tomio's reaction.

"We're all alone here, with no help from the Agency. God knows what Basil is dealing with back there in Britain, but I know that he would come if he could. Things are bad, Saxony. Don't you realize that?"

A spark of anger. "Of course I do."

"The future of the remaining mages hangs over our heads, not just Gage. If something had happened to you, it would have landed on my shoulders alone."

I crossed my arms. "I do know that, that's why I went after Dante. It was a chance to force him to tell us where Gage is. In the moment, it seemed like the right thing to do. I didn't know it was going to make you vomit."

He wiped his mouth. "It's a reaction I've had since I was kid. It only happens when I get really scared. I can fight it most of the time, keep things down, as long as I don't try to talk or explain myself until the nausea passes. It's been a long time since I've been that freaked out."

"How did you ever make it through all those fights then?"

He shot me a withering glare tinged with affection. "It doesn't happen when I'm frightened for myself, you numpty. It happens when someone I love is in grave danger and I'm not able to help them."

Someone I love.

The words echoed in my ears like a call into a canyon, then hung in the air between us. Tomio's eyes took me in, so big and dark and beautiful I thought I might fall into them if I didn't look away.

I looked at the floor.

My laptop dinged and the screen lit up.

Tomio and I met each other at the table, bumping shoulders as we read the text that came in from Ms. Shepherd.

N LANDED AT NAP 13:35, IDENTITY CONFIRMED.

A photo loaded and the pixels cleared. The shot had been taken from a security camera hanging in a high corner of a terminal building. A jet plane that looked a bit like the one Targa's shipping company used stood on the tarmac with its passenger door lifted and locked open. A man in a baseball cap and dark glasses had been stepping down onto the tarmac when the image was snapped. An airport worker stood off to one side, along with two security guards. A metal detector hung from one guard's hand.

Tomio and I moved closer to the screen.

"Is that him? How do they know? He's too far away," Tomio asked, giving voice to the precise questions I had.

Another photo loaded, this one blurry but growing clearer by the second as the pixels refined. This image was taken by the same camera, presumably after the security check since Nero was closer to the camera and the guards were now behind him. He looked to the side and had a toothpick clamped between his teeth, which made him look like he was grinning nastily. This time there was no mistaking his identity. He was the same man we had seen in the batch of photos Mehmet had shared with us.

"It's him," Tomio and I spoke in tandem.

We looked at one another. My pulse was racing. Would Nero think there was anything fishy in Janet's behavior? Would she get the secret out of him? If she did, would she get it in time to make a difference? What would Tomio and I be required to do once we had Nero's next move?

"Why do I suddenly feel like this is a crazy plan?" Tomio asked, tugging at his hair again.

"We need help," I replied, agreeing with him.

He looked pale and thoughtful. "We can't rely on the Agency, but..."

"But, what?"

He raised his eyes. "What about Ryan?"

I snorted. "I already told him Gage got taken. He didn't believe me. Besides, how can we trust him? He's buddy-buddy with Nero now."

"We don't know that for sure. It looks bad, I agree, but blood is thicker than water. Ryan is ruthless, but if we can convince him that Gage really is in trouble, he won't turn his back on his twin."

"You have a lot more faith in him than I do. That's one Wendig I've been lied to and manipulated by too many times to reach out and ask for help."

"Even for Gage's sake?"

I threw up my hands, exasperated. "I told you, he doesn't believe me. Basil said that even his parents can't get a hold of him."

"But—" Tomio pulled his cell phone out of his pocket and woke the screen, scrolling through his photos and videos. He selected the one we took of Nero's subterranean lair and of Janet. "He might believe this."

It took me a second to realize what he was saying. If we sent Ryan the video to prove that we met Janet and we'd been to Nero's place, Ryan should figure I hadn't been lying.

But there was another problem, in my mind. "Ryan is loyal to Nero now. If we alert Ryan that we've met Janet and know Nero's secret location, our cover could be blown."

I could see from his expression that Tomio disagreed. "I know you and Ryan have had your differences—"

I scoffed and rolled my eyes.

"But he's Gage's twin. He would never throw Gage under the bus."

"Why not?" I shot back. "He's done it before. He heavily drugged his own brother to get him out of the way when he tricked me into helping him Burn."

Tomio sliced a hand through the air. "A horrible, rotten thing to do. But aside from a hangover when he woke up, Gage was fine. I still believe that Ryan would never intentionally hurt Gage."

I gaped. "You're mixing the brothers up. It's Gage who would never do anything to hurt Ryan. He's loyal to a fault. Ryan can't even spell the word."

Tomio frowned. "I think you're wrong, and if we don't try to get Ryan in on this then we're depriving ourselves of our most powerful ally."

I felt my eyes grow warm. "Are you willing to stake

Gage's life on Ryan's loyalty? Because he hasn't exhibited any in the past."

Tomio didn't hesitate. "Yes. I'm telling you, Ryan has made a lot of bad calls in his life, but he will never betray his brother. My bet is that he was out of the country before Dante and Nero made their nefarious little deal and he doesn't even know that they have Gage."

"And if you're wrong, our only chance to save Gage and stop Nero will be blown."

He straightened and spoke louder. "I'm not wrong."

My face flushed with the heat of frustration. How could Tomio not see what was so obvious? My volume increased. "I think you are, and I've had more run-ins with Ryan than you have. I know how his mind works. Nothing will get between him and his thirst for power, not even his own family. He stole from his own parents, don't forget."

Tomio spread his hands. "Something they didn't care about and couldn't use. It was stuffed in the back of a seacan for over a decade."

My mouth dropped open. "I can't believe you're defending him."

Tomio let his head fall forward and took a breath, then looked at me. "I'm not defending him or saying that what he did was right. It clearly wasn't. All I'm saying is that stealing that orb from his parents' collection is one thing, letting Gage lose his fire or die is another thing entirely. That is a line he won't cross."

"I'm not willing to take that chance." I crossed my arms and let my eyes blaze with fire.

"Are you pulling rank?" Tomio asked, eyes wide.

I flushed but couldn't deny it. "Yes. We disagree

and we have to have someone in charge to make decisions. I won't compromise this operation by bringing a viper into our nest."

Tomio looked at me with some wonder, his mouth twitched with humor. "Wow. Operation? You sound like a real agent. Is it wrong I'm turned on right now?"

I picked up a pencil from beside my laptop and threw it at his head. "Ha ha."

Tomio ducked, laughing, and snagged the pencil out of the air. Just like that the tension between us diffused.

"Fine. We'll do it your way," he said.

I nodded and turned to fill a glass of water at the sink. "Thank you."

Tomio murmured something under his breath.

"What was that?" I turned off the tap, the cup hovering under it, half full.

"I said: for now." Tomio smiled, his eyes sparkling in an unrepentant way as he left the kitchen.

EIGHTEEN

A VIPER IN THE NEST

"Vole to Surfer, Vole to Surfer!" The radio blared from the table beside my bed. "Are you there?"

I lurched to sitting in the dark bedroom, blinking bleary-eyed at the clock. It was twelve minutes past one in the morning. The curtains fluttered with a soft breeze at the open windows. Heart climbing the inside of my neck with panicky claws, I reached for the radio and misjudged, knocking it with the back of my hand and sending it onto the floor with a clatter.

With a curse I threw the covers back, terrified that I'd broken the thing. "That would be just what we need," I muttered, snatching up the radio and scampering for Tomio's room as I depressed the button.

"Surfer One, here," I said into the walkie-talkie. "I'm waking Surfer Two."

The radio crackled several seconds later. "Copy."

Pushing through Tomio's partially open door, I found he was already rising to sit against the headboard of his narrow bed. The thin sheet fell away from the smooth musculature of his naked chest and I almost forgot what I was doing in his bedroom.

"I heard the crash," he murmured, reminding me I was here on official business.

I nodded and sat on the bed beside him with the radio in my hand. "Surfer One and Two here," I said, clearing my throat. "Go ahead, Vole. We're listening."

"It's happening tonight. Nero just left ten minutes ago. I only waited this long to tell you to make sure he wasn't coming back. Everything is quiet down here. He's meeting Dante, who has Gage, at a place called Il Cono tonight, rather, this morning. Now."

Tomio and I exchanged a spooked look, eyes big in the dark.

"Did you get an exact time?"

"No. I just know he's gone and he won't be back until the job is done," Janet said. "You'd better hurry."

"What's Il Cono?" Tomio asked.

"The Cone," I replied at the same time as Janet's voice came through the speaker.

Tomio rolled his eyes. "Yeah, I got that. I do have some Italian. What the hell is 'The Cone' and where is it?"

There was no answer for several seconds, then: "I don't know. I thought you would."

"That's it? You don't have any other information?" I couldn't keep the incredulity out of my voice.

"Sorry. That's it. I was lucky to gather that much. I don't know if I'm being paranoid but I think he might suspect something."

My stomach clenched and Tomio's face seemed to go pale in the gloom. "What makes you think that?"

"Just a feeling," she replied. "Like I said, I might

just be paranoid." She gave a nervous laugh. "You'd better go figure out what Il Cono is. Don't worry about me, I'm fine. Just like old times down here."

"We'll come for you as soon as we can," I said into the radio. "Thanks, Vole."

"I know, and you're welcome. Good luck, Surfers. Over and out."

"Over and out."

I headed for the laptop on the kitchen table as Tomio followed. Setting the radio down, I woke the computer up and did a quick search for 'Il Cono, Napoli, Italia'.

Tomio hovered at my shoulder as the search engine returned a single result. We leaned in to peer at the screen as a location pinned on the map of Northwest Naples appeared. A business listing along with a cheerfully colored logo and some photographs of a quaint establishment greeted our eyes.

"An ice cream shop?" I blinked up at Tomio, his face close to mine, eyes troubled. "Is it just me or does that seem really implausible?"

"It's weird, but that's what she said and I think we're lucky there isn't more than one location. It must be a cover. Come on. Let's go."

As we scrambled to dress in dark clothing and pack some water, our phones and some food, I sent Basil a text message updating him on the information Janet had shared. Tomio and I threw possibilities back and forth as we locked the flat and made our way to the Fiat, one of many cars lined up in a row on the street.

A shadow slipped underneath the small car's frame as I pressed the unlock button. Pausing at the driver's side door, I bent over to look under the front bumper.

The eyes of a frightened feline curled up under the car's axle stared unblinkingly back at me.

"Come on out from under there, kitty," I said in a soothing tone. "We're short on time here."

"Just go. The engine will frighten it away," said Tomio opening the side door.

I opened the door and slid into the driver's seat, leaving one foot out on the pavement. Turning on the engine, we waited a second and were rewarded when a dark streak shot from under the car to behind a dumpster across the street. Closing the door, I pulled away from the curb as Tomio pulled up the directions to Il Cono on his phone.

Piloting the car onto the Nuovo Via Marina and heading northwest toward an area of Naples we'd never visited, I mulled over how much time we might have.

"They still have to start the dehydration process," I said, my hands tight on the wheel. I was grateful for the near zero traffic on the roads.

"Unless they're coordinated enough that Dante started it already and Nero is joining him toward the end of it," Tomio answered. "Take this road, where it curves to the right."

We began to climb through a cramped residential area. A full moon gleamed crisp and bright from a vast night sky. Under other circumstances I would have admired the display of stars and constellations set so starkly against the smooth, cloudless backdrop of violet.

"That would be risky though, right? What if Nero got delayed for some reason? They only have one shot. If Gage dies, they won't have another crack at it."

"I don't disagree, but Janet's hunch also plays a part. If Nero really does suspect her, they have reason to hurry. If not, then they probably would take their time and be careful."

The lights of Naples appeared below as we gained elevation, cutting a sharp half-moon arc across the coastline and contrasting sharply with the blackness of the bay.

"So how much time should we assume we have?" My fire crackled eagerly in my torso, thinking of Gage lying there slowly burning from the inside out. Once I got to him, I could see what state he was in using evanescent vision.

"None," Tomio replied as he gave me another instruction and I turned the car left onto a narrow winding road. A few small businesses sprang up here, tabbacherias, pizzerias, banks, a few restaurants and clothing shops. "It's six minutes up this road. Right-hand side. It's not wise to assume we have any time at all. We just have to find him as fast as we can."

I nudged a little more speed out of the Fiat, taking a curve fast enough to send Tomio's shoulder into the door. A scooter buzzed into sight, its single headlight blinding me temporarily.

Tomio swore and grabbed for the handle over the door.

The scooter droned by with a single, angry beep.

"It will add a whole new dimension of difficulty to this operation if you kill us. Slow down," Tomio said as I took the next turn while accelerating. "It's three-hundred meters to Il Cono. Park here and we'll run the rest of the way. We don't want to lose the element of surprise."

I piloted the car to a side street and went two more blocks before squeezing up onto the sidewalk with a mish-mash of other tiny cars. I turned off the engine as Tomio grabbed our backpack of supplies. I locked the car and pocketed the key fob in the zippered chest-pocket of my jacket as Tomio zipped up his own thin, black windbreaker and shrugged on the backpack. It was far too warm for coats of any kind, but we needed to be as invisible as possible, so that meant long sleeves. Tomio drew a line when I suggested toques and bala-clavas just in case we needed to hide in the shadows. He accused me of over-dramatizing, I argued we should be prepared for anything and it wasn't like I was asking him to wear war-paint. He argued that if someone spotted two kids in face-masks, they'd for sure call the police. In the end, since I'd pulled rank about Ryan, I'd let him win on the balaclavas. Plus I thought he had a point about someone calling the police.

"What's the plan," Tomio murmured as we approached Il Cono from behind.

"We break in as quietly as possible. Neutralize any resistance. Now's the time for you to exercise those killer martial arts skills."

We crossed the road avoiding the coins of light thrown by the streetlamps. Il Cono was on a corner, so we approached it from the side street. A door fifty yards ahead might be its back door access.

"And if it's just the two of them? I'll take Nero and you take Dante?" Tomio whispered.

"I should take Nero, you should take Dante," I said, stomach prickling with the feet of a thousand ants marching. The anticipation of this confrontation was worse than the action itself. I wanted to get this over with as quickly as possible. A fleeting memory of what Basil had said about the mage who possessed an orb whispered through my mind like a gust of wind through a broken shutter. I wished I knew the nature of the power and if Nero had indeed accessed it. I was Burned and Tomio was a champion martial artist, but what was Nero?

"I'm the fighter," Tomio whispered, as if reading my mind. He put a gentle hand on my shoulder. "Wait. Let's settle this before we get any closer."

I stopped. "I'm Burned. Nero is Burned. It won't be a fair fight if you take him. Besides, you've been coaching me for a year now. Where's the faith?"

Tomio frowned and for a startled second, then: "Fine. I'll take Dante. Does he have any training at all?"

I thought back to our confrontations in Venice. Dante had sucker punched me once, but after that his violent strategies had relied upon taking one of his own family members hostage with a blowtorch. I didn't recall any evidence of fighting know-how. "I don't think so. He's a coward at heart, and a bully."

"Boring," Tomio breathed.

"Still. He's the son of a mafia boss and no stranger to violence. Plus he's desperate, and that makes him dangerous."

Tomio nodded. "Noted. Let's do this."

He moved quietly on cat-like feet and I stayed on his heel like his shadow as we closed the distance to our target.

SLINKING along the street and hugging the wall, I followed Tomio to the side door. Once there we hesitated. An address to the right of the doorjamb suggested it was actually a private flat, not the ice cream's shop's rear access, if it even had a rear access. We moved forward to the edge of the shop's window, leaving the door untouched. The front window—decorated with hand-painted frolicking gelato cones with happy faces—was dark. No interior lights. No sign anyone was inside.

A cat wailed from some distant street, lifting my hackles. Another cat answered with a deep, mournful cry. We shrank back as a car passed.

"There's no one here," Tomio whispered, taking another furtive glance through the window and then turning to me. "There's no access to any back room. It's not right. This can't be the place."

I rested my back against the wall and let my head tilt back, thinking. Liberating my phone from my pocket, I opened a search engine and did another search. No other 'Il Cono' appeared. My heart sank. I expanded the search limits to include the Amalfi coast and the cities there. One more Il Cono appeared but it was in a busy main street of Ravello, several hours drive away and surrounded by other businesses. From the photos, it was an even smaller ice cream shop than the one we were standing beside. The cool hands of panic began to wrap themselves around my neck. I shivered and turned to Tomio, realizing that he too was on his phone but he wasn't doing a search, he was texting someone.

"Who are you texting?" I leaned in close, hope rising in my breast that Tomio had thought of someone who might know, but he turned the screen off before I could get a good look.

"No one," he muttered, then moved past me

heading for the car. "Come on. Let's see if we can get a hold of someone at the Agency."

I slipped my phone into the inside pocket of my jacket and took out the keys to the Fiat as we walked down the slope to the car. As I slid behind the wheel, my phone vibrated. Leaving the door open, I pulled my phone out and stared at the screen. I was still staring at it in disbelief as Tomio sat in the passenger's seat and the car's shocks protested.

"Who is it?" Tomio asked, then leaned over the console to see it for himself. "Oh, wow."

A cauldron of bats took flight in my stomach, twisting and churning and making me feel nauseous. The name on my phone's screen was Ryan Wendig.

"Answer it," Tomio hissed with urgency.

"Why would he call me back now?" My hands quivered and I let out the breath I'd been holding.

"He'll tell you when you answer it."

My thumb hovered over the answer button but I could not bring myself to press it. After I let it go for another two rings, Tomio took the phone and I didn't stop him. I was too paralyzed to know what to do.

"Hello?" Tomio sat back in the seat looking far more comfortable than I thought he should, considering who he was talking to. "Hey, Ryan. Yes. She's right beside me. Hang on."

Tomio held my phone out and I stared at it. Impatiently, he nudged it further into my space. Finally, I took the phone.

"Hi," I husked, then cleared my throat.

"I'm sorry I didn't believe you," Ryan said, raising his voice above some steady background noise that sounded like a diesel engine. It was difficult to read his tone. "Where are you?"

I opened my mouth but couldn't form words, at least not fast enough for Tomio.

He leaned over and pressed the speaker button. "Ryan, you're on speakerphone. Go ahead," Tomio said, sounding eager.

It hit me like a flour sack to the side of the head. Tomio had texted Ryan, prompting him to call me. All the air felt like it was sucked from my lungs as the realization of his betrayal sliced into me like a letter-opener between the ribs. Lifting my eyes to Tomio's face, I stared at him in horror, accusation all over my face.

Tomio withered a little under my glare and looked away, but I sensed no regret in him.

"Where are you?" Ryan repeated.

Tomio opened his mouth but I got there first, the words snapping out. "Where are *you*, Ryan?"

"I'm parked outside my rental flat with the engine running, waiting for you to tell me where you are so I can come meet you. You'll never free Gage without my help, and I'll never free him without yours. We need to work together, and fast. It may already be too late."

"Why now? I told you Gage was in danger back when he was taken over a week ago and you didn't believe me." I pulled my leg in and shut the Fiat's door.

"I know, if you were listening, I already apologized for not believing you. I was sure it was a ruse you and Gage cooked up to trap me. I believe you now." Ryan's voice cracked. Either he was fighting for control over his emotions and he really was terrified for his brother, or he had superior acting skills. I didn't doubt the latter, but I greatly doubted for former. Still... Gage, Nero and

Dante were clearly not here to do their dirty business inside a tiny gelato shop. We had no idea as to their whereabouts and time was running out.

"I just got back into the country today," Ryan was saying. "I tried texting Gage's phone but he didn't answer. He doesn't ever not answer me. Still, I thought you might be playing a long game. But when Tomio texted me with a recent photo of himself and you here in Naples..."

I shot daggers at Tomio a second time. He patted the air as if to say, just wait, don't be mad.

"...I knew Gage was in trouble. Tomio wouldn't be there otherwise."

"What about you and Nero?" I asked. "You have a deal."

Ryan's tone turned into a growl. "As far as I'm concerned, he trampled any agreement we had when he allowed your piss-ant ex-boyfriend to kidnap my brother."

I gasped with fury. "Dante is not my ex—"

Tomio rolled his eyes so hard the irises totally disappeared. "Guys, focus. Ryan, where the hell is Il Cono?"

Ryan seemed startled into speechlessness for a second, then he answered in the tone of someone newly enlightened. "Of course. It's so obvious."

He laughed suddenly and without humor. In fact, it was a cold and frightening sound. Tomio and I exchanged a nervous look.

"Listen carefully. You need to go through a suburb just outside of Naples called Portici. Get on the SP19. Climb until you reach the turn off for SP140—"

Tomio scrambled for a pen or pencil in the Fiat's dashboard console, but there was nothing there but tissues and the car's rental agreement. He sent a desperate look that said, *we'd better not forget this*, then glared at the phone so hard I half expected it to light on fire.

"—when you see a sign for Oservatoria Vesuviano, pull off to the right side of the road. There's a rest stop behind some trees. Quite hidden so keep your eyes peeled. I'll meet you there. I'm driving a black Alfa Romeo Giulietta. Go slow. The road is not well lit up there."

The road is not well lit up there. Where was he taking us?

"Are you wearing sneakers?" Ryan's voice was clipped and business-like, all emotion and concern for his twin stowed away in the face of a job to be done.

"Yes," Tomio answered, since I was too busy still wondering how we'd suddenly found ourselves in partnership with one of my least favorite people in the world, against another of my least favorite people in the world, whom I was supposed to be bringing back to his father safe and in one unburned piece. I closed my eyes and forced myself to inhale slowly. I felt claustrophobia lurking at the edges of my consciousness, not from the tiny Fiat we occupied, but from the metaphoric walls closing in around me, funneling me into an outcome I could neither control nor influence.

"Good. We need to go off-road and on foot, and the ground is treacherous there."

My skin prickled as my mind caught like a minnow in a net on what Ryan had said about the sign we were to watch for. I lifted my eyes to the hulking shape in the distance, towering over the smear of city lights below and blocking out the stars like a menacing black hole.

"Vesuviano?" I asked with a croak. "As in... the volcano that buried Pompeii and Herculaneum?"

"Yes," Ryan replied smoothly, the certainty in his tone coming in clearly through the cell phone's speakers. I felt like someone had laid a lead blanket over my shoulders. What were we walking into?

"Il Cono is an affectionate term for Mount Vesuvius," Ryan continued. "They've gone inside the volcano."

NINETEEN

IL CONO

Tomio put the Mount Vesuvius Observatory location into the GPS on his phone and set it up where I could see it. We were a long way from the mountain top. The ice cream shop gaffe had cost us. According to the GPS, it would take us over an hour to reach the Observatory, but it was the wee hours of morning and the roads were quiet.

Driving fast through the narrow residential streets of Naples was treacherous and risky, even at night. Parked cars jutted into the street, the occasional car or scooter loomed suddenly around blind corners, street animals ran across the road at the last second, narrowly avoiding tires, and hairpin corners were frequent and confusing to read, even with directions. But once we were back on a main road, I pushed the Fiat to the speed limit of ninety kilometres per hour, then crept over one-hundred, then to one-twenty.

At one-thirty, Tomio said, "I get it, but let's try not to get pulled over, eh, speedy Canadian?"

I slowed the Fiat to one-ten, hoping the Italian cops

gave that much leeway. We had to slow again when we reached the town of Portici and pick our way through a confusing mass of one-way streets, dead-ends not marked by the GPS, and the occasional cluster of partiers on the corners of small and dirty piazzas. When the road began to climb, things grew quiet again. Apartment buildings became farmhouses and streetlights grew infrequent until they ended all together. Darkness swallowed the Fiat save for two circles of light illuminating the dirt road in front of us. The city dropped away and grew small. The temperature gauge on the car's dashboard indicated we'd lost three degrees Celsius since we'd left the city limits. I dropped the car into third gear to keep momentum as we climbed, the engine working hard as mud-holes and washboard rolled by underneath us.

The SP140 was narrower, rougher and windier than the SP18 and I had to slow the vehicle to forty just to manage the potholes and ridges. Thick trees lined the roadway on one side, while a steep slope dropped off to our left. The glow of Naples appeared in the rear-view mirror, then vanished altogether.

The forest grew sparse, then patchy. A swath of stars against a duvet of blue-black infinity opened overhead, taking my breath away. The moon bobbed into view as we curved around the backside of Vesuvius, hanging like an ornament on an invisible line, casting shadows behind the scrubby bushes and hillocks as it washed the rough terrain with cold, white light.

Tomio leaned forward as the observatory sign loomed. I slowed the Fiat further, creeping along until the copse of trees Ryan mentioned came into view. The rest-stop's narrow entrance would be easy to miss if you didn't know it was there.

Piloting the Fiat into the rest stop, we were swallowed by the shadows of scrubby evergreens. Our headlights swung across the rest stop as I pulled the car into a parking space, bouncing off the chrome of a pretty, black Giulietta. There was no sign of Ryan.

Tomio and I let out a synchronized exhale as I turned the Fiat's engine off. A lonely wind whistled around the rest stop, though we were protected enough not to feel it as we got out of the car. Tomio opened the car's rear door and grabbed the backpack from behind the passenger's seat.

Ryan materialized from the entrance for a walking trail leading past the rest-stop's toilet facilities. His black jacket, jeans and sneakers made him look like a floating head and pair of hands.

He greeted us with a beckoning motion. "Let's go. I'll fill you in on the way."

I locked the car and pocketed the keys, following Tomio to the trailhead. "How far?"

"Only a little over three kilometers but over rough, exposed ground." He eyed our black clothing with approval. "We can't use hand-lights, so watch your step."

Crickets and other night insects chirruped to one another as Tomio and I followed Ryan along the path leading to the toilets. Before we reached them, Ryan stepped off the path and into the trees, picking his way through until we emerged above the tree line.

It wasn't cold, but the wind threw grit against our legs and occasionally picked it up and threw it into our faces. Naples was a finger of dense but distant light to the west. It fell away as we climbed up and across the face of the mountain, leaving a smattering of lights visible from farmyards and country homes nestled in the valley around the back of Vesuvius National Park. The borders of the park were easy to make out, and the scar of the SP140, but that dropped away too.

Twenty minutes into the hike it felt like we were on a different planet. A lonely one, with no civilization or animal life at all. Even the insects were quiet up here. The terrain was dry, rocky, and loose; all the makings of a sprained ankle if one wasn't careful.

"You've been here before, obviously," Tomio said as we kept up with Ryan as best we could. He dodged treacherous spots and skirted loose scrapes of dirt the way only someone who'd done this trek—perhaps multiple times—could have. Tomio and I quickly learned that the safest thing to do was to literally step where he stepped. I brought up the rear and had to strain my ears to hear Ryan's answer over the increasingly rough wind.

"Nero brought me here before I left the country. No one is allowed to stray off the volcano's walking path so no one ever comes back here. The way inside is a tight squeeze initially, so I hope you're not claustrophobic."

"Isn't it dangerous?" I asked. "I've never been inside a volcano but it doesn't seem like a great place for, you know, creatures who need oxygen to live."

"There is oxygen inside thanks to multiple vents and suction, and it's not as hot as you might think, at least where Nero will be taking them. If you descend further, yes, it'll get too hot for a natural, and toxic." Ryan bracketed one side of his mouth as he explained over his shoulder, never taking a misstep as we scrambled over the alien terrain.

Even scrubby grasses were few and far between now, and the soil was so dark and sandy it was like walking on finely crushed ebony. Moon and starlight cast small pointed shadows across the ground, helping our eyes pick out obstacles.

"Why here?" I asked, shielding the side of my face as the wind lifted a sheet of grit to pepper our clothing and exposed skin.

Ryan gave a private, sour laugh I could barely hear. "Nero has a flair for the dramatic, as you'll see, and so must Dante, if he agreed to this. What better place to feel the contrast between your natural and your supernatural self than above a hot, lava lake that will kill you in one moment and be swimmable in the next?"

My mind went to Gage as a cold prickle of fear traced up my back like a witch's finger. What would they do with Gage if they successfully made the transfer?

"Hurry," I said, trying to swallow down rising panic. My fire inadvertently sent power down my legs without me consciously commanding it to. I put my hands against Tomio's back and pushed. He surged forward and did the same to Ryan.

I knew from reading the tourism brochures the city of Naples produced, that Vesuvius was always in danger of erupting. The last major one had happened in 1944. It blew my mind that Italy still allowed people to make their homes around its base, even with the incredibly fertile farmland the volcano produced. In spite of popular belief, the pamphlet had read, volcanic eruptions were not a fast process. A buildup of increasingly heavy smoke and ash happens before any lava is actually spewed, as happened in 1998. Even for fire magi, a volcano wasn't a friendly place to be, yet here we were heading toward a vent. I couldn't decide if this was something I would ever tell my parents about or not, but to make that decision, we had to survive first.

No ash or smoke had been seen issuing from Vesuvius in recent years, and in fact the only thing to stain the blue sky over Naples was smog from the city itself. Still, the volcano was only one unpredictable aspect of this task, Nero was the other.

A sharp cliff looming against the sky seemed to appear out of nowhere, jolting me out of my thoughts and bringing me to a sudden halt. Ryan and Tomio had apparently not been lost in their thoughts as badly as me, and were swallowed up by the near impenetrable black shadow beneath the cliff.

"What's this?" I heard Tomio ask as the shadow swallowed me as well. I reached out a hand to feel his back. The wind immediately stopped its battering of our clothes and hair.

"It's a remnant of a much older volcano called Somma," Ryan replied, his voice hushed now that the wind had been cut off. "It collapsed after the Pompeii event, and now it cradles the Vesuvius cone. See?" He pointed to the shadow of a concave curve arching toward the sky, which was cut off at the top like someone had sliced across it with an ax.

"Do we have to climb that?" I asked.

"Nope. The vent is in the side of the old Somma."

I felt more than saw Ryan gesture that the vent was ahead of us, but I couldn't see anything now that the moonlight was behind the cliff face.

It was impossible to run here, with fire-power or without it. The ground was a treasonous conglomerate of razor-sharp rocks and shifting rubble. We needed to brace one hand against the cliff to the right of us just to pass along the seam without falling down. I longed to light a hand-torch, but I knew that was out of the question. If the dastardly deed was already done and we were too late, there was a chance we could meet Nero and Dante as they emerged.

Pain sliced into my left ankle as a rock rolled beneath my sneaker and I turned my foot, hopping at the last second to prevent a sprain. I closed my eyes and clenched my teeth against the pain. It passed quickly without Tomio or Ryan realizing how close I'd come to injuring myself.

Ten minutes of this treacherous walking in the windless dark and my armpits and lower back were soaked with sweat. I longed for solid ground beneath my feet, and a light to see what lay ahead.

A faint sulfuric smell reached my nostrils, the first fume I'd detected since this pursuit had begun. I was about to ask about it when Ryan stopped and held up a hand. He pressed himself against the cliff wall to let us see what was ahead.

I had to strain to make it out, but my eyes had adjusted enough to see a narrow crack in the cliff face ahead. My heart fell into my shoes as I realized how much Ryan had downplayed the size of our entrance. Entering Vesuvius meant getting down on hands and knees, maybe even crawling on our bellies, underneath many tons of volcanic rock.

Without even stopping to warn us about what we'd encounter once we did get inside, Ryan gracefully dropped to his hands and knees in front of the crack and crawled in.

Tomio, who'd been so nervous to swim under the wall in the cistern underneath Naples, appeared to have zero qualms about tackling this particular obstacle.

"Wait," I hissed, then bit my lip when Tomio didn't pause, but shuffled into the crack behind Ryan. A second later and I felt completely and utterly abandoned.

Taking a big breath of outdoor air and trying not to think about the fact that it might be my last, I stuck my head inside the crack and went totally blind. My ears and my sanity latched onto the sound of Tomio and Ryan moving up ahead of me in the hellish blackness. I had to move forward, that was all I could do.

We're coming Gage, I thought. *Hold on.*

Closing my eyes since they were no good to me for the moment anyway, I began to crawl forward through the outer crust of one of the most dangerous volcanoes on earth.

TWENTY

INTO THE FURNACE

Army crawling on my elbows, the clinking almost musical sound of hardened cinders moving beneath me echoed off the walls of the tube we'd entered. Desperate for light, I had to restrain myself from sending fire into my hand to illuminate my fingertips. Surely I would not be visible inside this pitch dark tunnel. How long was it anyway? Still, it wasn't worth the risk. If Ryan wasn't doing it up ahead, then I shouldn't either.

I could hear the sound of my own breathing as the tunnel narrowed and pressed down from overhead. I bumped my head three times on the hardened magma above before I finally learned to keep my face close to the floor. Dust particles went up my nose as I pressed my lips together to keep from inhaling it fully. The sound of Ryan and Tomio scraping along ahead of me in the dark and occasionally uttering a quiet grunt—probably as they bumped their own body parts against the walls like I'd been doing—actually kept me from going into panic mode.

I heard my clothing rip and felt a pull at my knee,

and another at my right elbow a moment later. Something caught my hair and I had to reach up and back to untangle it, causing my shoulder and neck to cramp. It felt like we'd been crawling through this horrific tunnel for a day already. I lay my cheek against the ground and told myself everything was fine. Ryan knew exactly where he was going, and this tunnel would soon end and we'd be able to stand up like proper bipeds. I allowed no inner voice to interrupt, argue or question, just like a proper dictator.

How had we gotten ourselves here? Another surge of gratitude for Tomio rose in my breast. If I was feeling on the edge of a panic attack with him here, how could I have done this without him?

Somehow, I unlocked my mutinous muscles and kept going, squirming along like a little blind mole.

"Just a little further, Saxony," Tomio half-whispered.

His words echoed so strangely down the tube that it sounded like he'd said them right beside both of my ears. I hadn't been aware that he'd reached the end, but relief surged through my blood the way sunlight pours through a window when the blinds are pulled up. I increased my speed.

"Watch your head at the end, there's a sharp rock jutting from the right side," he said from somewhere in the darkness ahead.

Ryan whispered something I couldn't hear and suddenly there was an illuminated pink hand glowing in the dark above me.

The diffused wash of red-tinged light lit the tunnel. It was no more than thirty inches wide. Pitch-black hardened cinders and broken magma littered the lava tube with refuse. A few sparkles caught my eye as Tomio's hand-light caught flat edges and reflected.

When I reached the end and Tomio helped me to my feet, a new sound impinged my heightened senses. A prehistoric rumble from far below, soft but constant and menacing, like the steady snore of some huge dragon sleeping deep inside the earth.

A faint glow was visible ahead, but it was still so dark beyond Tomio's hand that my eyes couldn't pick out anything solid to fix themselves upon, which gave me vertigo. How was Gage faring in this suffocating, disorienting darkness? I reached out for Tomio to steady myself and got his forearm. He turned his hand up and grabbed my forearm back, like he knew exactly how I was feeling with all the blood tumbling down my body to find its proper place. He gave me a few moments to stabilize, then put out his hand-light and doffed the backpack to take out a bottle of water. We took turns drinking.

Ryan was a dark shape against a barely perceptible amber glow. A glow I realized was not coming from his body, but from something ahead and around a corner.

Since Ryan hadn't protested Tomio's hand-torch, I lit mine. My vision cleared. The illumination painted highlights and crescents of shadow across Tomio's handsome features. His eyes looked enormous in his face, huge and black and full of wonder and excitement. He was... smiling. His dimple, usually soft and almost invisible, was a crater in his cheek.

"Are you enjoying this?" I half-squeaked as he turned to follow Ryan.

He shushed me and crept along faster to catch up, shouldering the pack again. The ground was less treacherous here than inside the tube or outside the volcano, soft yet solid, like a layer of dust over uneven stone. A smell registered in my brain. I don't know how long I'd been able to detect it before my mind gave it due attention. The odor grew thick as we journeyed deeper through the now large lava tube, and something happened inside my chest as a result. The temperature and humidity had both risen, making the air feel cloying and close, leaving a coating on my skin and inside my mouth and throat. But thirty seconds later the feeling passed, though I knew the atmosphere had only grown more toxic.

The smell was unpleasant. A mixture of gases like sulfur and methane. I knew with objective certainty that too long in here and a human would die, but not a mage. A mage could breathe this air for a long time before it affected them, just like Mehmet had alluded to. How was it Dante could even be in here? It was hot, but not so hot a natural couldn't bear it, but surely he'd pass out from the fumes within a few minutes, if not sooner. Even if there were vents letting in a flow of air from outside, unless he was sitting right next to an intake, he would not benefit.

Ryan's shape paused at the edge of a vertical black shadow—a cliff—and peered around the corner, then he slipped around it. Tomio followed him, and I followed Tomio.

We'd stepped out onto a wide, flat ledge and into a brighter amber glow. Ryan walked to the edge to look down. As Tomio joined him, he dropped his hand and his hand-light went out. I followed. My own light went out from pure amazement at the view before us.

Vesuvius was dormant, that much was apparent

from the outside. But inside, standing high up within the ribs of the deadly giant and looking down, I could sense the power of this natural wonder. I had never seen anything so incredible in my entire life. Even Targa's descriptions of the ancient ruins of Atlantis, or Georjie's account of Queen Elphame's castle in the fae lands of Stavarjak could not compare.

I felt like I'd slipped through a portal into an alien universe, or maybe stepped into an artist's depiction of hell. The air rippled with heat and purgatorial fumes, though there was very little smoke.

Some two thousand feet below and laying mostly open before us was what could only be described as the world's most bizarre cavern. Not yet visible was the source of orange light from far below, the sleeping engine of roiling lava that was the heart and guts of Vesuvius.

Ledges and walkways of varying thicknesses and depths—from a few feet wide to as wide as a freeway—could be seen running around the inside of the volcano, all the way to the bottom, but so uneven and littered with detritus that taking these ledges would be more like scrambling than hiking, where one needed to use both hands to get along. Deep, dark shadows hid much of the interior, keeping its secrets away from the light. The rumble was louder standing here at the edge of the mountain's rib, but still distant and almost soothing. There were no other sounds, no voices, no signs of movement.

"Come on," Ryan said, turning from the ledge to take a curved path to the right. "They'll be further down."

Further down meant hotter and closer to the source

of the gas, but neither Tomio nor I protested. A ripple in my lungs made me press a hand to my chest and pause. Ryan glanced back and happened to see me with my hand on my breast.

"It's just your lungs dealing with the gas," he murmured. "You'll feel dizzy in a few minutes, but that will come and go in waves. You get used to it. Eventually."

Tomio suppressed what might have been a belch or a hiccup, then nodded, thumping the side of his fist on his own chest.

More of the volcano's core came into view as we followed Ryan along the craggy inner wall. When a perfectly round amber eye appeared far below, my breath was stolen from my chest and my legs stopped moving. A single massive pool of lava churned beneath a black layer of cracked and shifting cooled magma. I had seen video footage of bright orange lava spewing from within the earth like a fountain, sending sprays of molten rock in all directions to blacken and harden into super fertile newly formed land.

This was not like that, but it explained the low rumble.

Vesuvius' great engine of heat and liquid rock was very much alive, but it shifted slowly and sleepily, its top layer cooling rapidly as little jets of steam and vapors spouted from the cracks. From this great height above, the eye looked small, but a person standing next to it on its flat rim would be a tiny figure indeed.

A wave of dizziness passed through me like a specter had passed through my body. I bent over and put my hands on my knees, closing my eyes until the feeling passed. I felt Tomio's hand on my back. I understood why Ryan hadn't been moving faster now. My lungs and brain had enough on their plate processing the atmosphere in here. If I had to run while feeling this whoopsy, I risked falling off an edge.

The dizziness passed, as Ryan had said it would, and I stood, nodding to the boys to let them know I was okay. They looked like they might be fighting their own vertigo. A moment later Ryan continued on, scoping the strange landscape ahead.

The cavern was not entirely hollow, but had a main column of open space above the mouth. From there countless caves and lava tubes broke from the central space to run out like veins to the skin of the monster.

When we passed a vent we knew it, and stopped to breathe in the less toxic air current as it flowed softly across our path from one invisible intake vent to an outtake vent. I knew from Ryan's movement when one was coming, he'd slow and turn his face into it to take a breath before moving on. Then Tomio would pause and do the same, then it would be my turn.

I had to suppress another jolt of near-panic when I looked behind at where we'd come from and realized that I was hopelessly lost. Without Ryan, we would never find the way we'd come in. Unless one of the airflows entered through a vent large enough for a human to pass, the only way out without our navigator would be with fire-power, straight through the side of the volcano's walls.

I shoved the unpleasant feeling of claustrophobia lingering at the edge of my mind violently away, and concentrated on what my eyes could see. This wasn't much more of a comfort but at least it gave me something to do.

We began to descend a long slope of smooth, powdery rock, and the feeling of being infinitesimally small returned with a vengeance. It was like being in the dwarf's underground city, but without the mining railways, or the huge carved columns holding up the ceiling. One could imagine the sound of singing echoing through this place. A companionable and comforting way to pass the time and keep one's mind off the fact that one was basically enclosed in a super-heated stone womb that could fill with molten rock at any moment.

"There." The whisper jarred me out of my reverie. I followed Ryan's pointed finger and at first saw nothing out of place.

Then the light shifted and brightened, as one of those big black blocks of hardened lava rolled over.

Not quite directly across from us but close, and further down, two small figures moved slowly along a narrow ledge, then disappeared a moment later as a shadow swallowed them up.

My heart surged and my lungs gave that weird fluttering sensation as my mind processed what I'd seen: two people, the one in the lead larger and misshapen. The second followed so closely there was almost no space between them. The leader was weirdly shaped because he was carrying a body.

There was no way they could hear us, as far away as we were and against that low rumble of Vesuvius' guts, still the three of us crouched at the edge of the cliff and kept our voices low.

"I'll get ahead of them by traversing that ledge," Ryan gestured to a narrow ridge, "you keep going and get behind them. Wait for me to distract Nero, then deal with Dante and get Gage out of here. Looks like they've knocked him out or drugged him."

Ryan took a step but Tomio stopped him with a loaded four words. "Shouldn't Saxony distract Nero?"

My thudding heart swelled at Tomio's vote of confidence. Nero was the dangerous one, and while Ryan was also Burned, he'd only been so for a matter of weeks. I'd had a year of training with Basil and with combat coaches, and I could handle record levels of heat and power. It made sense to me as well that I be the one to distract Nero, though the idea of it made my lips feel numb.

Ryan bared his teeth, his white grin a specter in the gloom as we locked eyes in a way that gave me chills. "You want to sacrifice your life for my twin? Be my guest, but if I go after Dante, I will end him. That okay with you?"

"No!" I hissed. If anything happened to Dante, I would never be free of Enzo. I gave Tomio a look that said I was okay with Ryan's original plan. "I'm sworn to return him to his father in one piece. Neutralize him, but don't hurt him. At least, not excessively." I wouldn't mind if Dante came out of this with a few bruises, and somehow I thought even his own father wouldn't be too sorry about that either, after all the stress and frustration the young mafia don-to-be had caused.

We agreed and split up, Ryan tackling the volcano's terrain at a dangerous speed. He was gone from sight in a moment. Tomio and I moved like shadows over the strange blend of jagged rocks and smooth pathways covered in volcanic dust. We descended where we could to bring ourselves even with where we'd last seen our targets. Scrambling over sections of loose boulders, it was impossible not to disturb the rubble in such poor light and volcanic stone was noisy, with a glass against glass kind of clink. My heart sank as we approached. Unless we found a flat section, there was no way we could be totally silent as we crept up on them.

A voice bounced off the stone as I joined Tomio where he pressed himself up against a wall behind a short outcrop. The language was Italian, but it was still too far away and soft to pick out words I recognized.

Tomio's fingers closed gently around my wrist as I pressed against him and the wall. Ahead of us lay a narrow, treacherous path with a cavernous drop-off on one side, and layers of outcroppings, each standing proud of the next. In one way it was perfect for sneaking up on someone and staying hidden, but one wrong move and one might tumble into the abyss before us which had no visible bottom, just a yawning crack of darkness, hidden from even the volcano's low pulsing light.

With a quick glance around the outcropping, Tomio signaled he was about to move with two squeezes of my wrist. He slipped around the jutting feature and into the next shadow. I followed without giving myself time to think about what lay below. Volcanic dust puffed from our feet and I heard small clusters of grit and little stones tumble into the crevice. We moved along this way, like stop-motion characters, slipping from shadow to shadow until the murmur of Italian grew clearer.

Ryan had said to wait for him to distract Nero, but he hadn't said what that distraction would be, and nothing had happened yet. When Tomio and I breached the next outcrop it would be the last. The final section was open and without cover, the element of surprise would surely be lost.

We pressed our backs against the warm walls of Vesuvius and waited. Tomio's fingers, soft from coatings of dust, slipped around my wrist again but this touch was different. It wasn't meant to communicate, only to comfort. I was momentarily jarred at how clearly his touch communicated this to me. No fire passed between us, yet there was a bond, a strong one, one I might have been foolish not to have recognized earlier.

A pop of pink light exploded across my retinas, making me gasp and Tomio stiffen. With a squeeze on my wrist, Tomio lurched around the final outcropping. I followed, fire licking along my spine and ribcage, begging to be used.

As the scene materialized before our eyes, my mind struggled to make sense of it.

Nero's tall, lithe figure straightened as he looked around, seeing Ryan bearing down on him. Rose colored light cascaded across the terrain ahead of Gage's twin, illuminating a face straight out of a nightmare, nuclear eyes blazing like pink coals. But he was too far away for surprise to work in his favor, thanks to the broad open patch where Nero had chosen to stop.

Gage's form was seated on the rock. He looked boneless, like a ragdoll someone had propped on a shelf and allowed to flop over.

Dante had been kneeling before Gage, but sprang to his feet at the interruption. He turned and I caught sight of his face, or where his face should be. My heart turned over with horror and a scream lanced through my mind. Big flat round eyes like a bug, reflected orange and pink and black as he turned to behold us. A moment later I realized he was wearing a gasmask.

I expected Nero to move away from Gage and Dante to face Ryan, but instead he grabbed Dante's hand and yanked him into a crouch before Gage. Slamming one hand against Gage's chest and the other against Dante's chest, his body bowed under some force, flexing and tightening visibly.

An amber-white glow appeared under Nero's hand, moving from within Gage's body. He stiffened, his ribcage pressed outward as though pulled by Nero's hands.

It happened so quickly it took my breath away. Tomio and I sprinted, full in the open now, toward the threesome.

The light passed out of Gage's body and into Nero's hand. Flashing along like a sun, it traveled up Nero's arm, through his shoulder and across his chest. When it reached the middle of Nero's torso, Gage's body collapsed as though boneless and the light zipped down Nero's other arm and into Dante, where it paused and seemed to compress itself against him, like it had struck resistance.

Ryan was upon them. Screaming, he barreled into Nero and the pink light disappeared. There was an explosion of white light so bright I was momentarily blind.

Tomio tackled Dante. Flipping him over a leg, Tomio had him on his chest on the ground, gasmask turned to one side and muffled cries issuing from within.

Nero and Ryan tangled amidst explosions of light and color so bright it was impossible to make out who was doing what.

I flew to Gage's form, my trembling fingers searching for a pulse under his jaw. There was none. I prayed it was my own panic keeping me from finding it.

"Gage?" I called his name and slapped his cheeks as I lay him out on the rock. His head rolled to the side, limp and unresponsive.

"Is he alive?" Tomio called from where he held Dante down in the dust, a knee on his back.

"I can't tell," I cried, trying to detect breathing where there was none. I tried his wrists and his neck again, feeling for that subtle rhythm of life, the surge of blood through veins. No pulse. "Come on, Gage," I whispered, beginning compressions on his chest.

Some voice in the back of my mind was screaming, trying to get my attention. I shoved it away and focused on counting the compressions, sifting through memories of the CPR training I'd received in gym class in grade ten. Was it thirty chest compressions and then two breaths with the head tilted back? Did I plug his nose? I couldn't remember and that screaming in the back of my mind wouldn't go away. I ignored it as the voice of panic. Gage's body shook as I worked to wake up his heart, his mouth lax and open, his eyes closed.

He's dead, Saxony, whispered a cold voice from a dark corner, calm and detached. *They killed him. It's all over for Gage.*

"No," I screamed, feeling my lips and chin tremble as I leaned down to breathe into his lungs. They inflated beneath my hand and hope surged in my breast as I resumed compressions, but he was not breathing on his own.

Another scream in the back of my skull, it was

almost something I could understand, didn't want to listen to.

He's dead. It's no use, came that same steely reckoning.

"Gage?" Eyes glued to his face, I compressed, barely aware that somewhere in the distance, glows of light were popping from below. Tomio called again, his words as foreign to me as Farsi.

Gage inhaled and my heart surged with fresh hope, but it was a horrible choking sound followed by a cough.

The gasmask! Ripped the scream across my mind, finally clear. *Get the mask!*

I took a hot inhale and at Tomio, pale and wide-eyed. "Throw me the mask," I yelled, extending a hand. "Now, Tomio! Now!"

Understanding broke over Tomio's features. He yanked the gasmask off Dante, who immediately began to laugh and cough at the same time.

"You're too late, little Inferno," he wheezed, sending little puffs of dust up in front of his face. He inhaled and tried to speak again but only coughed as ash filled his lungs.

Snatching the mask out of the air, I pulled its straps over Gage's head and settled it into place. His chest rose and the mask's vents sighed as air passed through them. I put my fingers under his jaw and felt a thready, weak pulse.

"Gage?" I croaked, feeling a cold calm steal over me. The rising panic, the screaming voice and the cold whispers all ceased. I couldn't see Gage's face behind the mask, but behind the glass panels over the eyes, his lashes were down against his cheek. He was breathing and his heart was beating, but he was still not conscious.

The events of the last several minutes caught up to me. Like puzzle pieces sliding into place, the picture formed and I understood. Nero had not needed to dehydrate Gage to take his fire, he had the ability to take a fire by force. Gage was fireless, possibly still dying. We had no idea what forcefully taking his fire had done to him. We had to get him out of here.

TWENTY-ONE
A NEW HUMAN

One hand on Gage's gently moving chest, I looked at Tomio, whose eyes were so big they seemed to float in his face.

"We can't go back the way we came," I called, feeling my lungs butterfly as they dealt with the fumes.

"Even if Ryan wasn't busy—" Tomio gestured to the edge just beyond him and then seemed to be lost at how to finish the sentence as he peered down.

Leaving Gage's side, I went to the edge and felt my muscles lock as I found Nero and Ryan engaged in spectacular combat on the edge of the magma. They were two tiny figures throwing colored light as they tangled, almost dancing with one another, albeit violently. As we watched in dumb amazement, Ryan absorbed a blue flame Nero had hurled, seeming to carry its momentum into himself and using it to throw a spinning kick that knocked Nero sideways, directly onto the cracked surface of the magma.

"How did they get down there?" I breathed, but was too stunned to register Tomio's answer.

Small flickers of orange licked from Nero's clothing and shoes as he rolled over the dense half-hardened surface. His shoes flared and caught fire, burning away completely in seconds and leaving him barefoot. Unconcerned about what they were fighting on, Ryan tackled Nero and Nero received him as they seemed momentarily consumed by fire the color of limes. Buzzing and snapping sounds drifted up to our ears as rainbows of embers spiraled from the impacts of their bodies. Strange scents mingled in my nose, the volcano's gases mixed with the alchemy going on below. Ryan appeared to have no shoes now as well, and fire had burned away the bottom halves of his pant legs. They moved across the surface of Vesuvius' deadly core, unconcerned and unaffected by the barbecue pit they danced over.

How was Ryan, so newly Burned, able to do such alchemy and handle himself well enough to hold Nero, a much more experienced Burned mage, off? It struck me that whatever they'd been up to with all the traveling, they were not just Burned magi anymore, but something else. Something different.

"He's giving us time," I said, tearing myself away from the sight below. "We can't go back to the vent we came in, even if we could find it, we won't be able to get Gage through it."

Dante, still coughing and with his cheek pressed against the stone, said, "If you want to save his life, you have to get him to a hospital. He's a natural now."

Tomio fisted the back of Dante's neck, eyes blazing with fury. "Where did you come in?"

Dante tried to use his fire to rise, bucking under Tomio as he detonated, but he did it poorly. Lights popped in our vision as his badly-timed detonation made him jerk and then groan in pain. "It's hurts," he moaned, half-laughing, half-coughing.

"Of course it hurts, you idiot," Tomio sneered. "What did you think it would feel like? A foot rub? If you cooperate, we'll share some of our water with you. Where's the vent you came in through?"

Dante gave a few dry coughs, leaving off his efforts to escape Tomio's hold. "Up higher, there's more vents. Lots of them, where the walls are thinnest."

Tomio and I looked at one another, then at Gage. His chest rose and fell but he just lay there. Far below, the sounds of Nero and Ryan's fight continued.

"Will Nero come for you?" I asked Dante.

He gave that half-laugh, half-moan of pain. "I wish. Our deal is complete. As strange as it might sound, I'm on your side now. I want to go home."

I didn't know if we could believe him, but so far Nero was moving away from us, if he had even registered our presence. Either Ryan was leading him away, or it was as the don's son reported, their deal was finished.

Another peek over the edge confirmed two things: Ryan was using everything he had to keep Nero engaged in their fight, possibly even trying to kill him. Nero was mostly defending, and it didn't look like he was using a lot of effort to do it. At some moments, it almost appeared like Nero was enjoying himself, though it was difficult to tell as their facial expressions were obscured by distance, ripples of heat distorting the air, and the flash of fire-light issuing from their hands and their eyes.

"Straight up is the fastest way," Dante croaked.

I turned back. "What?"

He lifted his hand where it lay beside his head palm-down and pointed straight up with his finger. "Thirty feet up there's a lava tube. It starts big then narrows to a crack. That's the way we came in. You'll feel the air coming in."

Tomio and I agreed that he'd stay with Gage and Dante and I would find the vent as quickly as I could and make sure it was a suitable passage.

With my fire slipping into my joints and fueling my climb, I tackled the wall, funneling all of my focus into my fingers, arms, shoulders and legs. The sound of hand-to-hand combat grew distant, like it was part of some past dream and not this reality.

Hand over hand, foot over foot I climbed and the combatants dropped away below me. My heart thudded almost painfully with hope that Dante was right.

When a soft gust of fresh air brushed against my cheeks, I froze, trying to determine where it was coming from. Throwing my leg over a ledge and pulling myself up, I shimmied along a flat edge that widened and became an upward slope. Air moved along this slope from above.

Lighting a hand-torch, I threw back the shadows enough to see a natural set of rough steps over rounded, cracked lava rocks. Taking these steps up I discovered exactly what Dante had described. Ahead was a lava tube not quite large enough to stand fully upright inside, but wide enough to walk into. The air grew fresh as it blew against my face and hair. Darkness pressed back as I went deeper into the tube, which jogged in lefts and rights before narrowing further. It would be tight carrying Gage through here. It occurred to me to widen the vent with fire, but two problems emerged immediately, like a one-two punch. If I battered the walls to make a larger opening, the masses of stone above us might destabilize and collapse, crushing us as we tried to escape. Even my strength wouldn't be enough to keep a mountain from collapsing down on our heads. I could melt the volcanic rock, opening the vent that way but melting it enough to move it out of the way and then cooling it enough for Gage to pass through it without being burned by the heat would be a time-consuming process, he might be dead before I finished.

My mind worked these things over like a baker worked over dough as I shuffled along the vent. When a gash of faint moonlight appeared ahead, my heart buoyed. I snuffed my hand-torch and hurried to the exit. I had to turn sideways to skim through the crack, but if we kept Gage between us, Tomio and I working together should be able to extricate him. The question was whether we could control Dante while we did. I figured that as long as the mafia don's son went first, this shouldn't be a problem. It wasn't like he was in any shape to run away.

Emerging in the open night air was like taking cool water into my parched throat. A breeze had never felt so delicious. The light of a bloated moon, even behind a thin gauze of clouds, seemed like a floodlight after the darkness inside the volcano. The crack would dump us out onto rough terrain and a steep downhill, but not one we couldn't handle. After that we'd have to find the cars. To do that I just needed to catch a glimpse of the city lights below to make sure we were headed in the right direction.

Wishing I could luxuriate in the night air and the distant sound of crickets from further down the slope, I returned to the crack and began the journey back. From above, I was able to see the easier path Nero and Dante had taken down.

By the time my feet struck the ledge where Tomio, Dante and Gage waited, Tomio had allowed Dante to sit up and had given him a water bottle, which was now empty. He was leaning against the wall with a hand over his torso, a grimace twisting his face.

"There's a way out," I said.

"Told you," Dante mumbled, then coughed and groaned, squeezing his eyes shut. I wondered if he was hurting enough to regret what he'd done, or if Nero had prepared him for the agony of the first few days after receiving fire. It was a wonder he was even conscious after having it snap into place like that so forcefully. When I'd received my fire, it had passed slowly from Isaia to me and the pain had been bearable. It made some sense that a transition made so quickly like that would shock the bodies on either end of the transaction.

There were no more flashes of light or sounds of combat drifting up from below, only the low rumble of Vesuvius filled the cavern's spaces. I turned to Tomio. "Where did they go?"

Tomio lifted a shoulder before grabbing Dante and standing him up on his feet none to gently. Dante gave a grunt and swayed but stayed on his feet. "I don't know. Maybe they killed each other. Come on. Let's get out of this hell-hole."

I went to Gage, happy to see his breathing was steady, though he was still unconscious. In this state there was no way he would be able to swallow water.

Firing up the muscles in my back and legs, I propped him up to sitting, hoping I wasn't hurting him more by moving him. A muffled groan came through the gasmask's ventilators and my heart jumped.

"Gage?" I peered through the glass coverings over his eyes to see his eyelids flutter but remain closed. "I have to pick you up. I'm sorry if it hurts."

As gently as I could, I got one arm around his back and the other under his knees. Fire-power poured down my legs and across my back and arms as I lifted him off the ground and straightened. It would be less awkward and easier for walking if I threw him over my shoulder the way I had Ryan, but if Gage was natural now, then his internal organs might have been burned by the forceful way Nero removed his fire. If I threw him over a shoulder, it could hurt him further or even kill him.

There was a tap on my shoulder. "Let me take him."

I turned to see Ryan at my elbow. I almost dropped Gage in shock.

"Where's Nero?" I asked as Ryan folded Gage's form against his chest, as tenderly as a father carrying a sleeping child.

I half expected him to tell me he was dead.

"Gone," Ryan replied as I moved to follow Tomio and Dante along the ledge. "He was only toying with me. I guess he finally got tired of it. Thank you for putting the mask on Gage. I'm not sure I would have thought of that."

The way Ryan said it made it clear he understood that Gage was no longer host to a fire.

With nudges from Tomio, Dante led our macabre little line. Ryan followed in Tomio's footsteps, cradling Gage against his chest. I could feel the heat baking off

Ryan's back as he employed his fire to bear his burden. I stayed close, watching Gage's head where sections of the ledge narrowed and there was hardly room for us to pass. In this way we closed the distance to the vent, freedom, and whatever was next.

TWENTY-TWO

AN OATH FULFILLED

Gage was still unconscious and Dante was groaning almost constantly by the time our filthy, exhausted crew arrived at the parked cars. Tomio had tweaked a knee and Ryan had tripped twice on the way back, nearly dropping Gage. I began to walk in front, lighting the way with both hands held in the air until the rising sun dusted the terrain with enough illumination for us to see by.

Ryan lay Gage across the rear seat of the Giulietta while Dante collapsed into the front seat of the Fiat, begging for more water. Tomio rooted in the trunk for another bottle while I unearthed my phone and set up the laptop, perching it open on the hood of the car. Creating a hotspot, I opened the Agency's dashboard and typed out a text to Basil and Ms. Shepherd. The fact that Gage still hadn't awakened, even after we'd taken the gasmask off him and he'd been able to breathe fresh night air, was making me feel queasy with worry. He needed medical attention, but we couldn't just take him to the nearest hospital.

Ms. Shepherd answered, typing back that she would open a line for a video call in thirty seconds. I beckoned Tomio over. Dante was guzzling water and groaning while Ryan was leaning in through his car's rear door trying to get water into Gage.

Ms. Shepherd's face swam into view, bright against the blackness of the night. "Go ahead please."

"We've got Gage and Dante. Both of them need medical help," I said. "Ryan is also with us, he's looking after Gage."

"Where are you?" Her eyes tightened as she looked behind us at the now lightening sky.

"We're near the Vesuvius Observatory. Nero took Gage's fire and gave it to Dante. They're both alive, but Gage is unconscious and Dante is in a lot of pain."

"The pain will likely soon pass," she said, "but still wise to get him checked out. Gage will definitely need medical attention, and most importantly, water."

"Ryan's trying to get some water into him, but you should know that Nero did not dehydrate Gage before taking his fire. He just... took it. Forced it."

For the first time since I'd made her acquaintance, Ms. Shepherd expressed some emotion—astonishment. "Are you sure?"

"We're sure. We saw it happen." Tomio bent over briefly to check on Dante, who was still moaning in the front seat.

"That's... anyway, okay." She shook her head and her business face was back. "Do you have two vehicles?"

I nodded.

"I presume Gage is breathing okay on his own?"

"Yes."

"Okay, here's what I want you to do. Saxony, I want you to take Dante and Gage to a hospital called Azienda Ospedaliera di Rilievo Nationale Antonio Cardarelli. We have a contact there, a medical professional who has worked with supernaturals. Do not go to the main emergency entrance at the front, take him around the back of the hospital to Entrance C. You'll see a sign for the Burn Unit. Our contact is Dr. Burr, and she'll be waiting for you at those doors. Tomio, if Ryan is willing, you and he must go straight to Nero's underground place and fetch Janet."

I looked at Tomio, feeling stricken. Janet did need to be rescued, and immediately, but what if Nero was there?

Tomio just nodded and moved toward the Giulietta.

"Might that not be the first place Nero goes?" I asked.

Ms. Shepherd nodded. "Perhaps. It depends if he thinks Janet gave him away or not. Either way, she needs looking after."

I hated the idea of getting separated from Tomio, but Ms. Shepherd was right, someone had to take Gage and Dante to the hospital, and someone had to rescue Janet. "Should *I* go with Ryan, and Tomio take the men to the hospital instead?"

"I'd say yes," Ms. Shepherd replied, "except that Gage's mother is on her way to Naples as we speak. Her plane is landing in a little over an hour. She'll be needing to see a friendly face and she has asked specifically to see you."

"Me? Why?"

"I can't speak for her. That was her request to Basil.

Best not waste any more time talking with me. We can touch base again once Gage and Dante are checked in."

I agreed and we signed off. Closing the laptop, I went to help Ryan move Gage into the back seat of the Fiat. As soon as we had the two injured men settled, Ryan opened the trunk and rifled through his things, pulling out a spare set of sneakers. He didn't bother to change his ruined jeans. Closing the trunk, he gave Tomio a nod then got into the Giulietta and started the engine.

Tomio had one hand on the door handle when he looked over his shoulder at me, his dark eyes swimming with dawn's light. He must have read all kinds of emotions on my face because he left the door to stride over. Pulling me against himself, his mouth came down on mine almost violently. Inside my ribcage, my heart thundered very slow but very hard as he kissed me, each pulse as low and deep as a drumbeat. I wrapped my arms around his neck and held him close, glorying in the liquid warmth filling me in response to his sudden and savage affection. My senses swam at the scent of his body, a warm earthy smell.

"Please be careful," I whispered, my lips at his ear.

I felt him shudder as he cupped the back of my head and kissed me under the jaw. Then, he released me and got into the vehicle.

The Giulietta's engine growled as Ryan steered the car out of the rest stop. I got into the Fiat, found the hospital with my GPS, then followed the Giulietta's tail lights down the mountain, my body so taut I couldn't even sit back against my seat. Beside me, Dante groaned with a hand over his chest.

"Will you hush," I snapped when I thought one

more complaint might push me over the edge. "You asked for this."

Dante pouted and looked out the window. After a while he raised one hand and looked intently at it. A flicker of light appeared in his palm and down one finger, but he winced and gave another moan of pain.

The Giulietta turned north and I had to turn south. I watched their tail lights disappear into the traffic, breathing out a prayer that they would get Janet out without problems.

Pulling up to the rear entrance of the hospital marked with a huge black 'C', I was amazed to find four paramedics waiting with two trolleys and some equipment. A third person wearing a proper lab-coat, with a short trendy haircut waited off to the side with a tablet in her hand.

Dante and Gage's doors were opened before I even turned the Fiat's engine off. The blond woman came around to my side of the vehicle as I got out.

"Ms. Cagney, I presume?"

I closed the door and watched in amazement as Gage was transferred to a trolley by three of the medics. Dante declined the trolley and walked into the hospital by himself with his hand over his stomach and a grimace on his face. I caught a glimpse of a waxy cheek as he raked his long hair behind one ear.

I turned to the blond woman. "That's me. Dr. Burr?"

She gave me a bright and enthusiastic smile as she shoved the tablet into my hands. "Just a few questions for you to answer—"

"Do you mind if I make a phone-call first?" I asked. "It's important."

"Certo, certo. I'll see to the men. We'll put them across the hall from one another. This wing is quiet at the moment. You'll find us about thirty meters down C hall."

"Thanks." I pulled out my cell phone and opened an app that records phone conversations then dialed Enzo's number through the app. I took a deep steadying breath and held the phone to my ear.

The don answered on the second ring. "Success, Signora Cagney?"

"Pronto, Enzo. You should send a plane, train or automobile to pick up your son. He's at the…" I forgot the hospital's long name, looked around and spotted the sign over the door, "Azienda Ospedaliera di Rilievo Nationale Antonio Cardarelli."

"Ospedale?" Enzo's voice went hushed. "What happened?"

"Your son is the proud new owner of a fire that he stole from my friend Gage."

"Madonna. But, he is okay?"

Irritation sparked at his lack of interest in the victim. "No, actually. Gage is unconscious, thanks for asking. It's not clear whether he will survive. Your son may be responsible for the death of my friend, and if Gage doesn't die, he'll be responsible for the trauma of a forced plenary endowment. As far as I'm concerned, you and I are more than even. The medical staff here are checking Dante now. He's in pain, but I'm sure he'll recover. And you now have a magus back in your employ. I suggest you send someone to pick him up and take him home. Dante is your problem now. Do we agree?"

The other end of the phone was silent.

"Enzo? I don't think you should waste time. Gage's twin brother Ryan will arrive at the hospital in roughly two hours. I won't be held responsible for what he does to Dante if Gage is still unconscious when he arrives."

He coughed and let out a thick, phlegmy sigh. "Very well. I will arrange a helicopter as soon as possible."

"I'm sorry I couldn't stop Dante from taking a fire. You'll never know how sorry. But your son is alive. He is not Burned and won't be attempting a Burning any time soon. That was the objective you gave me: I was to return him alive. I need to hear you say my debt is fulfilled."

"I would like to propose—"

I closed my eyes and spoke slowly. "I need to hear you say my debt is fulfilled."

After a moment's pause, the don admitted the words I was dying to catch on a recording. "Your debt is fulfilled."

I smiled and felt some of the tension drain out of my neck and shoulders. "Good. Shall I give your number to the hospital so you can arrange transport?"

"There is no need. I have their information. Thank you, Signora Cagney."

"Good bye, Enzo."

"I would like to propose—"

I hung up the phone and saved the recording.

WALKING DOWN C HALL, I found Dante and Gage's names already posted on their doors, which were both closed. Peering in on Dante, I saw him lying on a bed, facing away from a nurse who was sliding an IV needle into his arm. He had his other hand over his torso as he spoke to one of the medics while he took notes.

Crossing over the hall to peek in on Gage, the situation was similar, only Gage wasn't talking to anyone because he was still unconscious. Worry set heavy hands on both my shoulders. Surely he should have woken up by now. Dr. Burr stood at his bedside taking notes as a nurse arranged Gage's IV. She looked up and saw me in the window. She gave me a hand with all five fingers up and mouthed, "Five minutes."

I nodded and strolled down the hall to a dark green leather couch with a coffee table scattered with outdated Italian magazines. I went to the vending machine across from the couch and contemplated the snacks and drinks. My throat seemed to close up at the idea of anything but water, so I bought a bottle and sat down.

A tall blond woman wearing leather pumps and a tailored short-sleeved blouse appeared at the end of the hall. She looked tired and overstimulated at the same time. She looked around, read a sign, and decided this was the hall for her. Her footsteps grew loud as she approached, high-heels clopping on the tile. She read the names on all the closed doors as she came, and peeked into the rooms with open doors. Something about the way she moved and the angle of her cheekbones reminded me of the twins. She had a softness around the mouth that was pure Gage. I'd never met Angelica, but Gage spoke about her in reverent tones.

I got to my feet and called softly. "Mrs. Wendig?"

She looked up and took in my face and blazing hair.

Her breath came out in a rush and she came down the hall toward me at a near-run. She swept me up in a hug that smelled like faded Chanel No. 5 mingled with a hint of spaghetti bolognaise. She must have gotten off the plane and come straight here. When she pulled back and held me at arms' length, I jacked a thumb over my shoulder. "Nice to meet you, Mrs. Wendig. First room on the left."

"Bless you, Saxony," she said, squeezing me again.

"Why?" I asked, idiotically.

She only laughed and brushed at moisture rimming her eye before striding to Gage's room and looking through the window. She let out a distressed 'oh' as she peered through the glass, then turned the doorknob and walked in.

I followed her to the doorway, but hesitated to enter. Dr. Burr introduced herself to Angelica as she bent over Gage and put her hands on his cheeks, murmuring to him. She looked up at the doctor and straightened, now looking down at the shorter woman.

"I'm his mother. How is he?"

Dr. Burr's face lit up. "Ah, you've arrived. Did you fill in paperwork at the entrance?"

"Yes. There was a rather fierce nurse there who wouldn't let me pass without it. How is my son, please?"

Dr. Burr glanced at me and hesitated.

Angelica followed her view and saw me standing at the door. She extended a hand to me. "Come in, Saxony. Please. You should hear this, too. If it wasn't for you, he'd be dead by now. Basil told me everything."

I entered Gage's room and stood at the end of his bed. He was the color of paraffin, and a heart-rending sight. He lay there with an oxygen mask over his nose and mouth, an IV in one upturned arm, and a heart monitor beeping not far from his head.

"At this point," Dr Burr said, losing her smile, "Gage is suffering from what we call 'burn shock'. The best we can do for him is manage his fluids. We can't open him up to take a look, and burns caused by a supernatural fire are unpredictable at best, but we believe that he's sustained lung damage as well as internal blisters and edema. He may also have broken ribs from the CPR. We aim to resuscitate him by restoring adequate oxygen and fluid. We hope to maintain tissue perfusion and prevent his burns from deepening."

"When will he wake up?" Angelica wove her fingers through Gage's limp ones.

"I'm afraid we don't know, but his heartbeat is regular, if not as strong as we'd like. We'll monitor him for the next twenty-four hours and will give you an update tomorrow."

"Have you seen this before?" I asked. "I mean, someone who had their fire forcefully taken?" I was trying to ignore her comment about how I might have broken ribs.

Dr. Burr shifted her tablet to the other hand and put her stylus into her pocket. "I'm afraid not. I've seen three plenary endowment patients in twelve years of serving supernaturals, but they were all on the receiving end. I've never seen a mage like this before. I'm sorry to say this will be new for all of us. But, I have an expectation that Gage will survive it."

In spite of this positive news, Angelica seemed to wilt. I went behind her and moved a chair from the corner to where she could sit and still hold Gage's hand. "But who and what will he be if he does survive?"

A stream of Italian came over the hospital's intercom, which included a mention of Dr. Burr.

"I can't speak to who," she said, slipping her tablet into the deep pocket of her lab-coat. "But I can tell you what. Your son will be a natural, and if he's lucky, he'll have a normal life without a fire. If you'll excuse me, I'm being paged. I'll be back to check on Gage as soon as I can."

Dr. Burr headed for the door as Angelica and I exchanged a heavy look.

"If he takes it the way Chad has taken it, it will break our family," she said softly.

I felt a wash of cold realization splash over me. "What?"

"Chad lost his fire ten days ago, the same day Gage was taken. He hasn't spoken since and barely gets out of bed. He's a shell. I tried to get him to come with me, thinking he'd pull himself together for Gage but he's just a blank." She waved a hand in front of her face and widened her eyes, making them purposefully empty in a chilling imitation of someone who'd vacated their senses. "He's just gone. His mother has already arrived from England and moved into our house while I'm gone to take care of him while I'm away. And now this—" She gestured to Gage and her chin and lower lip wobbled. She put her face in her hand. "It's too much. I can't cope."

Heart thudding almost painfully, I moved to sit on the other side of Gage. I took his hand. "What can I do? Please tell me how I can help."

She looked up, her expression fierce. "Basil told me

that fires are going out because of Nero, though he couldn't explain how or why." She leaned forward, eyes earnest and hopeful. "Gage brags about you so much. Ryan too, in fact."

I recoiled in surprise.

"Oh yes. They do. Especially Gage. They say there hasn't been a student like you at Arcturus in its entire history. They told me—Gage specifically, told me—about the games, and your amazing abilities." Her eyes turned pleading and she reached across Gage's still torso for my hand.

I gave her my free hand and wondered if she could feel my fingers trembling. "Mrs. Wendig—"

"Please. The Agency is in a mess, we can't rely on them, though I know Basil is trying to pull together some competent mages. Look at what you've done already."

"But, I didn't—Gage is still—Look at him!"

"Yes, but he'd be dead if it wasn't for you."

"I'm not saying I don't want to help, I do. But... you should have seen Nero and Ryan—" Explosions of colored light and Ryan's blazing fists and eyes flashed from my memory. Somehow, he'd managed to leapfrog past me with hardly any time to adjust to his Burned abilities.

The door slammed open, startling us out of our conversation.

Ryan rushed into the room, face smudged with dirt, hair matted. Tomio followed, pausing at the door when he saw Gage lying there hooked up to oxygen, EKG and IV.

Angelica stood as Ryan came forward, expression stricken. He opened his arms for her.

She lifted her hand back and swung hard, striking his cheek with a resounding open-handed slap so loud Gage's heartbeat seemed to speed up momentarily in response.

Ryan's face jerked to the side. He was frozen like that for a few seconds, then straightened to stare at his mother in horror. I'd never seen such an expression on his face.

It was as if all the air had been sucked out of the room, then Angelica yanked Ryan into a violent hug and burst into tears.

Tomio and I shared an uncomfortable look as Ryan brought his arms around her and held his weeping mother, burying his face in her neck and shoulder. I moved away from Gage toward Tomio, beckoning him to leave. The poor Wendig family needed some privacy.

Taking Tomio's hand, I led him from the room. As he closed the door behind us, I noticed that Dante's door was open, the room empty. He must have been picked up by his father's envoy. I looked at Tomio and he looked at me as he expelled a long exhale.

"Where's Janet? How is she?" I asked as I moved down the hall to get away from the sound of Angelica crying.

Tomio shook his head. "Bad news. I've already called Ms. Shepherd and Basil."

I felt rooted to the ground. "What?"

"Nero got there before we did. He cleared the bunker of artifacts, and took Janet."

EPILOGUE

Tomio's hand tightened around mine as the small plane hit turbulence somewhere over the Mediterranean. Across Tomio, Ryan's hands gripped his armrests as he pressed his head back against the seat. Rain lashed the windows of the Bombardier Challenger the Agency had arranged to fly us back to England. Basil and Ms. Shepherd awaited our arrival at the London City Airport.

I caught a reflection of Ryan's face in the black screen of the entertainment center installed in the back of the seat in front of him. He looked a million miles away. I wondered what he was thinking.

After their private family breakdown, Angelica and Ryan had emerged from Gage's hospital room. Her eyes were puffy from crying while Ryan appeared to have slammed a door on his emotions. His expression sent a lance of apprehension through me, the cold eyes and hard mouth.

While Ryan had stood quietly by, Angelica explained that as soon as Gage was well enough to travel, she'd be taking him home to Canada. She was hopeful that his presence would help pull Chad out of his apathy.

"But you three—" she looked meaningfully from Ryan to me to Tomio and back to Ryan. "Sometimes responsibility comes before we are fully ready for it, and for you that time is now. Your species is under attack. You have the most experience with the enemy of any mages alive. You *must* work together with Basil to stop what is happening." Her eyes flashed and her voice grew steely, all her maternal softness stowed away. "If he is not stopped, I fear there will soon be none of you left." She nailed her son with a look. "Then what will it all have been for? All your tricks and cunning strategies to elevate yourself among your kind."

I looked at Ryan, trying to decode his expression but I could read nothing, just the cold hard wall he'd put up.

"Do it for your father," Angelica said to Ryan, taking his hand. "Do it for your brother. And maybe, one day, they will forgive you for what you've done."

A crack appeared in Ryan's veneer at these words, small and brief but unmistakable. For a moment I thought he was going to break down.

I moved to Ryan and took his other hand, unable to stop myself from offering comfort to the stricken, even if he had been my enemy. Our mage-bond flashed up my arm and he looked down at me solemnly. I couldn't offer him a smile, but I could look him square in the eyes without wincing or looking away. What'd he'd done for us inside the volcano had gone some distance toward softening my dislike for him. I wasn't sure if what Angelica thought Ryan needed forgiveness for was the same thing I thought Ryan needed forgiveness for, but it was clear that she thought Ryan's actions had led to the loss of Gage's fire, and maybe Chad's as well. It was also apparent that Ryan knew a lot more about what Nero was up to than anyone else did. We needed him.

Tomio closed our circle, taking my hand and Angelica's hand and looking at Ryan. "I'm in. No matter what comes."

"Me too," I said, squeezing both Tomio and Ryan's hands. "I'm all in. For Gage, for Janet, for Chad and for the magi. As long as there is breath and fire in me, I will fight."

Angelica nodded and looked at Ryan, Tomio and I followed her gaze. "And you, Ryan? Will you take this opportunity to redeem yourself?"

Ryan's faced worked but his eyes did not tear up, his mouth did not tremble and his voice was strong and steady. "Yes. There is nothing else. Let's go to war."

ENDNOTES

Here you are at the end! Thank you for coming along on this, the penultimate adventure in the *Arcturus Academy* series, with me. I hope you enjoyed it. Thank you to my editors Nicola Aquino and Victoria Knorr, thank you to my ARC team readers and members of my VIP Readers' Lounge and Audiobook Review Team. You make me feel so supported. No book materializes from the work of just one person, it seems to take a the proverbial village, even if its a hamlet.

Naples is a city I have visited several times. I have hiked Mount Vesuvius and probed the underground city, I have swum in the bay and roamed the streets of the historical centre and the fringe community of Portici. All of the places Saxony visits in this book were inspired by real life, although I haven't actually descended into the volcano itself. I don't think anyone has or can, although there are other volcanoes that humans can and do visit, and watching videos of those sweaty adventures was great fun during the research phase of this story.

As I type this my mind is full of all the coming events for the final story in the series, *Source Fire*. Oh what fun, what danger, what romance and what revelation is coming Saxony's way, and by extension (hopefully) yours. I do hope to see you at the end of the final instalment, and thank you again for coming all this way with me. It means so much that you choose to spend some of your precious time with me.

Naturally, the end of a book wouldn't be the end of a book without a request for reviews. They help an author find their readership, and a reader find their favourite author, better than any other marketing. If you pen a review on Amazon, Goodreads, Bookbub or anywhere else, I thank you from the bottom of my heart.

Love, Abby

Antalya, Turkey

Feb, 2021

COME A LITTLE CLOSER, MY DEAR...

Want to be kept updated on new releases, be the first to know about sneak peeks and 'read by yours truly' audio snippets? I'm no Judi Dench but I do try not to make too many swallowing sounds. I host the occasional sale and sometimes join themed multi-author promotions that are good fun. Join my newsletter at www.alknorrbooks.com or request access to my private VIP Reader Lounge on Facebook (don't forget to answer the three questions to get in). I also have Instagram for those who are curious about the life of a traveling fantasy novelist. I tend to visit a lot of ancient places, there's inspiration to be found there, doncha know. See you in them virtual hills!

ALSO BY A.L. KNORR

The Elemental Origins Series

Born of Water (Targa)

Born of Fire (Saxony)

Born of Earth (Georjayna)

Born of Æther (Akiko)

Born of Air (Petra)

The Elementals

Earth Magic Rises Trilogy

Bones of the Witch

Ashes of the Wise

Heart of the Fae

The Siren's Curse Trilogy

Salt & Stone

Salt & the Sovereign

Salt & the Sisters

Elemental Novellas

Pyro, A Fire Novella

Heat, A Fire Novella

Rings of the Inconquo

Born of Metal

Metal Guardian

Metal Angel

Mira's Return Series

Returning

Falling

Surfacing

The Kacy Chronicles

Descendant

Ascendant

Combatant

Transcendent

Visit www.alknorrbooks.com to sign up for AL Knorr's
newsletter. Get notifications for new releases and free stories.

www.ingramcontent.com/pod-product-compliance
Lightning Source LLC
Chambersburg PA
CBHW011033190726
48290CB00011B/2832